#40 in the incredible adventures of the

DEATH MERCHANT
BLUEPRINT INVISIBILITY
by Joseph Rosenberger

PINNACLE BOOKS   LOS ANGELES

DEATH MERCHANT #40:
BLUEPRINT INVISIBILITY

An original Pinnacle Books edition, published for the first time anywhere.

First printing, August 1980

ISBN: 0-523-41018-2

Cover illustration by Dean Cate

Printed in the United States of America

PINNACLE BOOKS, INC.
2029 Century Park East
Los Angeles, California 90067

This book is dedicated to
K. v L-R
Korbach, West Germany

True, the one thing you can't saw is sawdust; yet anything remains possible: whatever man can dream, man can achieve. The laws are there. They always have been—

Only waiting to be discovered. . . .

Richard J. Camellion
Votaw, Texas

Chapter One

Insomuch as a wise man only expects the unexpected, Richard Camellion was not surprised when an ONI agent, in one of the cars trailing Shiptonn, called on the radio and reported that Shiptonn had turned off Oregon Avenue onto Wise Road and was taking his two-door Mustang into Rock Creek Park.

The Death Merchant, sitting next to Rex Civalier, who was driving, spoke into the microphone. "Very well. We're on Oregon. Keep us informed." He removed his finger from the button and returned the mike to the set below the dash.

"Any park is dangerous in D.C.," Rex Civalier said. "I guess Shiptonn doesn't know that the nickname of Rock Creek Park is 'Muggers' Haven.'" He slowed the Dodge Aspen, his face showing annoyance at the thick stream of traffic ahead.

"He's not going to meet anyone in there; he's only taking the long way around to his real destination," Camellion said to Civalier, who was not yet 35, was dressed in a light blue summer suit and had a nose like a Malibu stork.

"He's not going to his home in University Park," Civalier said. "It's too far east. But he's up to something. There wouldn't be any point to all this driving around if he weren't —damn this traffic."

"It could be nothing more than a test run," Camellion said. "The people pushing the buttons are not fools."

Civalier reached up and pulled the overhead sunshade to the left, to protect his eyes from the setting sun, and increased speed as the cars in front pulled ahead.

1

"You're convinced that Shiptonn's a 'robot' that's been programmed?"

"At this point, I only know that Shiptonn is our very best bet, in fact, the only bet."

"We're only a quarter of a mile from Wise," Civalier said resignedly. "I suppose we turn off?"

"Of course. Among us and the other five cars, we should be able to keep track of Shiptonn."

He reached into the glove compartment, took out a special receiver—preset on 49 MHz and containing a field strength, or S-meter—and switched it on. Instantly the tone came through: *beep, beep, beep, beep.* A glance at the S-meter showed that the strength of the signal was five points below maximum, indicating that Shiptonn's vehicle was less than two miles away. *He probably turned off Wise and is coming back south through the park on Beach Drive.*

The communications radio buzzed. The Death Merchant switched off the bumper beeper transmitter, put it back into the glove compartment, picked up the microphone and pushed the button. "Cherry Wine here."

The voice came through the small speaker. "This is Blue-1. The target is moving south on Beach Drive. We're going to drop back and have Blue-4 take over. What is your position?"

"We're about to turn off onto Wise. We'll make better time once we're in the park."

"Don't go over the speed limit," the ONI man warned. "The park police operate like the Mafia. They're all over the place and will grab you in a minute. You'd have no way of explaining the electronic equipment, and you're both armed."

"We're not planning on going to jail—out," Camellion said and released the mike button. *Not here in Hot-Air City.*

Turning onto Wise, Civalier made a disgruntled face. "He's right on both counts, especially about guns. Jesus Christ couldn't get a permit to carry a gun in the District of Columbia. Of course, the trash has never worried about such minor technicalities. Since the no-gun law went into effect, crime has tripled, particularly stick-ups."

"I gather you're not for gun control," Camellion said.

"If I were I'd be against protection and self-defense. I'd also be a first-class idiot, like the gun-control halfwits who seem to operate on a misguided interpretation of the religious injunc-

2

tion of 'be good to those who do evil to you'—another piece of nonsense."

"There's no fool like a gun-control fool," Camellion said. "The gun-control advocates would have every citizen in the U.S. turn the other cheek and get it slapped like the first one."

"A lot of things don't make sense," grumbled Civalier, glancing in the rearview mirror. "Like this deal. Personally, I don't see why we couldn't ID ourselves as ONI in case of trouble. Undercover is one thing, but operating without any legal authority on a trailing assignment is carrying secrecy too damned far."

Camellion settled back in the seat and folded his arms. "I agree. After today there are going to be some changes."

Mason Shiptonn drove south through the park on Beach. He turned east on Park Road, then north on 16th Street, which became Alaska Avenue as, just west of Walter Reed Army Medical Center, it moved northeast. Alaska Avenue ended in Silver Springs. It was in Silver Springs that Shiptonn stopped. He parked on Jefferson Street, walked a block and a half and went into the Silver Slipper Restaurant. Ten minutes later, Philip Moore and Sandra Jukasta went into the Silver Slipper and were politely informed by the *maître d'hôtel* that it would be an hour or more before a table would be available. After all, most people made reservations.

Sandra Jukasta hurried to the ladies' lounge, went into a stall and, after making sure that the stall on either side was empty, took a walkie-talkie from her shoulder bag and contacted Cherry Wine, who was in charge of the operation. Quickly she explained the situation.

"Where are the others?" asked Camellion who, with Civalier, was just pulling into Silver Springs.

"Rice and Henderson are watching the front entrance," reported Sandra. "Woodside and Yesley are watching the parking lot. Gann and Foutch are keeping an eye on the rear entrance. Any special instructions?"

"That's a good spread-out," Camellion said. "All you and Moore can do is watch the subject. We'll join Woodside and Yesley in the parking lot."

3

"What do Moore and I do when a table becomes available?"

The Death Merchant smiled. "In that case, you and he have dinner."

"At the prices they charge at this place?"

"Charge it to a rich relative, say your Uncle Sam."

Sandra hesitated. "Is that an order?"

"It is. I'll see that Moore is reimbursed—out."

Mason Shiptonn, having spent 52 minutes at the dinner table, was paying his chèck as a waiter was showing a fuming Sandra Jukasta and Philip Moore to a table. Shiptonn, however, did not return to his car. Instead, he turned the corner, walked a block on Hudson Street and went into the Romantic Melody, a fancy cocktail lounge. An impatient John Rice and Lincoln Henderson sauntered in—separately—a short time later, Rice going to the end of the bar closest to the door, Henderson taking a booth, both watching Shiptonn who was sitting alone toward the inner end of the bar.

In the meanwhile, Sandra Jukasta again hurried to the ladies' lounge of the Silver Slipper and again contacted Richard Camellion, who was parked half a block from Shiptonn's car on Jefferson Street. John Rice made contact with Cherry Wine from the men's room of the Romantic Melody.

Shiptonn left the Romantic Melody at 8:37, walked back to his Mustang on Jefferson Street and drove to St. George Square. After turning on the square, he headed north on Georgia Avenue, which was actually the multilaned Route 97. A quarter of a mile behind Shiptonn were agents Yesley and Woodside. Next in line were Rice and Henderson, Gann and Foutch, then Camellion and Civalier and finally Moore and Jukasta.

In each car, each agent next to the driver wore a very special pair of glasses. The reason was that the bumper beeper, no larger than a bean and dropped into Shiptonn's gas tank at 4:45, was powered by the action of the gasoline on a certain type of silicon chip, this form of power giving the tiny transmitter a working life of only 3 hours and 14 minutes. The bumper beeper in Shiptonn's car was now dead. However, it was the Death Merchant who had foreseen the possibility that

4

Shiptonn might take longer than 3 hours and 14 minutes to get to where he was going. Accordingly, the tires of Shiptonn's Mustang had been coated with a special substance that, when viewed through the special Ouffa glasses, glowed with a greenish phosphorescence. Now the Death Merchant and the other agents wearing Ouffa glasses saw luminescent tracks where the Mustang's tires had rolled over the pavement.

Driving leisurely, Shiptonn went only half a mile on Georgia Avenue. He then made a left turn onto Colesville Road, a two-lane blacktop, driving southwest until he reached 16th Street. At this point, as Shiptonn turned north on 16th, agents Yesley and Woodside dropped back.

Shiptonn drove the short distance to the East-West Highway, turned left, went another half-mile, then made another left on the local blacktop that led to Rosemary Hills, a rather secluded village favored by retired military men. Agents Rice and Henderson now continued to drive west on the East-West Highway, while Gann and Foutch tailed Shiptonn. The Death Merchant and Civalier speeded up.

Eighteen minutes after Mason Shiptonn drove into Rosemary Hills, Foutch contacted the Death Merchant on the radio, his voice low but containing notes of excitement. "He finally stopped. He parked his car in front of a house at 314 Elm Way."

"But you didn't see him go into the house?" Camellion asked.

"No, but he must have. The houses are set far apart, big yards on either side. He'd hardly park in front of one house and go into another, although he could have, as a precautionary measure."

"OK. Park several blocks away. Mr. C. and I will take over."

Rex Civalier glanced anxiously at the Death Merchant who was hanging up the mike. "What's our next move?" he asked. He felt slightly uneasy when Camellion opened the glove compartment, took out a silencer and began to attach it to the extended barrel of a Smith & Wesson 9mm auto-loader. Every now and then Camellion glanced at the phosphorescent tire tracks, to make sure that he and Civalier were on the right course.

"I'll have a look at the house," Camellion said, iron in his voice.

A deep frown was born on Civalier's forehead. "You mean, get out of the car and go into the yard? Isn't that pretty damned risky?"

"Do you know of a better way?"

Civalier didn't; he didn't reply either.

"When we get to the house, go on down half a block and park," Camellion said. "I'll walk back." He finished screwing on the silencer, shoved the S & W auto-pistol into a custom-made shoulder holster, made specially to receive a silenced pistol, took off the Ouffa glasses and handed them to Civalier, who put them on.

It was comparatively easy for Civalier to follow the glowing tire tracks and find Elm Way. Soon they were passing number 314 and saw that the two-story house—its front facing south—had light green siding, a dark green roof and a columned front porch that extended the entire width of the building. On each side of the large front yard tall bridal wreath hedges served as boundaries, separating the grounds from the properties next door. In the front, just beyond the public sidewalk, was a red-leaf barberry hedge. Four sugar maples were in the front yard, their luxuriant foliage already tinted orange, gold and scarlet by the autumn temperatures. Several lights were on downstairs. The upstairs was dark.

"I can go a block and turn off," Civalier suggested. "That way we'll be parked on another street. How about it?"

"Good idea," said Camellion. "All I want to do is make sure that Shiptonn is at the house. Then we can start an investigation of the owner and put a twenty-four-hour watch on the place."

"Two men are better than one," Civalier said. "I should go with you."

"Two men would appear more suspicious," Camellion said. "Besides, I want you to act as a monitor. Once I leave the car, if I'm not back in a half-hour, you call the other boys and come on in—and I mean come inside the house."

"Oh boy," sighed Civalier, "and us without a search warrant. That could be sticky, more sticky than fly paper."

"Let me worry about it," Camellion said, smiling. "There's a lot going on you don't know about. Don't ask me to explain."

* * *

Five minutes later, Rex Civalier had parked on Vine Street, Camellion had walked around the corner and was headed toward number 314 on the opposite side of the street, which, with lights in the middle and at each end, was well lighted. Cars were on both sides of the street but, as far as Camellion could tell, were devoid of occupants.

He crossed the street at an angle, wishing he had brought a light topcoat, for the air was chilly. He decided that there was only one way to approach the house—the direct method. *If I get cute on this creepy-crawler caper and go sneaking through backyards, someone might see me, or I might run into a barking dog. At least there isn't any moon.*

Walking at a moderate pace, Camellion reached 314 Elm Way, as indicated by the large white numbers on the green mailbox atop a wooden post. Nonchalantly, he turned into the opening between the red-leaf barberry hedge and started up the flagstone walk.

The danger now was that someone inside the house might see him. Drapes were pulled over the lighted windows downstairs, but who was to say that someone wasn't watching from the darkened windows, upstairs and downstairs?

What do I do if the drapes are pulled on the south side? I can't go inside. Even if I could get away with it, I'd tip my hand.

Six feet from the stone steps of the low front porch, he darted to his right and ran to the southeast corner of the large dwelling. He paused and listened: nothing, only the normal night noises. He looked around: cool darkness, the outlines of clump birch trees between the house and the bridal wreath hedge. Confidently he moved through a flowerbed of mixed-color petunias and approached one of the narrow Colonial-type windows. Drapes had been closed over all three windows. However, the drapes were not completely together in the center of the middle window, the result of which was a half-inch crack.

Carefully, his feet trampling the petunias, Camellion moved toward the center window. He was totally unprepared for what happened next.

"Do not move and do not turn around," the voice behind him said in English that was heavily accented. "If you move

7

before I tell you to, I will fire. No one will hear the shot. My weapon has been silenced."

Damn! The position of the voice indicated that the man was at least six feet behind him. *Too far for me to execute any kind of disarming tactic. But why is he waiting?*

He quickly found out why. The man behind him began speaking in an Oriental dialect. *Mandarin Chinese! I'm almost certain!*

Another voice answered in Chinese, a voice with a kind of tinny quality. The Chinese behind the Death Merchant was speaking into a walkie-talkie, reporting his catch and receiving orders from another agent inside the house.

"Move backward," the Chinese ordered. "When you leave the flowerbed, you will turn to the north and walk very slowly. You will place your hands on top of your head. Do not attempt any sudden moves. I can see you clearly and am an excellent shot."

The damned Chinese's a pro! Camellion thought. *He's keeping his distance and not taking chance one. Fate—do something!*

Fate was sound asleep, because the Chinese gunman forced Camellion to the rear of the house, then made him stand three feet in front of the door on the back porch. Silently the door opened from the inside. There, against the background of light, stood two white men, each joker holding a gun, the big man with a big mouth and tan suit clutching a Colt Trooper .357 Magnum, the other man, who had a double chin and a beer-barrel gut, holding a Smith & Wesson stainless steel .38.

The two hoods backed away, and the gunman behind Camellion ordered, "Inside."

A few minutes later, the Death Merchant, the two hoods and the Chinese gunman were in a study that had floor-to-ceiling bookcases on the west and the north walls. A zebra-skin rug was in the center of the hardwood floor. A cream-colored couch was by the east windows, a beige velvet divan in front of the south-side windows. Three comfortable, cream-colored, stuffed easy chairs were grouped in front of the two couches. Close to the west-side door between the bookcases was a television set, with a Sony videotape viewer on top of it.

Mason Shiptonn sat toward the west end of the beige divan,

looking as normal as the average man on the street. If he had been programmed, he certainly didn't show it.

Another Chinese sat in one of the easy chairs. He stood up and turned around the instant Camellion and the three other men entered the room. Middle-aged, he had a moon-round face, intelligent eyes, thick black hair, neatly combed and tinged with gray at the temples, and wore an expensive dark gray sports coat, with shirt and trousers to match. He could have been a prosperous Chinese-American businessman, from New York, L.A. or Frisco. The Death Merchant would have bet his 2½ square inches in hell that he wasn't.

Moonface looked at Camellion with a cold stare beneath heavy eyebrows and rattled off a stream of Chinese at the other Oriental. He then regarded Camellion solemnly. "Your coming here was most unwise," he said, without the slightest trace of an accent. "Naturally you are an agent of the United States Navy's Office of Naval Intelligence—and keep your hands on your head. Or Mr. Yang will be forced to shoot you in one of your legs."

He turned and looked at Mason Shiptonn.

"Do you know him? Have you seen him before?"

Shiptonn shook his head. "He's a total stranger to me," he said.

He sounds normal, too, the Death Merchant thought. Could it be that he's not programmed? On the other hand, if he knowingly and of his own free will stole the invisibility file on the U.S.S. Eldridge, he couldn't have passed the narcohypnosis[1] test with such flying colors. Grojean and Stavover could be right. Maybe the Commies have found a way to 'manufacture' the perfect Manchurian Candidate!

During that very short time, Camellion's mind had been racing for a solution. Moonface, who was evidently the boss, stood in front of him, between two of the easy chairs. To Camellion's right, five feet in front of him, was Big Mouth and his .357 Magnum. At the same distance, to the Death Merchant's left, was Beer-Barrel Gut. Behind Camellion, Yang had moved in closer. Camellion, estimating that Yang was less

---

1. The use of drugs to induce hypnosis. One of these drugs is Thorazine.

9

than four feet away, did some quick thinking. He was lightning fast and knew it. *All I need is the opportunity.*

Moonface turned back to face Camellion. "I think you will be only too glad to tell us what we want to know after Yang is finished dislocating your bones. He's a specialist at the art of extracting the maximum of pain from the human body, and oh yes, this house does have a soundproof room in the basement."

He glanced at the man to Camellion's right. "Search him for weapons."

Yang spoke up. "Keep your hands on your head and don't move."

Camellion, sensing Yang moving slightly closer, tensed himself, kept his hands on his head and didn't resist as the big man with the big, wide mouth first shoved his .357 Magnum into a shoulder holster, then spread open Camellion's suit coat. The man's eyes widened as he pulled the Smith & Wesson, with its attached 4-inch-long silencer, from the special holster.

"Well now," he grinned, glancing tauntingly at Camellion, "look at what I've found."

Holding the pistol by the butt, the hood turned to show Moonface what he had found—and that's when the Death Merchant made his move.

Executing three movements, Camellion first shot out his left hand in a *Shito-Ryu* Karate *Yon Hon Nukite* four-finger spear stab. At exactly the same time that his four fingers stabbed into the side of Big Mouth's neck with such force that his hand was almost buried to its main knuckles, he executed his second and third movements: The thumb and forefinger of his right hand went to the back of his neck, he tossed himself to the right and spun to face Yang and Beer Gut.

Camellion had moved with such unbelievable speed that Big Mouth, who had dropped the pistol with the silencer and had begun to choke to death, had not yet had time to start to sink to the floor; nor did Beer Gut have time to fire the stainless steel .38 revolver in his right hand. During that mini-slice of a single moment, Beer Gut froze in surprise, his mind made blank by the unexpected.

Yang was slightly faster than the two hoods by a hundredth of a second. He fired by instinct, by sheer reflex, the silencer on the Chinese T-51 making a *bazitttt* sound, its 7.62mm bullet streaking within a few inches of Camellion's stomach. Continuing on its hot way, the slug zipped through the coat of Big Mouth, who was falling to the floor, narrowly missed hitting Moonface's left side, and struck Mason Shiptonn just below the left shoulder, causing the man to cry out in pain and alarm and fall sideways on the beige velvet divan.

While Moonface struggled to retain his composure, Yang did his best to swing the T-51 to the right, toward the Death Merchant. He was a fraction of a second too slow. Camellion had pulled the 8½-inch-long sheet metal punch from its holster on his back and now threw it by the handle when Yang was in the middle of the turn. Carried forward by the weight of its all metal handle, the ice pick-like blade buried itself in the right side of the Chinaman's chest.

"Uhhhhhhaaaa!" Yang gurgled out another cry, wobbled on his feet and, eyes bulging, made a final effort to raise the pistol. But he was attempting too much with too little.

As Camellion executed a perfectly timed Tae Kwon Do Hyung *Ap Chagi* front snap kick that broke Beer Gut's right wrist and sent the S & W .38 flying backward out of his hand, his left arm streaked out in a *Shuto Uke* sword-hand block that knocked Yang's right arm to Yang's left, away from Camellion. Again the silencer made a *bazitttt* sound, but this time the bullet bored harmlessly into the floor.

Now the Death Merchant's concern was Moonface, who had adjusted to the unexpected change of events and who, apparently unarmed, was moving toward the west door between the bookcases.

"*Hana! Dool! Set!*"—one, two, three in Korean—muttered Camellion. While his right hand jerked the Chinese pistol from Yang's dying hand, he jumped forward and this time let Beer Gut have a *Mawashi Geri* roundhouse kick squarely in the face. The man's double chin wobbled like a flag in a hurricane. There was a crushing sound as his lower jawbone snapped. Blood flew, teeth snapped off and the upper jaw was fractured. Demolished, Beer Gut staggered back, choking sounds pouring from his bloody mouth.

In another instant, Camellion spun around and snapped up the T-51 pistol, knowing that Moonface was only half a second away from getting a bullet in the spine. He pulled the

11

trigger as Moonface darted through the west side door. Nothing happened. The weapon had jammed. The Death Merchant dropped the useless pistol and darted over to where his own S & W silenced 9mm automatic lay on the floor. By then it was too late—Moonface had slammed the door and was gone.

The thought was a bitter one: *I've blown this deal*! He hurried across the room, picked up Beer Gut's stainless steel .38 and ran to the door on the west side. But he had more sense than to open it and go crashing into—what? Instead he put a couple of 9mm slugs through the door, just in case anyone was on the other side. Just as quickly he went across the room and stabbed the north side door with a couple of 9mm bullets, all the while wondering how many other people were in the house. Had Moonface gone after more men, or was he in full retreat?

Camellion glanced around the room. Shiptonn was lying on his right side, moaning softly, his face half-buried in a beige velvet cushion. Big Mouth, lying on his back, had a hideous expression on his face, the contorted look of a man who had fought desperately to obtain air and had lost the battle. Close by was Yang, the right leg of the corpse doubled under it. The dead man looked as if he had sat down, then toppled forward.

Fighting a hideous hell of excruciating pain, Beer Gut was on all fours, his head hanging down, blood pouring out of his mouth and nose onto the edge of the zebra-skin rug.

"You're going to talk your head off!" Camellion said just before he tapped Beer Gut over the head. "You're going to tell us every itty-bitty thing we want to know." He shoved the stainless steel .38 into his belt, went across the room, switched off the light, then walked over to the beige velvet divan. He first pulled out the end to his right, ignoring the moans of Mason Shiptonn, who almost rolled off to the floor. He then went to the left and and pulled it three feet from the wall. He was crouching behind the left end when he heard a car roar out of the driveway to the west of the house. *Unless it's a trap, there must have been only the two Chinese and the two hoods. No one else is in the house—maybe. Just the same, I'll wait for Civalier and the other ONI boys—and one woman.*

Waiting patiently, watching both doors in the semi-darkness, the Death Merchant speculated over the chain of

12

events that had brought him to this house in Rosemary Hills, Maryland.

Three months earlier, one of the top secrets of the United States Government had vanished, an ultra-secret file from the Master Safe Room of the Office of Naval Intelligence. Labeled BLUEPRINT: INVISIBILITY, the file was a complete report of an experiment that the United States Navy had conducted during October, 1943, an experiment regarding electronic camouflage—*invisibility*.

Scientists had made the U.S.S. *Eldridge,* a destroyer, disappear from the Philadelphia Navy Yard.

"It wasn't as if the vessel were still there but that no one could see it," Courtland Grojean had explained to Camellion. "They not only made the ship invisible, but they teleported it to the Navy base in Norfolk, Virginia, and made it reappear—all this within three seconds."

The experiment, conducted by the Office of Naval Research, had been a huge success. With one exception: the new kind of electromagnetic field had affected adversely the officers and crew of the U.S.S. *Eldridge.* When the destroyer reappeared in Norfolk, Virginia, some of the officers and crew were stark, raving mad.

There were delayed effects. A week after the experiment, one crew member vanished in front of his wife and two children and was never seen again. Two officers—insane and confined in a secret mental institution—and one crewman—sane and still on board the *Eldridge*—burst into flames and died of spontaneous human combustion on the same day.

Other officers and men would become "stuck in time," or "frozen in the green"—as had been stated in BLUEPRINT: INVISIBILITY. The unfortunate man would disappear; yet he would still be there, "frozen," unable to move.

There were three degrees to this "freezing." In a "slight freeze," the unfortunate man would become visible again within an hour, without any kind of outside help. In a "medium freeze," the victim could be brought back instantly if, when his body began to waver, as if in a heat-mirage, another crewman could reach him in time and "lay on hands." It was from these men that scientists learned that the "freeze in time" involved more than simple invisibility, but was actually

13

a netherworld in which time ceased to exist. The victims "in freeze" could still think and breathe and see, but were like statues in another time continuum, another dimension of existence. Some even reported seeing and talking to strange, alien beings. Ten of the men who had been stuck in slight and medium freeze gradually lost their minds. They too were confined to mental institutions.

"Deep Freeze" was the most hideous of all. These victims could not be brought back to the reality of this time continuum, not until seven months after the last man went into deep freeze—seven long months, $30-million worth of special electronic equipment and a special ship berth. They found the last man to go into deep freeze and returned him to visibility. He was a slobbering idiot. So were the two other men who had gone into deep freeze and were returned.

Other crewmen gradually lost their minds, the strain of not knowing if they would vanish or burst into flames being too much for them to bear. Five committed suicide. Even one of the physicists who had participated in the experiment took his own life, leaving behind a note saying that he was "atoning" for having helped open "the doorway to hell." Two weeks later, his wife and two teenage children died under mysterious circumstances in a "fire of unknown origin."

The Office of Naval Research discontinued the experiments with invisibility and teleportation—the instantaneous transfer of solid objects from one place to another—and tried to pretend that its scientists had not made still another discovery stemming from Einstein's $E = mc^2$, his Unified Field Theory, although there were those dissenters who insisted that, at all costs, the experiment should be continued. In contrast, there were those scientists and intelligence officers who were adamant that the formula and all written evidence of the experiment be destroyed. My God! The atomic bomb had come from $E = mc^2$. But this invisibility and teleportation program tore away the curtain to another universe, to another reality for which man was ill-prepared.

A compromise was reached: The experiment would be terminated, but a complete report would be filed away until such time that it was felt that science had advanced to a stage where the experiment could be reactivated with comparative safety.

Thirty-six years later, the BLUEPRINT: INVISIBILITY file was missing. *The file had been stolen. . . .*

The Office of Naval Intelligence went crazy with frustration, anxiety and fear. The Central Intelligence Agency, National Security Agency and the president's Advisory Board were given reports of the catastrophe, which was particularly serious for two reasons.

One—the vital file, now missing from Falcon-2-S, the Master Safe Room, contained the formula that would enable any foreign power to duplicate the experiment that involved hyperspace, that point in which space and time were reduced to "non-space" and "non-time"—totally annihilated. A billion light years could become a single second, depending on the strength of the hyperfield, and the universe reduced to the size of a pin head.

The CIA, taking over the investigation, grilled the top brass of ONI unmercifully, paying particular attention to the 14 Special Clearance clerks who had had access to Falcon-2-S. Even Admiral Chester Oliver Stavover, the Chief of ONI, was given six different polygraph tests and questioned under narcohypnosis. He and all the others passed with flying colors, including the 14 clerks.

Facts were facts: No one at ONI headquarters had *knowingly* or *consciously* stolen the invisibility file, according to Grojean. As a result of the questioning sessions, he and his staff of Counterintelligence experts had to conclude that an enemy power had perfected a method of manufacturing the "programmed spy," an individual who could perform a mission and not realize that he (or she) was doing it. *The perfect agent*! Even if he were suspected, no amount of questioning, including narcohypnosis, would be able to extract any information, much less a confession, because the information would not be in the conscious mind of the subject. They would beat him to a pulp and get nowhere. The subject himself would believe he was innocent!

Two—somehow over the years the Soviet Union had heard about the invisibility-teleportation experiment. But the CIA learned that the Soviets were convinced that the U.S. Navy had used a submarine and was investigating some magnetic version of the Moebius Strip.[2] The Soviets believed that the Moebius Strip was a powerful magnetic field. As the submarine pursued its course around this invisible strip—turning over completely in the course of each revolution—some electronic device was activated to cut the field in two, as if with a pair of scissors. At this point, the sub vanished, to reappear miles away.

Waiting behind the divan, the Death Merchant smiled a crooked smile. He had finally gotten it out of Grojean why the boss of the CIA's counterintelligence division was so worried: While the CIA was investigating ONI, the National Security agency was conducting its own investigation of both the ONI and the CIA.

Grojean's afraid that some of his own misadventures and CI projects will be dragged out of the dark cellar and exposed to the scorching light of day. I don't blame him. He has a lot of secrets.

2. The Moebius Strip is a "one-sided" ring of paper, and is easy to make. You simply take a long strip of paper, give one of its ends a half-twist and then glue the two ends of the strip together to form a ring. If you wish to verify that this strip has only one side, take a pencil and draw a line down the center of the strip. You will find that, without having to turn the ring inside out, you can continue the line until it has rejoined its beginning. If you take a pair of scissors and cut along the penciled line, the strip will unfold into one large ring.

Chapter Two

The world headquarters of the Central Intelligence Agency is located in the rolling countryside close to Langley, Virginia. The Company, however, does have numerous offices in Washington, D.C. Some of these are "open," i.e. undisguised and not behind a cover; others are "closed," i.e. disguised as being something else.

Ronk's Stationers, Inc. at 2116 Constitution Avenue was such a "closed" Company office, with the owner, four clerks and the two stock boys all working for the Company; but only Alvin Ronk, the owner and manager, was a case officer and/ or a career employee.

Used primarily for meetings between high-level officers of the various branches of American Intelligence, Ronk's Stationers had two entrances into the large meeting room concealed in the basement. A "customer" could go into Mr. Ronk's office and go down a flight of steel steps, the top of which was concealed behind a metal bookcase in the owner/ manager's office. Or one could drive into the large garage in the rear, open a section of the brick wall on the south side and use those steps. No matter which entrance was used, he or she always found himself—when he reached the bottom of the steps—in a small anteroom containing only a steel door. A red push-button was in the center of the door. Below the button was a horizontal slot 2½ inches long. Certain high-level agents did not have to press the red button and identify themselves to the man on duty. They simply inserted a card, on which was printed the fingerprints of the little fingers of their left and right hands, into the slot. They counted to ten, then removed the card. Five seconds later the door would automatically swing open.

Six days after the Rosemary Hills operation, an elderly gentleman—bald, wearing eyeglasses with plastic frames, walking with a limp and using a cane whose handle was a brass duck's head—walked into Ronk's Stationers, Inc. and asked to speak to Mr. Ronk. Five minutes later, having given Ronk the correct code phrase, the Death Merchant pressed the red button in the steel door.

Courtland Grojean and Admiral Chester Stavover had arrived 15 minutes earlier and had gone down to the secret room by means of the garage steps.

At the moment, Admiral Stavover was not the least bit pleased at finding out how he had been tricked by Grojean in order to lead the CIA to Mason Shiptonn, one of the fourteen clerks who had access to the invisibility file.

"The idea was Camellion's," Grojean said. He glanced at Camellion. "Go ahead. Tell him."

"It was a matter of logic, Admiral," the Death Merchant said. "Only nineteen people had access to Falcon-2-S—you, your four assistants, and the fourteen clerks. I worked on the premise that one of the nineteen had to be guilty."

"Why?" demanded Stavover. "All nineteen passed the narcohypnosis tests." Balding, almost six feet tall and spare of frame, Chester Stavover stared suspiciously at the Death Merchant with gray eyes. "Or do you believe Grojean's theory about a 'programmed' agent?"

Annoyed, Courtland Grojean interjected, "We were at a dead end, Chet. We had to start someplace—and it seems we were right. Shiptonn is programmed, although we don't have concrete proof, not yet. We'll get into that later. Go on, Camellion."

The Death Merchant toyed with the cup of coffee in front of him on the table. "I assumed that one of the nineteen was programmed and that the enemy would also have implanted an unconscious mechanism that would respond to danger. It was for that reason that Mr. Grojean told you, several weeks ago, that the CIA was very close to discovering who had stolen the file. We knew—"

"But I told only my assistants!" protested Stavover.

"I felt that one of them would gossip and that the vital

18

news of the impending arrest would reach the fourteen clerks. I was convinced that the news would trigger the unconscious protective mechanism in the guilty party and that he would seek instructions from whomever had done the job. As you may have guessed by now, the scheme worked."

"We were watched, kept under close surveillance, day and night," Stavover said, a slight smile on his thin lips.

"And we had all your home phones tapped and your homes bugged," Grojean said smugly. "My boys even tailed the wives."

Stavover tapped ash from his cigar and looked at the Death Merchant. "What occurred to point the finger at Shiptonn? He's been with ONI for thirteen years and has a Special Clearance rating."

"No one acted the least bit suspicious, until eight days ago," Camellion said. "On his way home, Shiptonn stopped and made a phone call from a public telephone booth. We figured he was reporting what he had heard, that the Company was about to close the net, and was getting instructions. After he made the call, he went straight home and stayed there. I concluded he'd make his move the next evening, after he left ONI headquarters. And he did. And we did."

"Yes, but we still don't have any actual proof that Shiptonn is our man," said Stavover cynically. He added quickly before Grojean or Camellion could respond, "I agree that something damned strange is going on and admit that it's more than likely that Shiptonn underwent some mental metamorphosis."

"So what else is new?" asked Grojean.

"We gave Shiptonn five different polygraph tests yesterday," Stavover said, "and they proved he's telling the truth. He doesn't remember going to the house. He doesn't remember the two Chinese. All he remembers is leaving ONI headquarters after work. He acts like he's in a dream world."

"When are you going to try narcohypnosis?" Grojean wanted to know.

As usual, the 60-ish boss of the CIA's CI Division was dressed in an expensive suit and vest of European cut. His loafers, imported from Great Britain, were of oryx gazelle skin.

"We can't use drugs until the doctors give us permission." Carefully, Stavover placed his cigar in the slot of the large

19

green ashtray. "I'm told it will be another two weeks. As you know, we have Shiptonn in one of our hospitals, and there's three men with him, day and night."

His curious eyes went to Camellion, who sat across from him at the table, then swung back to Grojean. "Why did you use ONI agents instead of your own case officers on the Shiptonn operation? I'm curious."

Grojean's voice was flat and accusatory. "You insisted on keeping Uncle out of it if something went wrong and the regular Washington Bluecoats or the Maryland state police got into the act. I wasn't about to place any of my COs in such a compromising position."

Stavover tried to shrug off Grojean's resentment with a big smile.

"Camellion didn't seem to mind the risk," he said. "I don't know why—"

"I'd have terminated any cop who might have butted in," Camellion interrupted. "I wouldn't have wanted to, and I wouldn't have enjoyed killing them, but I would have had to. Grojean's case officers would have had second thoughts about wasting civilians."

Stavover stared distastefully for a moment at the Death Merchant, then said in a clipped tone, "Fortunately, everything went smoothly."

"Yes, 'fortunately,'" Camellion commented, thinking of the risk that he and Civalier and other ONI agents had taken. Rex Civalier and four other agents had parked out in front of the house and crept into the dwelling, after shooting off the front and the rear locks of the front and the back doors. Two of the agents had supported the dead hood between them, as though the corpse were a drunk, and had "walked" him right out the front door and down the front flagstone walk. Two other agents had supported the hood with the kicked-in face. Rex Civalier had lugged Yang, but only after the Death Merchant pulled the metal punch from the dead man's chest and wiped the blade on the coat of the corpse.

Camellion had carried out the wounded Shiptonn.

No one had called the police. Either none of the neighbors had attached any importance to so many men going in and out of the house, or else they didn't give a damn. Camellion and the agents had piled into cars and driven back to D.C.

Grojean finished lighting one of the Virginia Circle cigarettes he bought regularly from Nat Sherman's in New York and said enthusiastically, "We know where we have been. Now let's decide where we're going from here."

He glanced at Camellion, who was sipping coffee and munching candied apple slices. The Death Merchant seemed to be amused but tolerant.

Admiral Stavover, engrossed in a ten-page report that Grojean had brought with him, didn't answer. He wouldn't find anything in the report that Grojean and Camellion didn't already know.

Identification found on the dead Chinese indicated he was Huan-yi Yang, a minor official of the People's Republic of China's delegation to the United Nations. Officially, he was one of the assistants to the Red Chinese's Attaché of Agriculture. Unofficially, he was probably a member of Communist China's 3rd Bureau, the Red Chinese intelligence service, as indicated by the fact that the delegates at the U.N. hadn't reported him missing.

Fingerprints of the two white men identified them as New York gangsters. The dead man was Frank "The Boot" Gerstein, a thug who had specialized in kicking his victims to death. The man still alive, whose jaws were now wired together, was Karl Huse. Both men were associates of members of a non-Mafia mob headed by Charles "Blackeye" Franzese.

The bodies of Gerstein and Yang had been secretly cremated.

Karl Huse had talked. Four days after he had been taken to a secret CIA hospital, a "rest home" in Wheaton just north of D.C., Camellion and three other CIA agents had gone to Huse's room, shoved a pad of paper and a pencil into the frightened man's hands and given him the blunt, brutal facts of his situation. He could either talk—in this case write—and tell them what they wanted to know, or he could face the results of his refusal.

Huse quickly scribbled on the pad: *Where am I?*

"You might as well be in hell," Camellion said. "Will you cooperate with us?"

Huse shook his head. No, he would not.

"Suit yourself."

Camellion, reaching into his coat, nodded to one of the

CIA case officers, who quickly jerked back the sheet covering Huse's legs and stomach. Camellion pulled a .22 Ruger auto-pistol, with a silencer attached, and shot the astonished mobster through the instep of his left foot. Huse made a strangled noise of agony and his body jerked as blood began pouring from the top of his foot.

One of the CIA men rang for a nurse. Another said, "The bullet didn't come out through the sole. It's still in his foot."

Camellion looked down at the agonized gangster, who was twisting in pain. "We'll be back tomorrow. If you still refuse, I'll shoot you in the right foot. The next day I'll start on your kneecaps, then your elbows. After that, you'll probably be dead of shock."

A young and pretty nurse came into the room, walked over to the bed and looked at Huse's shattered foot. "Oh my! I see he's had an accident. I'll get the doctor."

"See you tomorrow, old chap," Camellion said as he and the other COs left the room.

The next day, Huse couldn't write answers fast enough.

He was not acquainted with the two Chinese; he had never seen them until he and Gerstein met the two men in Washington, at Union Station, just off Massachusetts Avenue. The four of them had then driven to the house in Rosemary Hills.

Why had the two men come from New York to Washington, D.C.?

Huse wrote furiously on the pad—to meet the two Chinese and follow their orders. Barney "The Pig" Gindow had given each of them $1,000 and had told them to meet the two Orientals and follow their orders. The Chinese wanted a man hit, and Huse and Gerstein would do the job. Gerstein was a licensed pilot. He and Huse would rent a private plane, fly out over Chesapeake Bay at night and dispose of the weighted body in the Bay.

Barney "The Pig" Gindow was the right-hand man of Charley "Blackeye" Franzese, who was the lover of Soraya Duncan, a beautiful woman who operated a high-class "escort" service in New York. At this point the report became more interesting. For over a year, CIA men had observed, with keen interest, various members of U.N. missions wining and dining the lovely young ladies who worked for Soraya Duncan and her Olympia Escort Bureau.

22

*　*　*

Admiral Stavover closed the blue file and pushed it toward Grojean.

"I am somewhat amazed at the vulgar nicknames many of these hoods have," Stavover said. Smiling slightly he reached for his cigar, which had gone out.

"Back in World War Two I knew a fellow named Marvin Mantlemann," Grojean said. "We ended up calling him 'Marvin Mantelpiece.' "

The Death Merchant crumpled the empty box of candied apple slices.

"When it comes to nicknames, most mobsters are like children. The nicknames children bestow on each other can confer power. Like ancient Rome, the playground marks off the inner core of citizens from the barbarians and those of lesser social standing To be nicknamed is to be seen as having an attribute that entitles one to social attention within the group, even if that attention is unpleasant. Those who haven't any nicknames have no social existence. They are the non-people."

Stavover breathed deeply through his nose, and his mouth broke into a full smile. "Perhaps. But names like 'The Pig' and 'The Boot,' or 'Blackeye!' Ridiculous!"

"In our world, but not in the world of the mobster," Camellion pointed out. "Most mobster trash have great egos. Take Gindow for instance. He's a big eater, a glutton, and proud of it, and proud of his sobriquet, 'The Pig.' Or Gerstein, 'The Boot,' which signifies his ability to kick an opponent to death. As for 'Blackeye,' Franzese acquired that cognomen because he wears dark glasses constantly, day and night. He has to. He can't stand light. For years he's suffered from *retinitis pigmentosa*, an eye disease that slowly destroys the light-sensitive cells of the retina—the rods and cones."

"We've done a lot of high-powered investigating these past four days," Grojean said. "Franzese will be blind in four or five years." He laughed deeply. "Provided Camellion here doesn't kill him within the next few months."

Stavover, who suspected that Camellion was a "contract agent," didn't laugh. After reading an earlier report of what Camellion had accomplished in the house in Rosemary Hills, he had concluded that Richard Camellion was a one-man crew on a ship of death.

He reached out and tapped the blue folder. "There wasn't anything mentioned abut Philip Armstrong, the owner of the house in Rosemary Hills. Or is Armstrong a blind?"

"He's real. He owns the house. He's a retired psychiatrist from Los Angeles," Grojean said. "He and his wife are vacationing in Paris. They'll find quite a surprise in store for them when they return to the States, provided the Red Chinese don't have them both killed."

"You mean killed before your 'street boys' in Paris fail to put the grab on the Armstrongs?" Stavover said wryly.

Grojean's slight laughter was only a coverup for the black worry eating at his mind. . . . Those damned snoops in National Security were asking dangerous questions, questions that were on the fringe of probing into the CIA's own mind-control experiments, which had begun in 1956. Of course, there was no denying that the Company had been deeply involved in behavior modification experiments. Those big-mouthed, half-witted liberals, who were convinced that every citizen should be privy to CIA secrets, had seen to that. In 1978 the Company had been forced to release 50 documents to the ridiculous Center for National Security Studies. Ha! What did college professors, many of whom were sympathetic to Communism, know about Counterintelligence, about the real world of Intelligence and Espionage? Those documents had been very damaging. They contained such headings as PROGRESS ON BLUEBIRD: AN ANALYSIS OF CONFESSIONS IN RUSSIAN TRIALS: EXPLOITATION OF PRISONER OF WAR RETURNEES; ARTICHOKE CONFERENCE, 21 MAY 1953: CONVERSATION WITH GIBBONS; MKULTRA FILES: INFLUENCING HUMAN BEHAVIOR: FRANK R. OLSON.

Particularly damaging was the report that told of Olsen jumping out of a hotel window after a case officer slipped LSD into his drink. The sob sisters had had a field day. Had Olsen committed suicide because the LSD had driven him crazy, or had he been murdered because he was about to reveal those who had tried to make him crazy?

Blue pencils flew all over the place at the Center in Langley. What? Too many deletions, for reasons of "national security?" No problem. Burn the documents.

24

Grojean was very worried: The same thing was happening all over again, only this time it was much more serious. This time it was NSA doing the snooping—NSA, whose highly trained agents were not as easily fooled as those egghead professors who couldn't have found their own behinds with both hands in the Hall of Mirrors at Versailles. These NSA agents were wondering why the Company was so intensely interested in hypnotism, in such things as the Thematic Apperception Test and the Hypnotic Induction Profile. Grojean could have told them the reason. He hadn't because it was none of their damned business. He could have told them that with hypnotism any intelligence service could be sure of its own private messenger—or assassin. A man could be hypnotized in say, Washington, and given a certain message. The message could be both long and intricate, since an intelligent individual, under hypnosis, could memorize an entire book if necessary. A posthypnotic suggestion could be implanted in the subconscious of the subject, by which only a certain person could "dehypnotize" him and obtain the message.

Grojean wasn't too concerned about the files on hypnotism, mind control and assassination. They were safely hidden on microfilm in the secret archives of Q-Department, which officially did not exist. Not even the president of the United States was aware of those files.

Grojean wished certain other files were as invisible. So far the director and the deputy director of the CIA had blocked the efforts of NSA to probe U-SEN-OPER-F.[3] But suppose the president intervened? All hell would break loose and there would be a general investigation of the CIA, especially the covert operations section.

For almost seven years, Grojean and a special group of trusted case officers had plotted and planned to steal the contents of BLUEPRINT: INBISIBILITY. It was vitally necessary. Much to the Navy's embarrassment—the scientists working for the Office of Naval Research didn't realize that men would become invisible while not aboard the U.S.S. *Eldridge* and not under the hyperfield's influence—it had stumbled upon a tremendous secret. Either by accident or design, the scientists had succeeded in creating a very special kind of

3. Ultra Sensitive Operational Files.

force-field invisibility and teleportation. Without realizing it, the Navy had opened the door to an infinite number of possibilities that were mind-boggling.

Did the results of the experiment indicate the existence of other dimensions in time and space? Apparently this was the case. The hyperspace quality and/or factor could be a practical way for man to reach the stars—literally any star anywhere in the entire universe!

Another possibility was that continued work with the experiment could provide the answer to any mysterious disappearances taking place in such deadly areas as the Bermuda Triangle and the Hell Sea near southern Japan.

Grojean's thoughts flashed back to one scientist the CIA had tracked down several years ago—Doctor Hugo Plogg, Ph.D., a physicist who had taken part in the highly secret experiment.

"I wasn't on board the ship," Plogg had told the three case officers. "I can only tell you what the men who *were* later reported. They said that when the hyperfield started to be felt, a hazy green light became evident. Soon the entire vessel—the inside as well as the outside—was clouded in this green haze, and the ship, along with its personnel, began to disappear from sight of those watching on the dock. I was one of those watching. I'm convinced that the basis of what happened will eventually be proved through Einstein's Unified Field Theory."

Green haze? Survivors of incidents in the Bermuda Triangle often spoke of a mysterious green mist that appeared before the disappearance of ships and planes. Some pilots had even reported outrunning such a mysterious green-tinged mist.

Was it possible that all the ships and planes that had vanished were "stuck in time," with passengers not even realizing what had happened to them? Were the ships and planes and people condemned to sail and fly on forever, to a destination they would never reach? It was possible. Non-space and non-time! Forever could be a single second.

Grojean finally answered Admiral Stavover. "The last report I received from Paris was this morning. My men haven't found the Armstrongs. But they're far down on the list of

26

priorities. How and when and where Shiptonn was programmed is our number-one problem."

He swung half-around in his chair and looked at Camellion, who had left the table, crossed the bunker-like room and was pouring another cup of coffee from an automatic drip coffee maker on a small table.

"Camellion, bring me a cup—black, if you please," Grojean called out.

The Death Merchant nodded and reached for another cup. "How about you, Admiral?"

"Thank you, no." Stavover sounded sad. "I've an ulcer and coffee is on the 'No' list."

With a mug in each hand, Camellion returned to the table, placed one of the mugs in front of Courtland Grojean, then sat down, saying, "Speaking of priorities, I think we're in agreement that it was Shiptonn the two dirt-bags from New York were supposed to snuff?"

"I'd say so," Grojean said. "The only reason Shiptonn was alive when you arrived was that the two Chinese hadn't had time to complete their questioning. Clever the way that bird Yang was stationed outside. They were professional all the way."

"It's also safe to deduce that their system of programming, be it hypnosis or whatever, is limited," Camellion said. "Otherwise they could have programmed Shiptonn to commit suicide."

Admiral Stavover shifted his weight in the chair and leaned forward, a gloomy expression on his face. "I agree that Shiptonn was no doubt the target of the two hoods, but I'm leary of the theory that Charles Franzese and Soraya Duncan are operating a sort of American 'Swallow'[4] ring for the Red Chinese. Why, such an operation would be too obvious. Even if the escort service were a legitimate enterprise, some

_____

4. A female KGB prostitute spy. The male homosexual spies are known as Ravens. These agents are recruited and trained by the KGB's Second Chief Directorate, which concerns itself with the subversion of foreign visitors and the regulation of the lives of Soviet citizens at home. There are 12 departments in the Second Chief Directorate. The first six are concerned with Soviet-based foreign diplomats. It's the First Department that deals with American diplomats. For obvious reasons, it is the largest.

27

suspicious-minded foreign agent would see the young women with various delegates and think the worst. No way. I can't buy it."

Grojean's eyes darted to the Death Merchant. "You know, he has a point. Just imagine what the KGB, or MFS[5] or STB[6] would think if they saw one of their nationals living it up with an American woman, much less a 'capitalist' whore from an escort agency?"

"You're absolutely correct," Camellion said. "However, both of you are forgetting that what is true of the Commies isn't true—unfortunately in this case—of our allies. A lot of U.N. delegates from Western nations are only too happy to have a roll in the hay with a good-looking American woman, prostitute or otherwise. No doubt that's how the Red Chinese got to Shiptonn when he was in town, in New York, nine months ago. How remains to be seen."

Admiral Stavover cleared his throat and his face fell. He didn't like the implication that one of his people could have loose morals.

"It's difficult to accept," he said. "Shiptonn is a family man. There isn't anything in his Psychological Profile Index File to indicate he could be subject to immoral behavior."

"Ostrich crap!" Camellion said. He smiled and made a motion with his left hand. "Shiptonn's only human. Any man can be lured into the sack by the right woman. Let's be practical. Shiptonn's not any saint."

"Perhaps. But in this case, Shiptonn must have called the escort agency and made an appointment. That would be completely against his character. If there's any truth to Duncan and her girls being end-of-the-line agents[7] for the Chinese, then Shiptonn was probably suckered in somehow. Even that is difficult to believe: He didn't go to the security conference alone. Four others were with him. Three were men. One was

5. *Ministerium für Staatssicherheit.* Ministry for State Security, in East Germany.
6. *Statni Tajna Bezpecnost.* The Czech intelligence service.
7. CIA jargon for a man or woman who carries out an actual espionage operation. These agents work under career intelligence officers and are usually nationals of the nation in which they live.

28

a woman. They and Shiptonn were only in New York for a week."

"So what?" Camellion put down his coffee cup. "Their nights were free, and I'm sure the five didn't hang together like hicks on their first visit to the big city. Somewhere along the line, the enemy got to Shiptonn. And forget about the dolls who work for Duncan. I feel intuitively that they don't know what is really going on. Duncan employs forty-one dolls—far too many to keep that kind of secret."

"At this point, it's all academic," Stavover said, slowly crushing his stub of a cigar in the ashtray. "When are you leaving for New York?"

"Tonight. I'll get in late and get organized before midnight." He smiled at the curious expression that slid over Stavover's face. "It's a matter of circadian rhythms, involving the science of chronobiology. I'm one of the 'Night People. ' But don't expect me to get the file back. By now it's been carted back to Red China by some Chinese diplomat."

"I'm not concerned about the file," Stavover said. "I want the riddle of how it was stolen from ONI headquarters solved. Until we know how it was done, we can't be sure that the secrets in the Mountain[8] are safe."

"Like you said earlier, Chet: It's conjecturable for now," Grojean said. "I'm telling you, though, Mason Shiptonn was programmed. How it was done is just as important as how the file was stolen."

"When we find out how Shiptonn's mental faculties were engineered, we'll know how the file was stolen," offered the Death Merchant. "It's no big deal about how when it comes to the file. Shiptonn went into the room, stuck it under his shirt and walked out, or else he photographed every sheet in the room and then got rid of the original in the shredderburn."

"He couldn't have gotten the folder out of the building," Admiral Stavover replied. "Of that I am positive."

Grojean said, "The most puzzling thing is why he didn't just photograph the sheets of the file and smuggle out the

---

8. A complex on the East Coast, deep inside a mountain where vital documents are kept—in case of World War III.

film. That would have been easy, getting the film out. He could have used a Plan, a hollowed out heel, something on that order. If he hadn't taken the file, if the file hadn't come up missing, we wouldn't be the wiser. He had to have a reason."

"A blind," Camellion said. "The Red Chinese wanted us to miss the file. That's what we must find out. It's like life. You have to play with the cards you've got, and we have a pretty good hand."

"Sure, but only if we win the game," Grojean said bitterly. "The way things are now, we're ahead of the Commies in every way, especially in ELINT.[9] But if the Red Chinese have found a way to manufacture the 'perfect spy,' God help this nation!"

"God help this nation anyhow, considering the unrealistic dumbbells in command." Leaning back and tilting the chair slightly, the Death Merchant chuckled. "We're on a ship of fools whose captain acts more like a pastor than a president. He'd do a helluva lot better if he spent less time in the front pew of the National Cathedral and more time over at the Pentagon with the joint chiefs."

Grojean lighted another Virginia Circle, put the lighter on the table and said with a straight face, "Our leader is simply determined to demonstrate to the world that the U.S. has taken to heart the Christian injunction to 'turn the other cheek.'"

"Unfortunately, the Communists interpret such unrealistic behavior as weakness," Admiral Stavover said crossly. "We'll never keep ahead of them with a philosophy that stems from 'The wrong shall fail' and 'The right prevail.' A Born-Again Christian is no match for a realistic Communist."

Camellion looked at Grojean. "Who's handling this operation for the Company in New York?" he asked, changing the subject.

"His name is William Fieldhouse," Grojean said cautiously, more than realizing that Camellion was a fanatic about the men with whom he worked, especially the head case officer.

9. Electronic intelligence, i.e. the gathering of intelligence by means of satellites, spy planes, video monitors and other technological means.

"He's a young guy, but don't let his age bother you. He's had a lot of kill experience in Vietnam and an inborn talent for Intelligence."

"Just so he's not an ex-minister or an ex-agent of the ATF,"[10] Camellion said firmly. "The first don't want you to take a drink even to put out a fire—and no smoking even if you catch fire. Ex-ATF agents are no better than thugs who delight on stepping on human rights. I never work with liars and hypocrites; they always turn out to be cowards. You can't depend on them."

Camellion detected that special self-satisfied look that crept into Grojean's eyes. The same quality was in the CI chief's voice.

"You and Fieldhouse will work fine together. He also shares your great 'love' of liberals and trash in the Federal bureaucracy."

Grojean glanced at his wristwatch. "I've got to leave. I'm due at another meeting in an hour."

"And I've got to pack," Camellion said. He watched Grojean get up from the table, walk over to the disposal machine, turn it on, then insert the blue folder, containing the report, into the slot. There was a *werrrrrrrrrr*-ing sound as the report was shredded on its way to the acid dissolvent in the bottom of the machine.

Camellion got to his feet, knowing that his work was cut out for him. All he had to do was find out how the Red Chinese had programmed Shiptonn and how Shiptonn had stolen BLUEPRINT: INVISIBILITY.

All I have to do is accomplish the almost-impossible. . . .

10. The Bureau of Alcohol, Tobacco & Firearms.

Chapter Three

New York is one big cesspool! It's almost as bad as Athens. . . .

The Death Merchant looked through the slit in the parted drapes at the numerous pinpoints of light in the distance, thinking that he was not only in one of the worst polluted cities in the United States but also in one of the most unusual hotels in New York. In fact, the Payson Arms was one of the most uncommon of hotels in the entire country.

Located on Payson Avenue, in the northwest corner of Manhattan Island, the twelve-story hotel was neither the best nor the worst in New York. Due west of the hotel was Inwood Hill Park, through which ran the Henry Hudson Parkway. West of the Parkway was the Hudson River. Twelve blocks to the east was the Harlem River, which moved north, then curved to the west to flow into the much larger Hudson River. One left the Henry Hudson Parkway in Inwood Hill Park and crossed the Henry Hudson Bridge, after which one was in the Bronx.

However, it was not the location of the Payson Arms, nor the area, that contributed to the uniqueness of the hotel. The Payson Arms was uncommon because it was owned by the United States Central Intelligence Agency, although only a score of people knew it. On the surface, the hotel was owned by the Merrick Real Estate Corporation. In turn, Merrick was controlled by Denbow, Raines and Garvey—another holding company owned by Florida General, still another holding company that had been incorporated by Samual L. Kaine and Angela Mataska, two members of the CIA's Proprietary Operations Division.

Nonetheless, the Payson Arms was a legitimate hotel, for the Company preferred investment-fronts that could pay their own way. All sorts of people stopped at the Payson Arms—salesmen, small businessmen, wives with men other than their husbands and husbands with women other than their wives.

The Payson Arms, like many other hotels, had year-round residents. The entire 11th floor housed these elderly men and women, all retired Agency people without families.

The 12th floor was the operational headquarters of the CIA in New York. There were, however, two other regional offices: one on Duane Street, close to the Civic Center in lower Manhattan, the other in Freeport, Long Island.

The hotel had seven elevators. Four were manned, day and night, by operators. The other three were self-service. All seven elevators could go to the 12th floor; yet there wasn't any danger. Should some individual who was not a member of the Company make a mistake and go to the 12th floor, he would be spotted by hidden TV cameras the instant he left the elevators or emerged at the top of the steps. Burglars who specialized in hotels? Over the years, half a dozen goofs had tried to get into rooms on the 12th floor. All six had vanished. . . .

The Payson Arms was unusual in another way. Two of the bellboys—both were case officers—engaged in pimping on the side. If some man checked in and wanted a woman, either Tunney or Simmons could furnish the bed partner. This type of service was a must. Whoever heard of a New York hotel whose bellhops couldn't furnish hookers? Unthinkable! Even the better-class hotels made sure that class dolls "on call" were available. It was all very unofficial, naturally, with management looking the other way while the bell captain and his crew did the dirty work.

The Payson used girls who hustled only part time, the majority of them students from the community college which, east of the Harlem River, was only a short distance from the hotel.

Camellion pulled the drapes tightly shut and turned to William Fieldhouse who, well-muscled and nice-looking, was not yet 30 years old. Tall and quick-moving, Fieldhouse also had the trim waist of a man who kept in shape—*It all fits with*

33

what I read in his file. Fieldhouse was more than an expert in Thai boxing; he was also adept in Japanese Aikido and Pentjak-Silat, the national defense form of Indonesia.

"What's the rest of the security setup up here?" asked Camellion. He walked over to a brown Naugahyde couch, sat down and crossed his legs.

"Only God could get in here," Fieldhouse said, sitting down in a swivel rocker armchair. "Six of the rooms on each side of the hall are the originals. We can enter by means of panels in the rear walls. Other sections are just one big room, some having four or five doors facing the hall. From the hallway, all the doors are numbered in sequence and look like ordinary doors, but every door has a solid steel plate in the center and is equipped with pick-proof deadbolt locks, with extra long bolts. Just to be on the safe side, every door has an S-alarm that rings in Central Security. Three men are on duty at all times on this floor. The nine TV cameras are monitored from Central Security. Anything else?"

"What about contract agents?" Camellion said. "Do you ever permit any of them to come up here?"

Surprise flashed in Fieldhouse's brown eyes. "Of course not, Mr. Hafferton. You're the first. You must be something very special or Mr. Grojean would never have permitted your coming up here, or for that matter taking charge of the entire operation."

A wave of amusement rippled across Camellion's mind. As a cover he was using the name Jefferson Davis Hafferton, all the while knowing that Fieldhouse and the other Company people suspected the name was not his real one. As a further cover, to outsiders, he had a room on the 10th floor. And just in case any of the enemy tagged him and did some backtracking, they would find that Jefferson Davis Hafferton was from an old New Orleans family that had gone to seed. The danger was that the Red Chinese might suspect he was a *doppelganger*.[11]

"I'm nothing special," Camellion said easily. "I'm just the guy who gets the job done. By the way, nix the 'Mister' and call me Jeff."

11. A double and/or counterpart. In CIA parlance it refers to an individual who permits the Agency to use his identity. However, a *doppelganger* can be a deceased person.

"Good enough," grinned Fieldhouse, who proceeded to light a Vantage cigarette. "Call me Bill. Sooo . . . how and when do we start?"

The Death Merchant looked at the clock on the wall—3:30 A.M. He noticed that one of the two other agents in the room was yawning. He was a serious-faced black man, built like a linebacker, wearing a blue suit and smoking a sculptured Meerschaum pipe. His name was Gordon Hayes, and Camellion estimated his age to be about 40.

Dennis Float, the second case officer, had a heavy build, cynical dark eyes, smooth fair hair and a florid handsome face. He moved slowly and deliberately and was in his mid-30s.

"It's too late to do anything tonight," Camellion said, quick to notice that Fieldhouse held his cigarette in an unusual manner, between the thumb and the little finger of his right hand. He also wore his wristwatch on his right wrist, an indication that he was lefthanded. "We can pick it up in the morning. I'll be back up here at eleven. I want you and I to have a private conference. Have the files handy on Duncan, Gindow and Franzese. In the meanwhile, arrange for me and one of your people to meet Ewart Gremmill. Any questions?"

"Hundreds, but they'll keep until tomorrow," Fieldhouse said.

At five minutes after eleven the next morning, Camellion was seated in Bill Fieldhouse's private office, a tiny cubicle in the southeast corner of the 12th floor. The office, paneled in redwood, was soundproof and had just been checked for bugs. Three Company technicians were constantly checking the rooms on the 12th floor for hidden transmitters, one man taking the day shift, the other two the evening and night shifts. Always there was a technician walking around with a field-strength or grid-dip meter, looking for spurious oscillations.

Bill Fieldhouse, sitting on the corner of a plain gray metal desk, one foot on the floor, handed Camellion a thick green folder marked MOST SECRET, SUBJECT BIO-HISTORY, and said, "Maybe now you can tell me why the Center has suddenly developed such an intense interest in those cheap hoods and the Olympia Escort Bureau?"

Camellion told him about the missing BLUEPRINT: IN-

35

VISIBILITY file, filled him in on the details and finished with, "Our job is to find out if the Olympia girls lured Shiptonn into a position where he could be—and was—programmed. Plus *how* he was programmed, the methods used, and *how* he stole the file. This also invoves *why* he took the actual file, when just as easily he could have photographed the contents."

Fieldhouse looked stunned. "By God! They actually made a ship and its crew disappear," he said with quiet intensity.

"And teleported them as well!" Camellion reminded him.

"But it's something right out of science fiction! How could they do such a thing?"

"Don't ask me. I'm not a scientist." Camellion draped his left leg over the arm of the easy chair. "The whole business is part of Einstein's Unified Field Theory. The way Admiral Stavover told it, the experiment involved electric and magnetic fields. An electric field, created in a coil, induced a magnetic field at right angles to the first. Each of these fields represented one plane of space. But since there are three planes of space, there had to be a third field. This was a gravitational one. By hooking up electromagnetic generators so as to produce a magnetic 'pulse,' it was possible to produce this third field through the principles of resonance. Anyhow, that's how I understand it; and Stavover said he wasn't sure he was explaining it right to us.

"One thing is certain: Every advantage we have today, from cars to computers, from toasters to hair dryers, is based on interactions between electricity and magnetism. But there's a third side, or component, which forms the third side of the triangle that has eluded scientists. That's what the U.S. Navy stumbled on."

"Einstein's Unified Field Theory," said Fieldhouse slowly, looking up toward the ceiling. He paused, then swung his gaze to the Death Merchant. "What is it, exactly?"

"Exactly?" Camellion laughed. "I don't know. I can tell you that it's not possible to discuss the Unified Field Theory in non-technical terms. As I understand it, the heart and soul of the theory is that a single set of equations can explain mathematically the interrelationships between the three basic universal forces: electromagnetic, gravitational and nuclear. Scientists don't know whether such a 'field' would be interdimensional or have anything to do with time. But if we're to assume that such a field could be developed, it would have to incorporate X-rays, light, radio-waves, pure magnetism and even matter itself into the final equations. It's not difficult to imagine the insurmountable complexities involved, considering that Einstein spent the greater part of his life trying to perfect the idea and often was heard to complain that he didn't have enough math to complete the work. Whether he ever completed the Unified Field Theory is anybody's guess."[12]

An expression of uncertainty captured Fieldhouse's face. "I thought you said that the Navy made use of the Unified Field Theory in the experiment?"

Camellion smiled. "I said that the experiment had to include the Unified Field Theory. We still don't know if the scientists working for the Office of Naval Research were consciously making use of the theory or accidentally stumbled onto its results. Admiral Stavover himself doesn't know. Even if he had read the report, he wouldn't have understood it."

Fieldhouse thought for a moment, smoke curling from his nose. Finally he said, "Yet I get the impression that Admiral Stavover isn't too worried about the Red Chinese having the report. Why is that? Or don't you know? Or can't you tell me?"

"I know and I can tell you. But you're not to repeat it to any of the Cos here. Two reports of the invisibility and experiment were made. One report was put on microfilm and placed in the Mountain. The typed report was placed in the Ultra-Secret Safe Room at ONI headquarters. The one at ONI was doctored."

A trace of a smile crept across Fieldhouse's face.

"Then the one at ONI didn't contain the real formula?"

"It did, but more was added to it. It's possible that first-rate physicists could see through all the math chicken scratching, even though it's improbable. Anyway, that's what the brain

12. Even today, the majority of Einstein's work is beyond the comprehension of the world's most brilliant scientists. It is felt that the Unified Field Theory is still an *incomplete* structure, that is in the sense that the Special Theory of Relativity is *complete*. The Relativity theory is only a part of the Unified Field Theory.

boys have indicated to Stavover. Do you have anything else to do now?"

Fieldhouse first leaned sideways and crushed out his cigarette in an ashtray on the desk. He sat up then, put his other foot on the floor and looked at the Death Merchant.

"Why?"

"It's going to take me a while to read this biography report."

Fieldhouse stood up. "I do have some things to do. I'll be back in say . . . oh, forty-five minutes. We can go downstairs and have lunch at the Zebra Room, next door to the hotel. The food's not bad and the prices are reasonable."

"No dice," Camellion said firmly. "I don't want us seen together, not in this area."

"You're the boss," Fieldhouse said and left the room.

The Death Merchant settled back and started to read the report that had been put together by the Company. The rap sheets of Charley "Blackeye" Franzese and Barney "The Pig" Gindow were longer than the weekly grocery list for Boys' Town. Both men had been arrested scores of times, suspected of everything from burglary to murder. Franzese's last pickup had been by the FBI, in 1978, in connection with interstate theft. A Federal judge had dismissed the charge, claiming insufficient evidence.

A lot of arrests, a dozen or more trials, but not a single conviction! Franzese's legitimate interests included taverns, a junkyard, a warehouse and a small trucking company. The Mob's real money came from numbers, loansharking, selling stolen merchandise and prostitution. Occasionally, the Mob would work a swindle, such as a "bust out."[13]

The Death Merchant's eyes narrowed when he read, *The Franzese-Gindow combine is not a part of any of the five Cosa Nostra families operating within the New York City area. It is believed, however, that the Franzese-Gindow Mob pays tribute to the old Vito Genovese family and to the Carlo Gambino family in order to operate.*

13. One version is phony bankruptcy. More often than not, the business is "torched," burned down, after the merchandise is secretly taken out, in which case the mob not only collects the insurance but also profits from selling the merchandise through other outlets.

38

For a long moment, the Death Merchant studied the mug shots of Charles David Franzese and Barney Cyril Gindow. Cruel, calculating faces, faces that told Camellion that their owners were without mercy or compassion.

Cyril! What a joke. I think that maybe I'll have to liquidate those two pieces of sewer scum.

With interest, Camellion turned to the section on Rosalie June Fluggmeyer who, 31 years earlier, had been born in the coal-mining town of West Frankfort, in that part of southern Illinois known as Little Egypt. Only now she was Soraya Duncan, the owner and operator of the Olympia Escort Bureau.

There was a 5″ X 7″ glossy photograph of the woman. Below the picture was the remark that the Company man had taken the photograph from a Hostess Twinkies bread truck. *Bread truck or flying saucer. Duncan's put together better than a Playboy Bunny!*

Only very slightly blurred, the photograph revealed Soraya Duncan coming out of an apartment building, walking under the canopy to the front entrance. She wore a white tailored suit, white gloves with wide gold bracelets over them and white pumps. She wore no hat on her shoulder-length red hair.

Camellion began to read her bio. Duncan's life in West Frankfort had been all strife and bad news . . . her father a coal miner, when he was sober, her mother a worn-out woman with no will of her own. Rosalie had come to New York at the age of 20 and had first worked as a waitress in various hash houses. Within a year she had graduated to knocker-trembling in a topless bar. She then took the flesh milk-route. Read the CIA report: *In 1972 it is believed that she became a call girl, operating from an apartment in the East 60s.*

Uh huh. A class hooker. The high-class tailgaters still operate in the East 60s and 70s.

During this period, Rosalie June Fluggmeyer called herself Nadine Arden. But in 1973 she legally changed her name to Soraya Duncan. During that same year, she also achieved the goal of many a hustle slut: She became the kept doll of Joe John Wang, an American-Chinese importer. *At least she wasn't a racist,* mused Camellion.

In 1975 she broke away from Wang after becoming the lover of Charles Franzese who, among his other operations, was also what is known in the play-for-pay business as a "brown-nose pimp"—that is, a diseased bedbug, who walks like a human being and who procures girls for rich and powerful men (or lesbians, for rich and powerful women).

According to the report: *Soraya Duncan opened the Olympia Escort Bureau, employing not only white girls, but also Orientals and blacks. We believe that Charles Franzese is part of the operation.*

Olympia had never been connected with any kind of scandal. Nine different times the vice squad of the NYPD had investigated Soraya and her young ladies (none were under 20 years of age; none were over 25). Each time, an undercover man had engaged one of the girls for an evening—dinner, a show, etc., at a fee of $100 per hour. Each time, the man had done his best to get the gal between the sheets. Each time, he had been firmly rebuffed. Sex? There wasn't even a goodnight kiss.

The FBI, on the assumption that Soraya's girls had to be hustling and that crossing state lines might be involved, had also done some probing. They, too, had scored zero.

Camellion did some thinking. Line up a thousand people, and every individual will tell you that the United Nations is the biggest hot-air and wind-bag society in the world. The odds are that not one of them will associate the U. N. with prostitution. In reality, the U. N. is one of the largest users of hookers, with foreign diplomats and emissaries having the best "class" hookers at their disposal. For more reasons than one, the girls consider such johns worthy prizes. Foreign diplomats are exceedingly generous with their nation's money and give extra gifts . . . cash, cars, jewelry. Such men have tons of money, court the sluts extravagantly and are great leads for learning about the wealthier members of their countries who come to the United States now and then and want to meet free-and-easy broads.

If anything, Soraya's girls were overworked. While they dated wealthy businessmen, American millionaires, much of their business came from the United Nations, by word-of-mouth advertising. Delegates from the Arab nations and from the Latin countries were very good customers. They always wanted blondes.

The Death Merchant wondered, *How many of them have been programmed?*

He turned a page and saw the name at the top of the next page: Gregory "Steel Fingers" Gof. *Now comes the weird part!*

Soraya Duncan's assistant, Gregory Gof, was a dwarf, a very ugly man who was only four feet tall, but whose body was very thickset. *He's damned near as wide as he is tall!*

Gof was Soraya's brother, and he had been baptized Gregory Peter Fluggmeyer. In 1973, Soraya had brought him to New York and he had legally changed his name to Gregory Gof. For a time he had been a "midget" wrestler. However, after Soraya started her escort bureau, Gof had become her bodyguard and chief stooge.

There was a CIA notation: *Why the subject should have chosen the name "Gof" is not known. We feel that the name might have some deep psychological significance for the subject.*

It was Barney Gindow who had tacked the moniker of "Steel Fingers" on Gof. At the age of 17, Gof had slipped and fallen into a threshing machine. The accident had cost him two fingers on his left hand and one finger on his right. The missing digits had been replaced with porcelain fingers. After her brother came to New York, Soraya had taken him to a specialist who had replaced the porcelain fingers with steel fingers that had movable joints.

Bill Fieldhouse returned to the office at 12:15. By then, the Death Merchant had finished reading the report and had placed it on the desk.

"You and a case officer will meet Ewart Gremmill at two this afternoon," Fieldhouse said, picking up the report. He walked behind the desk and pulled a large photograph of John F. Kennedy from the right side of the wall. The left side of the frame was hinged to the wall. Behind the photograph, in the center of the wall, was the round front of a wall safe. Fieldhouse dialed open the round door, but instead of an opening there was another round door with a slot, a tiny bulb and a

41

handle. He reached into his pocket, pulled out a plastic card, inserted it halfway into the slot and waited until the bulb glowed green; then he turned the handle and opened the door.

"The report didn't say whether Duncan herself goes out on dating assignments," Camellion said, watching Fieldhouse put the report in the safe and close both doors.

"She does, but not too often." Fieldhouse spun the combination dial and closed the photograph over the wall. He turned and looked slyly at Camellion. "Is that what you have in mind—having Gremmill introduce you to Duncan?"

"There isn't any doubt about Gremmill? He can be trusted?" Camellion asked, stretching out in the chair.

"No problem," Fieldhouse reassured him, sitting down in a swivel chair. "Within the last year he's been out several times with her girls. He offered them four-bills for just a quickie; they turned him down. Maybe only two or three girls are in on the programming. Anyhow, you're not a diplomat. You're supposed to be an old whoremaster from deep down in Dixie. Even if you were posing as a wheel from the U.N., what makes you think you'd get anywhere with the boss lady?"

"I like to start at the top and work down," Camellion explained. "If I can date Duncan, the impressions I get from her might enable us to develop some leads."

"Reasonable but damned risky," Fieldhouse said, nodding his head. "Let me warn you, though, Franzese is a very jealous man. He wouldn't dare go after a foreign diplomat, but a rake from New Orleans, dating his favorite bed partner, is another matter; and you'll have some of those Foolish Bunch of Idiots[14] trailing you and her around."

"You sound very positive."

"We know every move the Feds make. We have one of their secretaries on our payroll. The Mafia is also paying her to feed them information. Hell, those garlic-snappers have feedlines into City Hall, the Police Department, even right up to the state Capitol. But so do we."

"Well, well, a secretary who's a kind of unofficial double agent," mused Camellion. "What's the world coming to? Any more surprises in store for me?"

"No, not a double," Fieldhouse said quickly. "She's always

14. CIA lingo for the FBI.

42

been with the Company." He got to his feet and half-smiled. "Come along. I'll introduce you to the case officer who'll take you to meet Gremmill. You and he can grab a quick bite on the way." And as Camellion followed him to the office door, he added, "Speaking of surprises, if you manage to get a date with Soraya Duncan, you might get a few from her. Don't underestimate that bitch."

I never underestimate anyone, Camellion thought. *Or I would have died years ago. . . .*

Chapter Four

By the way he handled the car in heavy traffic, James Nivens proved that he was an expert driver, so good that he could have given lessons to New York cab drivers. In the rear seat of the Ford Granada, the Death Merchant had not mentioned that he was almost as familiar with New York City as he was with the Big Thicket area of Texas; but he was curious to see if Nivens would take the same route that he would have taken had he been driving—*So far, he has.*

Soraya Duncan's Olympia Escort Bureau, only a short distance from U.N. headquarters, was on Third Avenue near East 48th Street, in a suite of plush offices on the 27th floor of a modern office building. Nivens had turned off Ninth Avenue onto West 42nd Street and had headed east. Going through Times Square, he had continued east.

The Death Merchant glanced out of the window. The day was overcast, yet muggy. To his right was Bryant Park and, next to the park, the Public Library, which was on the corner of 42nd Street and Fifth Avenue.

"We're not too far from Duncan's building," announced Nivens. "Around twelve to fourteen blocks, something like that. We'll use one of the parking garages on Lexington Avenue and walk the block or so to the Butler Building.

"You're doing the driving," Camellion said to the CIA man whom he has assessed as being pure professional with a lot of savvy in the trade-craft, despite his meek appearance. In his 40s, Nivens had a thin, arrogant nose, a firm mouth, watery blue eyes and practically no chin. From his chicken neck downward, the rest of him was so sparse that, in theory, he would have had to use guy wires to protect himself in a stiff wind.

In contrast, the man sitting next to Nivens was tall, tanned and good-looking in a jaded sort of way. Ewart Gremmill reminded Camellion of the better-class Dirty Old Man. Exceedingly well-dressed and smelling of expensive cologne, Gremmill had that fresh, just-steamed-into-shape ruddy glow. He was well into his 50s, and the fresh look wasn't natural. It wasn't because in his earlier years he had been a stud for wealthy women. When his body had started to go to pot, it had been a simple task to steam it, beat it and massage it for the required trim physique—almost a daily ritual for Gremmill, who worked for the Company because he had to, because in a fit of rage he had murdered a woman in Yonkers, in 1973, and the CIA had found out about it. The Company had given him a choice: Either work for them or spend the rest of his days in the pen.

Taking the car across Maidson Avenue, Nivens half-turned his head and said with a tiny laugh, "New York is really 'Pork City,'. Hafferton. In case you don't know it, the major Midtown hussy belt is bordered by Sixth and Eighth Avenues between 39th and 47th Streets. But stragglers can be found all the way up to 57th. The gals are thickest around Broadway and 42nd. Day or night, they'll grab you."

"That's one route Duncan never took," Camellion said. "She was never a streetwalker."

"No, she never was," Nivens said. "She did take the garment center route for about six months. I guess you know how those hookers operate. They just move in and out of the various offices of the cloak-and-suit area and perform right in the office at various hours for what some call the 'executive coffee break.' The garment men prefer not to become entangled with the showroom girls, reserving them for the customers."

Gremmill removed his homburg and commented in a well-modulated voice, "You'll also find a lot of hookers around Broadway and 72nd and Needle Park. That area is worse than Times Square as a sex jungle."

Nivens' laugh was a half-sneer. "Yeah, and you know what the main danger of picking up a woman in that area is? You

45

may not discover she's a *he* until it's too late—and how will you explain that to the boys in the office?"

Gremmill wrinkled his nose in disgust. "I think the worst is from 110th Street up. East and west of the park and the tracks there are whole platoons of floozies on round-the-clock details. They're generally the busiest with their suburban trade, you know, the men who drive down from Westport, Larchmont, Islip . . . anywhere that features lives of quiet sexual desperation. I tell you, that area is tops for degradation. The girls'll jump right in your car and degrade you with their very presence, whether you pay them or not—so I've been told."

The Death Merchant found himself liking Gremmill less and less and despising him more and more. He knew Gremmill for what the man really was: a human leech, a parasite who made a profit from loneliness, who preyed on elderly women who couldn't bring themselves to admit that Time does change all things, including sex appeal. Beauty gradually fades. The wrinkles come. The end is always the fine dust of the dark grave. . . .

"Gremmill, are you positive that you have your story straight?" Camellion said harshly. He watched the gigolo carefully pat his just-so hair, then carefully place the homburg on his head.

"Of course. We met a week ago in an adult bookstore, one of them on Times Square," Gremmill answered, a nervous twitter in his voice. "But if you don't mind my saying so, I think we're wasting our time. You're supposed to be wanting a girl to shack up with. Why should I bring you around to her escort service? She will know that I've told you I've been out with her girls and didn't get anywhere with them. And now I bring you around wanting a date with her, of all people! It's ridiculous—if you don't mind my saying so."

"He makes sense, Hafferton," Nivens said, with a deep sigh. "You'll both be lucky if she doesn't chase you out of the office."

Gremmill turned and glanced at Nivens. "You said a while ago that 'we'd' walk to her office building. How do I explain your presence?"

Nivens slowed for a red light. "You won't have to. I'm

going only as far as Doubleday's. I'll wait for you two in the bookstore."

Camellion remained silent. Nivens and Gremmill could be right. He might not get to first base with Soraya Duncan. Neither man knew what was really going on, nor could he tell them, much less reveal his own reasoning as to why he felt Soraya might agree to have a date with him.

The Red Chinese had not uttered a whisper about the missing Huan-yi Yang. Not a peep from the Communist Chinese embassy in Washington. Not a word from the delegation at the United Nations. The Chinese were up the creek without a paddle; they were afraid that if they made inquiries, the news of what had happened in Rosemary Hills might become public.

Logically it followed that 3rd Bureau agents in the U.S. would be on guard, to the extent that any activity connected with the mind-bending, mental programming technique would be triple-checked and that the least bit of anything unusual would be viewed with extreme suspicion.

The trouble with Grojean and Stavover was that they didn't know the Chinese mind. Infinite patience came naturally to the Chinese. The situation was now at a standstill. Grojean and Stavover would wait to see what Camellion might dig up. The Red Chinese would wait, then wait some more. They wouldn't dare make the first move. They couldn't afford to. For all the 3rd Bureau knew Huan-yi Yang could still be alive—and talking.

Camellion's plan was not complicated: Stir up the Chinese and anything might happen. His walking into Soraya Duncan's office—unusual to say the least—and asking her for a date—even more fantastic—should do it.

Unless she has Vacant City under that red hair of hers, she will have to suspect me of being an intelligence agent. With all her ego, she should accept out of sheer curiosity. Then again, she might not.

He called out to Ewart Gremmill, "Gremmill, you're positive the appointment is for four-fifteen?"

"Of course. The receptionist said four-fifteen." Gremmill sounded unsure of himself. "An appointment with Duncan herself. I told the secretary that I was bringing a good friend with me and that he—you—wanted to meet Duncan."

"Having second thoughts?" Nivens chided Camellion.

"I want to be positive," Camellion said.

"It's a waste of time!" the elegant Gremmill suddenly said. "In my opinion, Mr. Hafferton, Soraya will suspect you of being a cop." He turned his head to the left and half-looked over his shoulder at Camellion. "If that happens, she might even suspect me of working with you."

"Don't worry about it," Camellion said, thinking that if Gremmill's temples hadn't already been streaked with gray— *He'd be wearing detachable silver sideburns. He already has the Chevalier strut and the carnation.* . . .

"That's easy for you to say," protested Gremmill hesitantly. "I'm thinking of that despicable Charles Franzese. He's always around her, and he's a very jealous man. I don't want such a vicious thug looking me up and asking questions."

With equal suddenness, Nivens' voice became cold and threatening. "Listen, Gremmill. Don't blow this deal, or you'll end up in the Tombs.[15] I'm not kidding."

"Don't worry. I know what to do," Gremmill said quickly.

Camellion should have felt sorry for Gremmill. He didn't, even though he knew that the man's performance, in Soraya Duncan's office, would be the last one of his life. Whether or not Soraya accepted the date, the Death Merchant had to assume that she would suspect him of being what he was, an intelligence agent. She would also realize that the weak link was Ewart Gremmill. If she didn't, the Red Chinese would. *If anyone pointed a gun at Gremmill, he'd talk so fast and so long that they'd have to terminate him to shut him up!*

That night Ewart Gremmill would vanish forever, although for the time being only Camellion, Fieldhouse and Gordon Hayes knew that he was scheduled for termination.

"We're almost there, to the parking garage," James Nivens said.

The offices of Soraya Duncan's Olympia Escort Bureau looked honest and above reproach, the front of the reception room facing a wide corridor, a solid wall of tinted blue glass encased in highly polished bronze, the office beyond furnished in contemporary Danish and presided over by a receptionist

15. Part of New York City's prison system.

who was young and well groomed, shapely and perfumed, overly friendly and as efficient as an IBM computer. In key help, Soraya Duncan employed only the very best and was willing to pay for it.

Behind the reception desk were two glass doors, one opening to Soraya Duncan's private office, the other leading to the four consultation rooms where Soraya and three "counselors" conferred with clients in regard to the type of girls they might want. White? Black? Oriental? Short, tall, fat, thin? Blonde, brunette or redhead? Did a client desire a girl who could discuss world politics or a doll who was knowledgeable about the price of hog feed in Kansas? However, 99 clients out of 100 preferred to discuss sex.

The men who came to the Olympia Escort Bureau had one common denominator: Most were over the hill and in the icy years of life. On the first date, all expected sex from the girl and were astonished when they didn't get it. The result was predictable: Most men didn't come back for a second date. Who cared? Soraya Duncan didn't. New York was a vast city. The supply of hopeful suckers was inexhaustible.

However, human nature being what it is, Soraya did have repeat business. A small percentage of the repeats were masochists who derived a perverse pleasure in having their date tell them no. Others were elderly, totally impotent men who couldn't have risen to the occasion in a roomful of naked girls. These men simply liked to be seen in the company of a pretty and sexy young woman. They also enjoyed intelligent conversation. None of the girls in Soraya's stable were stupid. A dozen had college degrees; one even had a master's in astrophysics.

There was also a percentage of closet homosexuals and secret bisexuals who returned time and time again, who found it necessary to be seen in public now and then with a woman; there were the celebrity fags who had to play it as straight as possible when in public, and a smattering of transvestites who would insist that the girl dress in a certain manner and/or wear certain clothes. The girl would then become their fashion alter-ego.

The well-groomed, well-stacked, perfumed receptionist looked up at Camellion and Gremmill and flashed her best

49

Pepsodent smile. The name plaque on her desk read Yvonne Masters.

"Oh yes, Mr. Gremmill and Mr.—" She glanced at Camellion.

"Jefferson Davis Hafferton," announced Camellion, letting the words roll from his mouth with a deep Southern accent.

"Go right in, gentlemen," she said, her voice as sensual as the rest of her. "Miss Duncan is expecting you."

Gremmill, forever the perfect gentleman, nodded and murmured a polite "Thank you, Miss Masters." Camellion only winked at the pretty phony. Together, he and Gremmill walked into Soraya Duncan's private office.

Soraya was seated in one of those modern office chairs that any sane person considers a nightmare, the kind in which the seat slants sharply, so that the front is seven inches higher than the back. But Soraya Duncan wasn't part of any bad dream, not the way she was sunk down in the chair, her long legs crossed, the lower part of her left leg swinging back and forth. Camellion didn't even try to fake any pretentions at subtlety as he let his eyes roam up and down her well-favored calves, as well as all the rest of her, making it more than plain what was on his mind.

"Do I meet with your approval, Mr. Hafferton—you are Jefferson Davis Hafferton?"

Soraya's voice, low and tinged with faint mockery, was as sultry as the voice of a new bride calling her husband to bed.

"You'd better believe it," Camellion said loudly. "I'll give you a gold star any day of the week, except on Sunday." He put his hands on his hips and continued to undress her with his eyes. He enjoyed it, and she didn't seem to mind. Almost at once he realized she was the most self-possessed woman he had ever met. Her green eyes appraised him quite calmly, putting an exact value on everything he wore, even down to his $150 brogues imported from Europe.

She herself was wearing tweeds. Strangely enough, the business tweeds seemed to enhance rather than detract from her desirability.

Watching her smiling at him, her crimson lips curled slightly in amusement, Camellion decided that laying it on the line would be his best approach.

"My good buddy, Ewart here, he said you were the most

beautiful woman in all of New York," Camellion said in a well-pleased voice. He patted an embarrassed Gremmill on the shoulder. "He sure didn't exaggerate. I just had to see for myself. I told Ewee here— call him Ewee—that I had to meet you. I told him that before I died, I had to have a date with you."

"And now you have." Soraya opened an Egyptian cigarette box, resting on a small table to her left, and took out a gold-tipped Nat Sherman Fantasia cigarette. Rose-colored, the cigarette was 6½ inches long.

Instantly, Gremmill's fingers went to his vest and came out with a small gold lighter. He reminded the Death Merchant of a well-trained dummy as he lighted Soraya's cigarette.

"Thank you, Mr. Gremmill." She exhaled and smiled again at Jefferson Davis Hafferton.

"Let's have a drink, shall we?" A teasing smile still playing around the edges of her mouth, she got up and walked slowly across the office. Camellion didn't pass up the opportunity as he followed her, his eyes knifing the jutting rim of her moving buttocks, picturing them, pink-white, without the skirt.

She pressed a button in the wall, and slowly the bar moved forward from its compartment in the wall.

"Well-stocked, I see!" Camellion cracked, deliberately moving close to her and enjoying Gremmill's embarrassment. A faint perfume drifted to him, and he could see the voluminous push of her breasts in the blouse under the top of the suit.

Putting her lush behind on a stool, she indicated the other side of the bar and gave a tiny laugh, her upper lip rising to show the tips of small, regular teeth.

"Help yourself, gentlemen," she said, then watched Camellion and Gremmill move behind the bar. "Nothing for me. I consider drinking a weakness of character. I dislike weakness of any kind."

"A little wine for the stomach's sake I always say," Camellion said and placed a glass and a bottle of Scotch on the bar. Gremmill reached for a wine glass and a bottle of Sherry.

"Mr. Gremmill told my receptionist that you're from New Orleans, Mr. Hafferton," Soraya said, "from an old Southern family."

"We're in cotton, peanuts and sweet potatoes," Camellion said. "But I don't have much to do with the family business.

51

My older brother is the working man in the family." He sighed philosophically, moved from behind the bar and eased onto a stool to Soraya's left. "Wilfred is the businessman in the family. I was cursed with being a disciple of Wine, Women and Song."

Soraya made no immediate response, but Camellion knew that the wheels of her mind were spinning at maximum. He detected a tiny glow of self-satisfaction in her eyes, as though congratulating herself for being right about him. She turned and glanced at Gremmill seated to her right.

"How long have the two of you been friends?" she asked.

"It's like I explained to Miss Masters over the phone," Gremmill said, toying with the stem of his wine glass. "We met a little over a week ago, in one of the bookstores on Times Square. We were both . . . uh . . . browsing."

She laughed lightly, then turned and looked into the ornamented glass behind the bar, her eyes moving to the image of Camellion.

"Tch, tch. Shame on both of you, going into such a place that caters only to the baser instincts. Times Square is one of the cesspools of the city. The way those shameless prostitutes congregate! Their public displays of *gaucherie,* anatomy and costumes are appalling."

She swung around on the stool toward Camellion and placed a slim hand on his right arm, her expression a mixture of disdain and amusement.

"I'd advise you to be careful of Ewart, Mr. Hafferton. He's an old roué. Before you know it, he'll be dragging you off to a pop orgy in the Village, or to one on Park Avenue."

Camellion took a swallow of Scotch before answering Soraya, who was watching him with analytical eyes.

"This is my first time in New York," he said and returned the glass to the bar. "I guess I want to see all the things I've read and heard about. I sure know I want a date with you before I die." He grinned broadly. "Ewee said I'd be wasting my time. But you know what I said? I said, 'Ewee, you just give that escort bureau a phone call and make an appointment with that living goddess.' I said, 'Ewee, it never hurts to ask. After a date with her I could die happy.'"

Soraya raised a quizzical eyebrow. "You seem to be preoccupied with death, Mr. Hafferton." As patient as a creeping cancer, she didn't press for a reply. She merely sat there, studying Camellion the way a microbiologist would observe a newly discovered germ. The Death Merchant admired her caution and serpentine approach.

But she's used too much eyebrow pencil for my taste.

Camellion frowned for a moment, let a puzzled look creep over his face, then leaned out and looked past Soraya at Gremmill.

"You didn't tell Miss Masters when you made the appointment?"

"No, I didn't," Gremmill admitted sheepishly, acting his part masterfully. He had had plenty of acting experience over the years—lying to stupid but wealthy women. "It sounded well . . . too gruesome."

There was a surprised look on her lovely face, but her eyes met Camellion's with perfect composure. "What does he mean? What are you trying to hide?"

"I'm not trying to hide anything," Camellion said with sincerity. He sighed heavily. "I have what doctors call *myelocytic leukemia.* I've only got about sixteen months to live. I'll be bedridden in about a year. That's why I came to New York, to have one last fling." Very quickly he drew back, looked at her and said earnestly, "Don't worry. It's not a disease you can catch. It's cancer of the blood."

Very slowly, Soraya Duncan licked her upper lip with the tip of her tongue. She crushed out her red cigarette.

"You mean that you are actually dying," she said, her voice low, her brow furrowed. "Yet you still want a date with me! Amazing!"

"I sure do!" Camellion then took another long slug of Scotch, letting the booze wash his mouth and sterilize the area where his tonsils had been. *Either she suspects me of lying and of being an agent, or else she feels sorry for me. I've never seen a hooker yet who didn't have a soft spot in regard to death.*

Soraya smiled impudently at him. "When I go out with a client my fee is two hundred an hour."

Camellion rolled the booze around in his mouth. He was swallowing the Scotch when a buzzer sounded on Soraya Duncan's desk.

"Excuse me." She left the bar, went to her desk and flipped the switch on the box. "Yes?"

"The checks are ready to be signed," the voice said, a voice that was deep, but had a strange, odd, almost child-like quality to it.

"All right. Bring them in." She waited by her desk, her finger resting on the on/off switch of the intercom. In a very short time, a side door to another office opened and one of the weirdest human beings that the Death Merchant had ever seen waddled into the room.

Four feet tall, Gregory Gof was so muscular that he was practically square. His head was very large and slightly misshapen, as though, earlier in life, he had been a victim of *hydrocephalus*, or *osteitis deformans*. He was as ugly as a ten-car pile-up, the mouth large, the lips abnormally thick so that the teeth were hidden. The nose, enormous, twisted to one side. There was a black patch over the left eye, held in place by an elastic band over the high forehead and in the back of the head thick with dark, shiny hair. The right eye was small, the eyebrow heavy and fuzzy.

Gregory Gof reminded Camellion of a barrel walking on two legs, a barrel with massive arms too long for the rest of his body—*Why the black patch? He wasn't wearing it in the photograph.*

"Here they are," Gof said, his voice guttural, yet far too high for such a little/big man. He handed the checks to Soraya, cocked his head to one side, stared at Camellion and Gremmill and, in his swaying gait, left the office. Both Camellion and Gremmill had noticed the shiny stainless steel fingers on his hands.

Soraya placed an onyx paperweight on the checks and returned to the bar, noticing at once the odd expression on Gremmill's tanned, well-scrubbed face. He had not succeeded completely in concealing his abhorrence of Gof, although he had tried.

"Beauty is always in the eye of the beholder, Mr. Gremmill," Soraya said softly. "That was Mr. Gof. He's my accountant and sometimes acts as my bodyguard."

"Your bodyguard!" Gremmill said dumbly.

"Don't let his size fool you," Soraya said intensely. "He has the strength of several men."

She swung on the bar stool and turned to Camellion, facing him.

"As I was saying, I only go out with special clients. When I do, my fee is two hundred an hour."

Camellion pretended to think for a moment. "I'm trying to decide if there is any way I might qualify as a special client," he finally said.

"Why don't you assume that you could?" she said, a kind of sulkiness in her voice. "What could you lose?"

Camellion faked surprise. *She'll either say yes, or take sadistic delight in saying no. It's now or forget it.*

"In that case it would be a matter of whether I could afford you for five or six hours," he replied, forcing a worried expression to mask itself on his face.

She leaned closer and placed a cool hand on his arm.

"Could you?"

"Yes."

"What time do you want to call for me tonight?"

Chapter Five

At such short notice, it had not been possible for Camellion to obtain reservations at any first-class restaurant. In keeping with the character of Jefferson Davis Hafferton, he had apologized profusely to Soraya when, at 7:00 P.M., he had called for her at her Park Avenue apartment building. She hadn't minded, saying that she preferred places that were less crowded. "That's why I dressed casually. I should have told you not to wear evening clothes. I'm glad you didn't."

She chose to go to Kenny's Steak Pub on Lexington Avenue, a midtown hangout. After dinner, they took a cab to Sherry's 1890 Banjo Parlor on Vanderbilt Avenue and later went to an Off-Off Broadway theater on West 63rd Street, explaining that it wasn't the play in which she was interested; it was the audience.

"The plays are all alike," she said, with a wave of her hand. "Will the heroine eat the sunflower seed and find God or will she take an overdose of drugs and perish? It's the audience that fascinates me. Other than couples like us, people who are slumming, they're all from Freaksville."

"People seem to interest you."

"Life interests me—and death."

All the while, Camellion had his mental defenses up, constantly analyzing her words and mannerisms, her expressions and body movements. Not once did any of her gestures—chewing a lip, toying with her hair, etc.—tell him that she was ill at ease. Whatever she might really be feeling, she was a master at self-kinesic-censure. At no time did any of her movements indicate that she was lying.

Highly intelligent, she had an appreciation of the arts and

56

could converse, with wit, on any number of subjects. They discussed modern art and related subjects. She confessed an interest in Zen Buddhism and had studied—"off and on," as she put it—the works of Gurdjieff, and his more famous pupil, Ouspensky.[16] "But their philosophy of reality doesn't make sense to me. And their books are almost unreadable."

Proving to have that rare combination of beauty and brains, Soraya Duncan was a superb conversationalist, her choice of topics forcing the Death Merchant to double his mental guard, less he slip and make a comment that would indicate he was more worldly than J.D. Hafferton.

She loved New York, this indicating to Camellion that she had not done much traveling in the U.S.

"Even the basic look in New York is different," she said as they sat in Belmores, an all-night restaurant at Park Avenue and 28th, where they had gone for ham and eggs. "Other cities have *looks*, but the New York stare is unique in that it takes place only in New York. Basically, it's more devious. You see, many lookers don't want others to know they're looking. They think it would be childish and undignified."

Camellion pretended great interest. "I didn't know that!"

There was some truth in what she was saying, Camellion thought, regardless of the exaggeration. In Los Angeles and Hollywood, everyone stares. But their stares are always more direct. None of the New York coyness. In the Midwest, say St. Louis or Chicago, the stares are warm, friendly and direct. In Europe, an American usually gets a variety of stares. Open, inviting and friendly—until he spends his money.

Camellion was troubled by a possibility he could not afford to ignore: that Soraya was not involved with the Red Chinese. She could be operating a perfectly legitimate escort service, and only Charley Franzese and Barney Gindow were involved with the Communist Chinese 3rd Bureau.

In analyzing Soraya, Camellion considered her a paradox and compared her to a certain type of New York girl who is difficult to get into a horizontal position between the sheets. This type is too attractive to be an ordinary receptionist or secretary. Nor is she talented enough for a glamour career or

16. Two Russian mystics who still have a large following. Their basic teaching involves a fourth dimension of awareness of mind.

now-and-then hooking. No pitch works on her, the sex-connection depending on her flippant, unpredictable attitude at the time. Nothing you say, do or promise will influence her one way or another. She is governed by whim and mood. Your only hope for a romp in bed is to catch her when she's ready.

Damn it. Soraya is a problem. Camellion had to admit that the real annoyance was with himself, with finding that he was sexually attracted to Soraya. His only consolation was that he would have to be blind, or a fairy, not to be attracted to her, although he wouldn't have paid her a buck in Confederate money to see as little as her bellybutton. Only two kinds of men paid for sex: idiots and uglies who were forced to.

The fact that Soraya had been a high-class hooker on-call didn't bother him. A few of his best friends had once been "in the life." One still was. "Prostitution" had a lot of meanings. Millions and millions of girls gave it away, for reasons other than money. And what about the millions of "nice" women who used sex to hook a hick into marriage? Oh sure, they were legal and respectable housewives. But after all the moral frosting was licked off the social cake, it all added up to the same naked truth: Sex was sex; sex was still the acolyte serving the God of the Almighty Dollar. Camellion despised Soraya Duncan for another reason: If she were involved with the Chinese 3rd Bureau—*She's betraying her country. The Red Chinese at the United Nations are bastards following the god of hell, but they're serving their country. Soraya is betraying hers, or I've made a very bad mistake.*

In the cab, on the way to Soraya's apartment house, he speculated that she had dated him as part of a plan to lead him into a clever trap. He doubted it. Should the Red Chinese suspect him, they wouldn't dare try a snatch-and-grab job while he was with Soraya; they wouldn't want to involve her—*Not unless they wanted to terminate the both of us. Oh boy! And with me unarmed . . .*

He was positive that she was involved with some sort of violence and death. He sensed a strong negative thought-field around her.

It was 1:48 A.M. when the taxi pulled up in front of Soraya's apartment house and Camellion drawled with a just-right

58

Deep South accent, "I'll walk you to the elevator." He wondered what kind of response he would get as he got out of the car and walked around to open the door on her side.

"It's still early," she said softly, getting out. "Why not come up and have a nightcap?"

A trap! There wasn't, however, any warning from his sixth sense, only the loud whisper of logic that led him to conclude that it could easily be a trap, in that it was her apartment where the brainwashing and/or mental programming process was conducted. By means of drugs? It was highly unlikely that drugs alone were used. It was a method that was fast, that could be completed without the subject's being aware of it, within six or seven hours. Anything longer would interfere with the subject's schedule. He might not notice the lapse, but his associates would. Or even a programming method that was shorter. *How could Mason Shiptonn have stayed away from his companions for any length of time? It has to be a fast method.*

He wasn't concerned that he might be exposed in any way to the more subtle techniques of hypnosis. His own protective instincts made it impossible even for experts to hypnotize him by the usual mental methods. Despite his ability to even withstand efforts to put him into a slight trance, he could not fight narcohypnosis—*I won't have to. Whatever methods the Chinese are using, it's not narcohypnosis. Narcohypnosis doesn't last. The programming they are using does.*

"I'd like that," Camellion said in reply to Soraya's invitation. He pretended great pleasure and excitement, so much so that even the cab driver gave him a you-lucky-stiff smile when he paid the man and gave him a sawbuck tip.

Into the building, Soraya identifying herself to three security officers in the small lobby; into the elevator and up to the sixth floor, then on to apartment 621.

Once they were inside the apartment, Soraya waved her hand toward the living room with its pale pink walls and white furniture. "Go on. Mix yourself a drink. I want to change into something loose." With a cheerful smile, she hurried down a short hall.

His guard up, Camellion went into the living room and walked behind the short bar trimmed in leather. Wishing he were armed, he went about making one of his favorite drinks:

two parts Scotch and one part Perrier over two ice cubes. He looked around the well-stocked bar for Angostura. There wasn't any, but it wasn't all that important. Making the drink, he looked for answers—*This is worse than trying to eat lobster!* Fact: She had invited him to her apartment. Why? *I make a pass and she turns me down?*

Pure instinct informed Camellion that was not the answer. What to do was rather obvious. Use the method of any wise and prolific make-out artist—*I'll not make any pitch.*

Relaxing on the long sectional sofa, Camellion found it difficult to keep his eyeballs from popping out of his skull when Soraya returned. She might as well have been naked! Wearing a green-and-white print caftan, she sat down next to him, a cigarette in her hand, an amused smile on her face.

This has to be a come-on! No woman in her right mind would wear a garment of such sheerness that her full breasts, with their pointed nipples, are revealed more clearly than they would be in a medium twilight! Unless she wanted the inevitable to happen!

She snuggled closer to him. "Now, Jeff, what shall we talk about?"

Let's try to throw her a wild curve! "Well, let's see. I owe you . . . I figure twelve hundred and fifty dollars. I'll write a check and—"

"Say, you're not gay, are you?" Frowning, Soraya drew back in puzzlement. Her expression showed annoyance at what she no doubt considered a rejection.

"Not hardly," Camellion said, rather coldly. He leaned over, put his drink on the coffee table, turned and drew her into his arms. Her hands slid up to his face and then around his neck. The smooth, white skin came closer, the long upper lip pouting at him. There was that perfume he couldn't place; the green eyes, bright and pinpointed like a junkie's; the flame-colored hair down around her shoulders. The lips on his were warm and giving, and the wet tongue that moved into his mouth was a live thing trying to reach the fingers digging into his neck. Through his coat, he could feel the hard points of her nipples as her breasts flattened, cushioning him with their warm support.

With a burst of thought, the answer to why came to him. Soraya was that kind of woman who liked to give herself to a man she considered inferior, a man she considered beneath her. In that way, she was the aggressor and didn't have to consider the man an equal sex partner. Because it was she who decided, it was then she who was superior.

His desire for her had caught up in his chest as he crushed her against him. She breathed heavily into his mouth, squirming against him, while he let his fingers move through the side slit of the caftan and walk along the warm skin of her inner thigh. With his other hand, he unzipped the front of the caftan and pulled it down to her waist, the falling away of the garment exposing her full, round breasts.

Soraya moved her head back after many long moments, her eyes almost completely closed, her mouth remaining open. Camellion bent and kissed her neck, sucking in the skin so that an angry red mark appeared on the whiteness. All the while he fondled her breasts, thumb and forefinger going from nipple to nipple, rolling and kneading.

"Oh-ohhh," she gasped, pushed herself from him and pulled his head to her breasts. Her whole body shivered as he grasped one swelled teat and sucked the inflamed nipple into his mouth; and as he drew on the velvety redness, she rolled from side to side like a ship on a stormy sea, moving toward him and thrusting the protrusion deeper into his anxious mouth. At the same time, one of her trembling hands fumbled for the zipper of his trousers.

Suddenly, Soraya pushed herself from him.

"The bedroom," she gasped, her face contorting with lust. "Let's g-go to the b-bedroom."

With a quick movement, she stood up and let the caftan slide to her ankles. Stepping out of it, she turned and, stark naked, headed toward the doorway.

Camellion, with lightning speed, was off the sofa and after her. Catching her before she was halfway across the room, he pulled her into his arms, his hands going to her buttocks.

"P-Please," she moaned. "The b-bedroom . . . let's . . ." Her voice trailed off in a gurgle of pleasure as he squeezed each warm mound in his hands and pushed his own steel hardness against her.

She put her arms around his neck, and again their lips met. Carefully, Camellion slipped his tongue onto her lips and caressed them with warmth and wetness. At first, she resisted,

61

but only very slightly; then she entered into the partnership, parting her lips until his tongue was doing a tango with hers.

Camellion pushed her away and, with a swift motion, picked her up in his arms and gently placed her on the thick white rug. She didn't attempt to get up; she only lay there on her back, her eyes closed . . . her legs open . . . waiting. . . .

He undressed very quickly and was soon lying beside her, his eager hands exploring her body . . . feeling . . . massaging . . . permitting her passion to build, without being forced. Soraya lay as though in some kind of trance, her lovely breasts indicating her increasing passion, rising and falling with greater rapidity.

He stroked and kissed her eyelids, her fine-boned nose, moving slowly—his lips, tongue and fingers—over her body, down over the bared neck, the heaving breasts, down over her silken stomach and smooth belly. With deft fingers he probed the wedged-shaped area of curly red hair, at the junction of the inside of her thighs.

"Do me! Do me!" she panted throatily.

Carefully, gradually, Camellion edged over his body until he was above her and his legs between hers. Her hand went to his rigid hardness. But he did not enter—not yet.

"H-Hurry," she whispered. *"Hurry!"*

Both his hands enfolded her body and he again lowered his head to hers until his lips met her trembling mouth and she accepted his tongue. Then and only then did he arch forward, pushing the tip of his hardness forward, into her begging orifice.

"Not . . . n-not too fast," she whispered, her arms going up around his neck.

Camellion relaxed, allowing his organ to rest in place, letting her absorb the feel of it and to build her expectancy of what would follow. Gasping in delight, she pulled his head to hers, and the gasping mouth sucked on his tongue, pleading with him, begging him, to continue.

He did . . . holding steady for a moment, then slowly forcing himself all the way in. She gave a tiny cry of delight, her arms tightened around his neck, her legs over his. Carefully he began his in-and-out motions. His arms tightened around her, and her arms and legs tightened around him, a torrid bliss uniting their bodies, making them one. They were both hungry for the supreme moment, that final, explosive sensation, and rapidly the pace became more furious.

"Faster!" she gasped. *"F-Faster!"*

And Camellion gave it to her that way, increasing speed, her own loins thrusting up to meet his forward plunging.

"Ohhhh!" she cried. "Now! *Nowwwwwww!"*

It was *now* with him, too. The rapture of their two bodies had mingled flame and fire together, so that when it was time for one it was time for the other.

Surging, swaying, heaving, the frenzy stored up and burst forth, until tension and strength and pure naked passion overflowed and swallowed them both in a strange but beautiful exhaustion. They lay there, recovering their senses.

The doorbell rang!

The doorbell rang again—this time a long 6-second ring!

I'll be a bow-legged frog in a blue bottle! In a flash, Camellion rolled over Soraya, who got to her feet with equal speed, a look of astonishment on her face now dotted with tiny beads of perspiration.

"Down the hall! Into the bedroom—quick!" she gasped, panic in her voice. She glanced in fright at Camellion, who was picking up his clothes from the rug, and hurried to the front of the sofa to slip on her caftan.

All the while the doorbell kept up a continuous buzzing.

Clothes in hand, the Death Merchant raced down the hall. Behind him, in the living room, Soraya slipped the caftan over her naked body.

Richard cursed the capriciousness of a laughing Fate. Damn it! He would like to have spent the night with Soraya, whom he considered a well-oiled Sex Machine.

He reached the darkened bedroom, gently closed the door, switched on the light and began to dress. He had put on his shorts and was stepping into his pants when he heard muffled voices from the living room . . . muted, angry voices, but he couldn't understand who was saying what and to whom. And there he was, caught with his pants down—almost!

The circuits of his mind clicked furiously. Was the interruption planned, part of a convenient trap, part of the mental programming procedure? *Not a chance. Soraya's surprise was genuine. She was genuinely afraid. It has to be that damned*

Charles Franzese at the door. At least somebody well known to the security guards downstairs, or they would have phoned before permitting whoever it was to take the elevator.

Camellion had put on his shirt, tucked the ends into his pants and was buckling his belt when the door was jerked open and three men stormed into the room. Behind them was Soraya, looking as if she had been smacked in the face with a wet towel.

Charley Franzese stared at Camellion, who—when he had read the mobster's bio at the Company's N.Y.C. Center—had wondered how Soraya could be attracted to such an ugly.

Franzese looked like the Hollywood version of a goof—long hair, a ruddy and pimpled rodent-like face, the ears so large they resembled miniature sails, a nose that resembled a small red apple and beaver teeth. But what Franzese lacked in looks, he made up in brainpower. A man does not crawl out of the slums and become a bit-time mobster by being stupid.

It still doesn't make sense, Camellion thought, watching Franzese stare at him through dark glasses. *How can such a hunk of attractive flesh like Soraya be attracted to a bedbug like Franzese? Pish'n-tosh. I'm going to have to slap the hell out of him and his two goons.*

The other two hoods—all muscles and no brains—stood a little behind the Death Merchant, giving him the tough eye, their stares saying you're-going-to-get-yours-pal.

Soraya rushed up to Franzese and put her hand on his arm. "Charley, please. Let's not have any trouble." Her voice shook, all her composure gone.

Franzese, throwing her hand off, turned on her. She backed away.

"You Goddamn bitch!" he snarled savagely. "Like I said out there, I heard you had an evening's date with some sucker. I've been looking all over town for him and you. You damned slut! Don't tell me you two weren't fucking up a storm!" He turned and looked at Camellion. The two hoods grinned. "There's not going to be no trouble. I'm just going to beat this redneck to a pulp. That's all I'm going to do."

Camellion, enjoying himself immensely, pretended fear.

"L-Listen, Mister, I didn't k-know she was your girl!" He put a tremble in his voice and backed off—*Walk into it, you excuse for a cockroach!*

Charley "Blackeye" Franzese did just that. Thinking his victory would be an easy one, he advanced on Camellion, who stopped by the wall and let fear flicker all over his face.

With a sneer, Franzese tried to grab Camellion's shirt-front with his left hand and give him a cross to the jaw with his right fist. What he tried was one thing. What he succeeded in doing was another.

The Death Merchant grabbed Franzese's left wrist, blocked the right cross and let the flabbergasted hoodlum have a *Fumikomi* front snap kick directly in the stomach, applying a *Ka-soku-te* bottom heel slam with just enough force to have shock switch off the moron's consciousness.

The same lightning-quick leap carried the Death Merchant forward, toward the two other goons, who were too dumbfounded to have time to protect themselves. Even before Franzese had time to fall completely to the rug, Camellion was smashing the closest thug with a left *Seiken,* a left forefist that caught the gorilla on the side of the neck. With a loud gurgle, the man started to wilt.

The third gunman jumped back and tried to pull a snub-nosed .38 Colt revolver from a shoulder holster. The poor fool didn't even have time to pull the weapon from the leather. At the same time that Camellion—just to make sure—let the first hood have a dynamite rear thrust kick that snapped four of the man's ribs, he sliced the second dunce, who was trying to pull a piece, with a right *Haito*-ridge hand that broke the man's jaw. A cobra-quick left *Hira Ken* knuckle-joint blow to the side of the man's head sent him the rest of the way into dreamland.

Soraya, who had backed against the dresser, gaped at Camellion as though she were staring at Superman come to life.

"My God!" she choked out. "H-How did you do that?"

Camellion did some fast thinking—*Should the Red Chinese take time to check, they'll find that the real Jefferson Davis Hafferton is not a Karate expert.*

"Don't ask me," he said, giving her a dumb look. "Maybe I saw it in a movie!"

"And did the movie teach you how to do all that?" She continued to stare suspiciously at him as he looked around the bedroom. The two stooges were out cold. Franzese, his dark

65

glasses half off his face, lay on his side in a fetal position. A low moan escaped his mouth.

Camellion knelt down and rolled the man over on his back. He chopped the gut-battered Franzese across the jaw with a sword-ridge hand, then reached under the man's coat and pulled out a Detonics .45 auto-loader.

"What are you going to do?" asked Soraya, watching his every move.

Camellion almost said, *I'm disarming those poor fools.* But he caught himself in time.

He gave her a phony look of surprise. "Why, I'm taking their guns away from them," he said, hoping she wouldn't ask why he thought they were carrying iron in the first place. "I'm surprised that you associate with such people. Who is that man with the sunglasses—your husband?"

Beginning to regain her composure, Soraya quickly shook her head.

"No, not my husband," she said, an angry hint to her voice as she watched him pull the .38 Colt from one hood, then go over and jerk out a Smith & Wesson 9mm auto-pistol from underneath the other man's coat.

He stood up and looked at her. "Do you have a trash disposal?"

"In the kitchen," she said, her green eyes boring holes in him. "But why throw away those guns?"

"It's against the law to carry firearms in New York," he said simply. "By the way, aren't you going to call the police?"

"No," she said all too quickly, following him to the bedroom door. "There's no reason to involve the police and have a scandal over a . . . a jealous suitor," she added when they were in the hall and headed for the kitchen. "Forget my fee for the evening. That should make up for the trouble you've been through."

The Death Merchant didn't answer. They reached the kitchen and Soraya turned on the light and indicated the door of the trash disposal chute in the wall. The tile cold on his bare feet, he walked over to the wall, pulled open the square door and, one by one, dropped in the guns.

Ignoring Soraya, who hurried after him, he hurried back to the bedroom, sat down on her bed and put on his shoes and socks. All the while, Soraya watched him the way a farmer would look at a Little Green Man stepping out of a UFO in the middle of his wheatfield.

Charley Franzese and his two gunsels didn't move, although one of them moaned softly by the time Camellion had slipped on his jacket and was ready to leave.

He paused by the front door and looked at Soraya Duncan, thinking, *The bitch suspects I'm not what I claim to be!*

"Will you be all right?" he asked her, pretending concern. "That chap with the dark glasses? He won't beat you, will he?"

"Oh no," she said with a tiny laugh. "Nothing like that. He yells and shouts and uses filthy language, but he won't dare strike me. I'll be all right."

She put her hand on his arm when he reached for the doorknob.

"Tell me, how was I in there?" she asked anxiously. "On the rug? Did I satisfy you?"

He looked at Soraya and smiled. "The best. The best I ever had," he lied.

Seven minutes later, Camellion was walking through the quiet lobby, the three security men giving him an odd look, which he pretended not to notice. The evening hadn't been a total failure. He had scored with Soraya and had saved the Company almost three grand.

But now she suspects. She has to. If she didn't, Franzese would. *They'll report to the 3rd Bureau and the Orientals will check in New Orleans. It's time for Jefferson Davis Hafferton to go out of business. It's time now for a direct approach.*

He was on the sidewalk, hailing a cab, when he thought once more of Soraya. She had been good. After all, there was never any bad. Only good, better and best. He rated Soraya as better.

Getting into the cab, he had another thought: *I wonder if Ewart Gremmill is still alive.*

Chapter Six

Being one of those people who could easily get by on as little as four hours' sleep, Camellion could have been out of bed as early as 7:30 the next morning. Why bother? He didn't get out of bed until 10:00. By 11:30, his breakfast—black coffee, a small glass of honey and two vitamin pills—and yoga breathing exercises were over with, and he began to pack, in preparation for leaving the Payson Arms.

Bill Fieldhouse, sitting on a chair, drinking coffee and eating an apple turnover, watched him pack. Every now and then, Fieldhouse would think of Soraya Duncan and chuckle.

"It's too bad that Franzese and two of his goons had to show up," he said amiably. "You could have spent the night with her. You would have had Thanksgiving, Christmas and your birthday all rolled into one. Sex is like the plague, I always say. And like the plague it can only be cured in bed."

"If Franzese hadn't showed up, I wouldn't have saved the Company all that money," Camellion said, putting six folded shirts into one of the two suitcases. He wondered how Fieldhouse would take the news of his latest plan—*When I tell him*.

Wiping his fingers on a handkerchief, Fieldhouse nodded. "You're right about that. You're right, too, about moving out of here. But I don't think Franzese and his hoods will be around here looking to get even. As far as Franzese is concerned, this is just another hotel. He starts trouble here and he knows management would call the police. The police would be happy to grab that crumb on as little as a traffic ticket. The Third Bureau is another matter. They'll check on the *doppelganger*. When they find out he knows nothing

68

about Karate, they'll try to grab you, either here or on the street. They won't want to terminate you until they find out what you know."

Camellion closed and locked one suitcase. "Exactly. And if they attempted the grab-job here, there'd be a lot of TV and newspaper coverage. We don't want the Payson Arms to have publicity of any nature."

"You haven't said where you'll be staying," Fieldhouse said casually. "How do we contact you?"

"I'll get in touch with you," Camellion said. He leaned over the bed and looked into the metal case containing his makeup materials. "Where I am going must remain a secret."

Not expecting such an answer, Fieldhouse almost choked on the cigarette he had just lighted.

"Your secret!" he said, resentment evidence in his voice. "What's wrong? Don't you trust us? Or have you forgotten that we're on the same side? Yet I'm not even supposed to know where you're going to be!"

The Death Merchant closed and locked the cosmetic and disguise case, then sat down on the bed, turned and looked levelly at a half-angry Fieldhouse. "Bill, it's not a matter of trust, not in the sense that you mean it. It's just that I never break my own rules of security. Understand?"

Fieldhouse pondered for a moment and took another drag on his Vantage cigarette. "Frankly, I don't," he finally said. "I don't see how you'll be safer at another hotel. Even if you use another name, it's possible that agents of the Third Bureau will find you."

Sighing, Camellion sat down on the bed. *It would be better to explain to Fieldhouse. . . .*

"I won't be staying at a hotel. I have my own safehouse in the New York area," he said straight out. "Who knows the future? I might need that same house a year or two from now. Should I tell you the location, the rest of the men at this station would have to know. Now, do you understand?"

Fieldhouse gave a lopsided grin, his feelings appeased. "Yeah, it makes good sense. But there's still the problem of communication. Of course, you would use a regular 6-Y code over a public phone?"

"Communication is not all that important at this stage of the game," Camellion said curtly. "I can tell you right now that our next move will be in a week or so. You and I are going to have a look at Soraya Duncan's master files. No telling what we might find."

Fieldhouse stiffened. His eyes narrowed and he gave Camellion a *is-this-guy-for-real?* stare. "You're saying we're going to burglarize her office in the dead of night? How in hell can we accomplish that bit of magic? Her offices are on the twenty-seventh floor of the Butler Building, and the security in that building is first rate. Watchmen making their rounds on the hour and guards down in the lobby. We wouldn't even be able to get past the guards in the lobby."

The Death Merchant's laugh was sly and sinister. "The Butler Building is only a short distance southwest of Pan Am's heliport."

Fieldhouse looked puzzled; then he forced a short, bitter laugh.

"I suppose we're going to use a chopper and climb down a rope ladder to the roof?" he said with mock seriousness. "Naturally the guards won't hear the noise of the chopper."

"Oh, nothing like that," Camellion laughed. Getting up, he continued with his packing, talking as he worked. "I'll explain how the helicopter will be used—at the proper time. Before I leave here, I'll write a message I want you to radio-squirt to Grojean. He'll have to arrange to have an eggbeater at the heliport of the Pan Am building. It shouldn't take him longer than a week to make arrangements."

He placed a bundle of socks in one side of the second suitcase and padded them into place, while Fieldhouse, rubbing the end of his chin, considered all the numerous possibilities, the most dangerous being that he and Camellion would be caught burglarizing the offices of the Olympia Escort Bureau. The more Fieldhouse thought about it, the less he liked the idea. Why, damn it! They'd have a better chance of sticking up Chase National Bank! The hell of it was that this weird man packing his suitcases was the boss. Grojean had made that absolutely clear. No one in his right mind ever argued with the chief of Counterintelligence. Grojean was always as objective as a kangaroo court.

"In the meanwhile," Camellion was saying, "I want you to use your contacts within the police department to check out the security system at the Butler Building. And I'll need an up-to-date blueprint of the building, plus a schedule of how the cleaning people operate at night in the building. We've got to know if Olympia's offices are cleaned on schedule every night."

"You seem certain that we can pull off this New York 'Watergate,' " Fieldhouse said, sucking in his breath. "I don't suppose you've forgotten the Third Bureau?"

"The job will require split-second timing, but we can do it," Camellion said soothingly. "I've pulled off bigger projects than this." He closed and locked the suitcase, then calmly eyed Fieldhouse and shrugged. "What about the Chinese? They already know we're wise to them from what happened in Rosemary Hills. They won't reactivate their mental programming until they're sure they can operate with safety."

Fieldhouse moved a hand through his hair. "Anyhow, they don't have anything to do with the Butler Building," he said resignedly. "We don't have to worry about them on that score—or about the New York police. If we hit Duncan's office at three in the morning, ninety percent of the cops will be asleep—or else ripping off somebody."

The Death Merchant smiled, thinking that New York was the only city that had a skid row that was constantly moving all over town on the subway system.

Putting the suitcases on the floor, Camellion asked, "Has Gremmill been taken care of?"

"By now he's part of a foundation of a building being built in the Bronx," Fieldhouse said and stood up. "What name will you be using, or is that also part of your own personal security?"

The Death Merchant put on his coat. "I'm going out to rent a car. I'll write that message to Grojean when I get back."

He left the room and went out into the hall, the lock clicking as the door closed. Fieldhouse lighted another cigarette, sat back down and did some thinking. It was worse than a swan dive in a brick yard.

They still didn't have the first clue about the mental programming plot. Now they were going to burglarize a Manhattan office building—and somehow use a helicopter!

Chapter Seven

The desire for safety stands against every great and noble enterprise!—so Tacitus once wrote. The Death Merchant, an avid reader of the Roman classics, agreed wholeheartedly. Because he did, he had established various safehouses in certain cities in the United States.

Years earlier, in New York, he placed confidence in a safehouse on the corner of Vermilyea Avenue and Corbett in Manhattan, under the name of Corliss Durbenten. However, in fighting the KGB, he had been forced to blow it up.

Three years later, he had established another safehouse off Rockaway Boulevard in Brooklyn, less than a mile north of the John F. Kennedy International Airport. Once or twice a year, as Allen Marion Coleman, an elderly retired watchmaker, he visited the small brick cottage and spent a week or so there. During the summer months, a maintenance company kept the grass trimmed and the flowerbeds weeded. The same company paid all the utility bills, which were usually at a minimum. Three times a year, Mr. Coleman paid the company for its services.

Security? The windows had steel shutters painted white. The front door and the back door were wood on the outside and steel plate on the inside; triple bolt locks top and bottom. Both doors and all the windows were tied in to a microwave system that, should anyone try to break in, would touch off a 118-db-sound-level siren hidden in the attic. If by some miracle some crumb did manage to get inside, sensor plates by the doors and the windows would flood the five rooms with tear gas.

Strangely enough, in spite of all this protection, a thief

would not have found anything of value. The furniture, while not exactly from Goodwill Industries, was still the kind that one would buy on the installment plan from Sears & Roebuck. Another oddity about the tidy house was that there was not a single radio or TV set in any of the rooms. Nothing that a thief could fence.

In spite of the drabness, there were items of great value in the house. Hidden in one wall of the bedroom was a cache of arms, spare cosmetics, a $6,000 short-wave radio and numerous changes of clothing for any season of the year. There were also five pounds of RDX in the narrow space, part of the trap that Camellion had rigged. Should the wrong people accidently discover the hidden opening and not press the proper buttons, also cleverly concealed, the explosion would be heard for miles. The owner, Allen Marion Coleman? How could you prosecute a post office box in Phoenix?

After leaving the Payson Arms, Camellion drove to Broadway. He proceeded south on Broadway, finally made a left on Canal Street and soon was crossing the Brooklyn Bridge into Brooklyn. Bored with ribbons of traffic and wishing he were back in Texas, he went to a small hotel on Flushing Avenue and, once inside the room, went to work with his makeup kit. A change of clothing and the job was complete. Richard J. Camellion had vanished. In his place was Allen Coleman, an almost-bald man with a wrinkled face and long, white sideburns.

He left the hotel, ambling past a desk clerk who didn't even glance at him, drove three more blocks, parked, went to a public phone booth and called the Abberdaxx Maintenance Company. No, he cackled. He didn't know how long he would be staying at the house. A week. Maybe two. He would phone and let them know when he was ready to leave New York and return to Phoenix, Arizona.

Sometime later, he arrived at the brick house off Rockaway Boulevard and began carrying in sacks of groceries.

Every day, Camellion drove into Manhattan.

On the first day, dressed in expensive clothes and carrying a $400 imported Tacuchi attaché case, he strode into the Butler Building and took an elevator to the 38th floor, the very top floor. He walked around for a time and, when no one was

73

looking, ducked into the service room that contained the stairs to the roof. If worse came to worst and he met one of the building's maintenance men, he could always say that he had walked up to the roof to enjoy the view. There was, however, no one on the roof. He looked around. There was the usual assortment of ventilation pipes, but no place where one could hide. Evidently, the air-conditioning units were in the basement. He quickly took the stairs back to the 38th floor.

On the third day, Camellion met Bill Fieldhouse and Gordon Hayes—big-as-a-mountain black CIA case officer—on Liberty Street, just south of the World Trade Center, at the southern tip of Manhattan. In a briefcase, Fieldhouse carried blueprints of the Butler Building, as well as a 20-page report of how Maddox Security Systems protected and patroled the building at night.

Fieldhouse had not heard from Grojean.

On the fourth day, still in the disguise of Allen Marion Coleman, Camellion went to the Butler Building and rented a one-room office on the 37th floor, telling Mr. Ellsworth, who handled rentals and leases for the company that owned the building, Kessler Real Estate, that he was in the investment business . . . stocks and bonds, that sort of thing. Mr. Ellsworth glanced at the engraved card that Camellion had given him—JASON B. SWAIN. INVESTMENTS. 1640 TAHOE DRIVE. TYLER, TEXAS 63090. 716-555-4879. Ellsworth would never know it, but Jason B. Swain was another *doppelganger* that Grojean had set up for an emergency.

"I'll want the office for a year," Camellion said pleasantly.

"Fine," Mr. Ellsworth said. "I'll have the lease drawn up. It should be ready tomorrow afternoon about this time.

On the fifth day, Camellion signed the lease and paid a year's rent in advance, giving Mr. Ellsworth a certified check drawn on a Manhattan bank.

"I have other business to attend to," Camellion said. "I'm not sure when I'll have office furniture moved in. I'll let you know."

On the eighth day, the Death Merchant met Fieldhouse and Dennis Float close to the Metropolitan Museum of Art in Central Park.

Fieldhouse had heard from Courtland Grojean. The helicopter was ready. It was waiting at the Pan Am heliport.

"Good," Camellion said and proceeded to outline his plan. "I'll call Ellsworth on the phone and tell him to expect the furniture the day after tomorrow."

"Then it's settled," Fieldhouse said. "We do it Thursday."

"Affirmative," Camellion said. "The day after tomorrow."

Chapter Eight

At 3:10 in the afternoon, four workmen dressed in coveralls began moving large wooden crates into room 3721 of the Butler Building. BEDICKER OFFICE SUPPLY CO. was printed on each box. From the various stencils, one could see that the two largest crates contained desks, while the smaller wooden boxes were filled with files and other office equipment.

Breathing heavily from the effort of their labors, the four men unstrapped the last crate from the large hand truck, left the office and returned to the freight elevator.

Mr. Ellsworth took a last look around the office, then walked out and closed the door, trying the doorknob to make sure that the lock had snapped shut.

Inside the crate marked DOUBLE PEDESTAL DESK was Richard Camellion. Bill Fieldhouse was inside a large box marked FOUR-WAY MODULAR DESKS, SECTION ONE. The wait would be a long one, a full 11 hours, but at least they had plenty of room and could stretch out.

At exactly 2:15 A.M. the next morning, the Death Merchant unlatched the bolt that released one end of the crate. He then pushed outward, the end—really a lid—swinging upward on hinges concealed inside the crate. Dressed entirely in black, including black boots with thick rubber soles, Camellion crawled out of the crate, pulling a small suitcase after him.

Four feet away, Bill Fieldhouse was crawling out of one end of the crate marked FOUR-WAY MODULAR DESKS, SECTION ONE. He, too, was pulling out a metal case with his gloved hands.

The office was not in total darkness. The top part of the

outside door was thick, wire-reinforced frosted glass. The top part of the outside wall was also composed of frosted glass, and light from the hall filtered through the glass.

"I hope to God these schedules are correct," whispered Fieldhouse, opening the suitcase he had taken from the crate.

"Didn't your contacts tell you that the cleaning schedule and the watchmen schedule never change?" Camellion slipped a vinyl mask of Frankenstein over his head, and pulled a cartridge and two holsters from the small suitcase. The large, special holsters contained two Walther P-38 auto-pistols, a 5-inch silencer attached to each weapon.

"I meant that there could always be a last-minute change," Fieldhouse said. "You said yourself that we've got to be prepared for anything." He pulled a mask of Wolfman over his head, then took his own P-38s from the case he had pulled from the crate. "When will the watchman pass here on his next round?"

"At two-thirty." The Death Merchant, having strapped the P-38s around his waist, slipped into a shoulder holster that contained a Webber-4b dart gun, a "Company" invention that contained 26 steel darts, each the size of a regular straight pin, hollow and filled with a very powerful sedative-hypnotic. Any human being struck by one of those needles would be out cold in less than a tenth of a second and sleep for hours.

The two men put on shoulder bags. Camellion's bag contained three smoke bombs, a gas mask and six tear gas canisters. Who could say what might go astray? The best laid plans of mice and men and Company people often have a habit of falling apart.

Once Camellion and Fieldhouse's equipment was in place, they closed the suitcases, shoved them back inside the crates and closed the lids. Earlier in the day Fieldhouse had suggested that if trouble arose, he and Camellion might be able to sneak back to the office and hide inside the crates. "Who would suspect anyone being inside crates of office furniture?" he had asked.

"A smart cop would, that's who," Camellion had said.

Both Camellion and Fieldhouse checked their special PRC-8 radios. It was possible that their lives might depend on one of the radios. Each man also carried a special pair of gloves, the horsehide fingers and palms almost an inch thick, the palms covered with what appeared to be thick steel wool.

The two men waited. Crouched by the ends of the crates from which they had just emerged, they waited impatiently for the watchman to pass by the office on his rounds. There were four watchmen that made the rounds every hour on the hour, each man taking nine floors, except the fourth man who had to work eleven floors. Every night the four watchmen rotated so that each man got his turn at the two extra floors, the 37th and the 38th. In the lobby there were four more watchmen on duty, two always at the desk, the other two making rounds outside the Butler Building.

Each watchman, making a round, carried a time-clock on a shoulder strap. On each floor there were various "key-stations." At each station, the watchman would take the key, secured to the inside of a small metal box by means of a chain, insert it into an opening in the clock and give it a twist, thereby making an imprint of the time on the paper dial inside the clock—proof to the insurance company that he was making a proper patrol.

Like most private agencies, Maddox hired a lot of retired policemen and, in the main, men past their prime. Yet these men carried .38 revolvers and could still pull a trigger. And being a retired cop is like having learned to swim: Once you've learned you don't forget. There was also the danger of discovery because of Factor-X. Precautions had been taken: In an extreme emergency, Camellion and Fieldhouse would force the elevator doors and, with the special gloves, slide all the way down on the cables to the first floor, provided the elevator they might choose was not in use at the time.

Presently they saw a shadow outside of the frosted glass. The watchman was passing on his rounds. The Death Merchant took out the notebook in which he had written the various schedules in ink that glowed faintly in the dark. The watchman who had just passed would hit one more key on this floor, the one around the corner by the bank of elevators. He would then take the stairs, walk down to the 36th floor and begin his rounds on that level.

The cleaning crew, composed of 104 janitors, cleaned the floors one by one, starting with the ground level and working upward. The routine never varied. According to the schedule, they wouldn't reach the 27th floor until 3:45 A.M. By then, the Death Merchant and Fieldhouse would be finished with Soraya Duncan's office and be on the roof.

"Let's go," Camellion whispered. "By the time we get to the stairs, the watchman will be on the thirty-sixth floor. He can hit all those keys in less than five minutes. We'll give him seven minutes; then we'll go on down to the thirty-sixth floor."

"It's still damned dangerous," Fieldhouse said matter-of-factly, checking his own Webber dart pistol. "The watchman who just passed finishes his run on the twenty-eighth floor. We must go all the way down to the twenty-seventh. We can't say it's impossible that we won't bump into the watchman who's patrolling Duncan's floor."

"It's highly improbable that we will," Camellion said. "Each watchman uses an elevator to go to the top floor of his route. He then starts to work downward. The watchman on this floor started on the thirty-eighth floor; he's the poor guy who's working eleven floors tonight. He'll finish on the twenty-eighth floor."

"So—?"

"That means the watchman below him began on the twenty-seventh floor and will finish on the nineteenth. All watchmen begin their rounds at the same time. By the time we reach the twenty-seventh floor, the watchman who handles that floor will have finished up and be in his little cubbyhole, taking his twenty-minute break. We'll have more than enough time to get inside Duncan's office. We'll wait until the two watchmen finish another patrol, then we'll head for the roof—and we'll still be ahead of the cleaning crew. Now let's go do it."

Dart guns in their hands, Camellion and Fieldhouse left the office, looked around and began creeping down the carpeted hallway, hurrying past darkened offices. The only lights were the so-called "running lights," small lights that gave just enough illumination for one to see his way. Of course, the cleaning crew would switch on all the bright overhead lights.

Ahead were the darkened windows of the building's outside wall. Basically, the interior of the building was of simple design. Many small, one-room offices were positioned so that they did not have outside windows. These smaller offices were arranged in "blocks" toward the center of each floor, while the larger offices and suites were situated toward the outside and had windows.

They came to a corner. With Fieldhouse keeping an eye on the rear, Camellion looked around the edge. There, ahead of him, were the rows of elevator doors and the regular stairs to the 36th floor. In the southwest corner was a firedoor, a lighted EXIT sign over it. This door opened to the service stairs.

The Death Merchant turned and glanced at Bill Fieldhouse. Because of the Wolfman mask over the case officer's face, Camellion couldn't see his expression and accurately judge his true feelings. But his body movements were sure and steady— *I was right. In any emergency, he'll do his part. He's not the usual career officer desk dodo.*

Camellion again looked toward the front. The area ahead was clear, the distance to the exit door about 100 feet.

"Let's move," Camellion said.

At a half-sprint, while watching all sides, they crossed the area, came to the firedoor and Camellion tried the handle. The lock was of the key-in-knob lockset variety. The door was unlocked, in keeping with New York law that all exit doors remain unlocked at all times. It wouldn't have made any difference if the door had been locked; it would only have taken Camellion longer to open it. He carried not only lock picks but special invented-by-the-Company devices that could open any slide-action deadbolt manufactured.

In a short while, he and Fieldhouse were in the stairwell and moving down the stairs lighted by small yellow bulbs. On to the 36th floor, down to the 35th, a slight pause, then the race downward continuing. The 31st . . . the 30th . . . the 29th . . . the 28th . . . their rubber-soled feet not making any sounds on the steel-mesh steps. The hell with 7 minutes here and 5 minutes there. Such a time schedule would only be pure guesswork, and the service stairs were just as safe.

At length, Camellion and Fieldhouse were on the small landing in front of the firedoor that opened to the 27th floor. It was impossible to be absolutely certain about any of the watchmen. Some sort of small difficulty might have developed that would require the attention of one or more of the guards, in which case they would be in an "off-schedule" position. A sprinkler-head might pop. Any number of things could happen.

But if all was as it should be, the watchman who had made the rounds on the 27th floor would now be taking his break on the 19th. Camellion glanced at his watch. He and Fieldhouse had gained 13 minutes by going down the service stairs instead of using the regular public stairs. Couple that time with the watchman's break, some minutes of which were already gone—*Hmmmm, not too bad. We've gained some time.*

"We have not more than fifteen minutes to get inside Duncan's office," he whispered to Fieldhouse. "All set?"

"We'll never do it standing here," Fieldhouse whispered.

"Be prepared for anything," Camellion warned. "It's impossible to tell what we might run into."

Camellion opened the exit door and looked out. Silence. Low, yellow illumination of only the running lights. They crept through the door of the service entrance and hurried north along a corridor that, toward the center of the east side, became two sections. One segment continued north. The other part went west, past the elevators, then, at a suite of offices, turned and once more moved north. The Olympia Escort Bureau was at the north end of this corridor, where it merged with the east-west corridor on the north side of the floor.

In less than seven minutes, the Death Merchant and Bill Fieldhouse were at the thick, blue-tinted glass door, and one of Camellion's lock picks was probing inside the Mortise cylinder of the ordinary switch lock. It took Camellion only several minutes to arrange the tumblers into the proper sequence and open the door. Once he and Fieldhouse were inside the office, Camellion closed the door, taking care to make sure that the lock snapped shut, even though it wasn't likely that the watchman, on his next round, would shake the door again. He would have done that on his first round of the evening.

Now there wasn't any young and shapely receptionist in the area, only her desk and chair, the rest of the Danish furniture, the ridiculous-looking mobile and the artificial rubber plant in the reception area.

They hurried across the room, and the Death Merchant gently pushed open the frosted-glass door to Soraya Duncan's private office, an office that was quiet and empty. The drapes had not been pulled and the light from the outside made the office a place of soft twilight, with shadows drifting silently over Soraya's desk and the other furniture.

"I don't see any filing cabinets," whispered Fieldhouse, "or is there a file room?"

Camellion went to the door that led to the other office, the door he had seen Gregory Gof use. "Gof is Soraya's accountant," he said. "The files might be in his office."

He and Fieldhouse moved into Gof's office—a desk, adding machines, three large video terminal computers, two hideaway drawer files, a few Duo Data Processing rollaway files, one 20-drawer tab card file and, best of all, three rows of four-drawer-full suspension files, seven files to each row. Light, filtering in from East 48th Street, gave the room a gloomy appearance.

Fieldhouse made a motion of disgust with one hand, whispering savagely, "We're never going to find anything in here. There are too many files and too little time."

Looking around, the Death Merchant was inclined to agree with him. But he only said, "We're here; let's give it a go. Watch the beam of your penlight. No one can see it from the hall, but they might from the building across the way on Forty-eighth Street."

He moved to one of the regular four-drawer suspension files and saw that it was locked by a Proof Lock system. *Oh damn!* He could open a "burglar-proof" Proof Lock with the equipment he carried but it would take time. *Fieldhouse was right—there isn't enough time. I didn't expect any Proof Locks.*

"You keep an eye on Duncan's office while I open this first file," Camellion said. "We'll see what's in this first file, then call it quits. We don't have the time." He reached into the shoulder bag and took out a flat, black case, his fingers sweating within the thin rubber of the surgical gloves.

He was about to open the case and Fieldhouse was almost to the door when they both heard the loud noise from Soraya Duncan's office, the kind of crash made by a small piece of furniture that is accidentally knocked over. By pure subconscious perception, the Death Merchant knew that the noise had been made by the chrome bullethead tree lamp that stood next to an easy chair in front of Soraya's desk.

"That wasn't the wind, old buddy," Fieldhouse whispered grimly. Reaching the door, he glanced at Camellion, who had put away the lock-pick case and had pulled both the Webber dart gun and a silenced P-38 from their holsters.

"Open the door and take a look," he whispered. "If we've been discovered get behind one of the end files of the last row and put on your gas mask."

"Well, if we can't be a tree, we'll have to be a bush," muttered Fieldhouse. "Goddamnit! I knew we should have stayed home."

Standing to the right of the door, he reached out, turned the knob, pulled the door open, looked out, jerked back his head and slammed the door, from the outside of which *thud, thud, thud* noises were coming—bullets hitting the wood, slugs fired from weapons equipped with silencers.

"Hell, we've walked into a trap!" hissed Fieldhouse, deep fear in his voice. "The office is full of men, and they're not watchmen."

"Mercy, mercy, dear Mother Percy," murmured the Death Merchant. "We've been outsmarted and outmaneuvered."

As Fieldhouse turned and raced to the last row of files, Camellion ran to the right of the door, grabbed the knob and jerked open the door, quickly ducking back out of the line of fire. This time there were loud, screaming *zings* as high-powered slugs chopped into the front of the metal filing cases, facing the door, in the first row.

Camellion didn't bother to return the fire. Instead, he raced along the north side to the last row of files where Fieldhouse, crouched behind the last file on the northeast corner, had pulled off his Wolfman mask and was fitting a molded-rubber Sherwood M-17 gas mask over his face. He moved over and made room for Camellion, who reared up and triggered off three quick shots at the doorway. In spite of the situation, Camellion felt intense pleasure when he heard the damage caused by the 9mm projectiles and the angry curses of the men in the office.

One hollow-pointed bullet banged into a brass rubbing hanging on the west wall of Soraya's office—from a plate dating back to 1443 and depicting Sister Marguerite de Scornay, the Abbess of Nivelles, Belgium, being introduced to the enthroned Virgin and Child. Now the good Sister had a bullethole in her neck. Another bullet had bored into the wall. The third slug had struck one of 12 glass modules that were fastened together. Filled with water, each module reflected light. Now the other 11, impelled by the force of the bullet, fell from the table and crashed to the floor.

"Get the hell in there and get them!" yelled an angry voice.

"It's a trap all right," Camellion whispered, rage in his voice. "That's Charley Franzese out there. I recognize his voice—him and his gunsels. Keep them busy while I put on my gas mask."

Without a word, Fieldhouse reared up and fired a round from each P-38, a *bbbzzziitttt* sound coming from each silencer. He now realized why Jason B. Swain had opened the door: to lob a gas grenade through the opening.

By now, Franzese and the other five gunmen in Soraya Duncan's office had moved out of the line of fire and had positioned themselves on either side of the door. They had intended to use surprise, but Frank Hurt—the clumsy sonofabitch—had to go and knock over a lamp and foul up everything.

Barney Gindow, a roly-poly sadist with a fat face covered with a network of fine red veins, nudged Franzese in the side and whispered, "What the fiddler's fuck we going to do? We were supposed to have them knocked out by now!"

"Shut up and let me think," Franzese growled, angry with himself. The entire plan had been his, and Wang Ch'en-Yi had agreed that the scheme, while risky, had considerable merit. Franzese and his crew of cutthroats would wait in the consultation rooms and grab the man who called himself Jefferson Davis Hafferton and whoever might show up with him; they would inject them with a strong sedative and hide them in the closet in Soraya's office. Then they'd turn on all the lights, sit down, start playing poker and wait for the cleaning crew. There wouldn't be any problem with the building's security guards. The Maddox watchmen knew Franzese and Gindow, having seen the two men enter the building numerous times at night with Soraya Duncan. After Hafferton was unconscious and hidden in the closet, Franzese would phone the guards in the lobby and apologize for not telling them earlier that he and some friends were playing poker in Miss

Duncan's office, and had been there since the office had closed. Why hadn't the watchman on that floor seen a light? Oh, that? Because they were playing poker by the light of only one lamp—the one that idiot Frank had knocked over—and because there's an acoustical panel between the lamp and the door. Franzese had thought of every angle: Why, that very day a large half-square panel had been delivered to Honey-Bun's office, just for that purpose, so that the watchman could see it . . . just in case anyone would have checked after the phone call.

Getting the unconscious Hafferton out of the building had also been arranged. Franzese and his men, all pretending to be drunk, would simply carry out the "passed-out" Hafferton —supported by two men—out of the building. And the second man could be handled in the same manner, whoever he was. Probably a U.S. Intelligence agent. But first they had to get at Hafferton and his helper—and now they had to kill the two sonsofbitches. They'd never be able to take them alive.

Homer Reel whispered in his raspy voice, directing his words at Franzese, "In another five minutes the watchman is gonna pass. He hears some noise, he's gonna be in here. What the hell we gonna tell him?"

"We're going to have to kill them," Franzese whispered savagely.

"Yeah, how in hell are we going to get in there to do it?" demanded Clyde Wooten. "The whole thing has fallen apart. We should have done what Barney said. We should have grabbed them when they first came in."

"Hell, yes, we should have," Gindow growled, "but the 'Big Brain' here wanted to be certain. He had to wait until they were in Steel Fingers' office. We trapped them, all right. We trapped them so Goddamned good we can't get at them."

"Shut your damned mouth, Barney," warned Franzese, exerting his authority. The office was in a kind of twilight and he had removed his dark glasses. Now he reassuringly patted the handkerchief pocket of his coat where he had placed the sunglasses. Without dark glasses, the light from an ordinary bulb would force him to close his eyes. "I'll tell you yellow-bellies how we're going to get them. They're in there down behind the files. While three of us set up a fire and keep them pinned down, the other three can rush in and take them by surprise. See what I mean?"

The others glanced skeptically at Franzese. Yeah, they saw what he meant, and none of them liked it.

"Bullshit!" sneered Oscar Yehling, a creep who would have wasted his own mother if the contract price were right. "Which three are going to 'volunteer' to commit suicide?"

"Damn right," said Gindow. "Those guys are pros. They've got silencers and know their business. I'm not going in there and get my butt shot off!"

"Huh!" smirked Frank Hurt. "You'd be better off to lose fifty pounds from that fat ass of yours!"

"Listen, when I give an order—" Franzese never finished. The three *plops* of objects hitting the rug made him and the others turn and look behind them. A few seconds later there were loud hissings from the two smoke grenades and the multi-purpose tactical gas grenade. Instantly, thick clouds of violet smoke and gray-white CN gas began pouring into the office. Instantly, Franzese and his group were helpless. With the tear gas and the smoke pouring into their lungs, all that Franzese and his boys could do was flee. Choking and coughing, Franzese realized that the two men in the file room would charge out, but he was coughing with such intensity that he couldn't talk and communicate a warning to the others. Hardly able to see, gasping, he staggered toward Soraya's desk, knowing he didn't have time to reach the reception area; and to be caught in the open would be fatal.

Barney "The Pig" Gindow's highly honed survival instincts flashed the same kind of warning to him. But like Franzese, he too was racked with coughing and could not yell at the other men, some of whom were staggering through the outer door into the reception area.

Gindow and Franzese were practically falling behind Soraya's large executive desk when the Death Merchant and Bill Fieldhouse stormed into the office from the file room, a Walther P-38 auto-pistol in each hand. The gas masks protected them from the smoke and the tear gas; yet their vision was limited to almost 3 feet and wouldn't expand until they were out of the office. They had only one plan: to get to the roof and get the hell away from the Butler Building.

Camellion saw a man staggering through the smoke—6 feet

in front of him—and fired. A *bbbzzziitttt* from the silencer on the P-38, and Homer Reel cried out in pain and went down with a 9mm projectile that had stabbed through his stomach and lodged against his spine. A *bbbzzziitttt* from the silencer of the Walther in Fieldhouse's left hand and Oscar Yehling, who was going through the outer door to the receptionist area, spun around and fell back, a bullet having gone through both lungs, chopping his heart apart on its route. Stone dead, he crumpled against one end of a three-seat sofa.

Clyde Wooten and Frank Hurt, who were already in the reception office and feeling as if their eyes had been washed out with soap suds, were the next to die.

Tears streaming down his face, Hurt caught Camellion's 9mm bullet in the left side, the punch of the projectile throwing him against the artificial rubber plant.

Another *bbbzzziittt* from the silencer on the P-38 in Camellion's left hand and Wooten cried "UHhhhaaa!" and, a slug in his chest, fell across the receptionist's desk. He reminded the Death Merchant of a taco!

Out in the hallway, Henry Oestreicher, the watchman, gaped in utter astonishment at what he considered to be something straight out of the impossible. He had "hit-the-key" in the other corridor and had been passing the Olympia Escort Bureau office when one of the inner doors had been flung open and two men, gasping and coughing, had staggered out. With them had come a cloud of violet-colored smoke!

Oestreicher was still immobile from surprise when a third man groped his way through the door, then suddenly spun and fell. The next thing that Oestreicher saw was two more men coming through the door.

Oh, my God! The two men had guns in each hand and were wearing gas masks!

A retired beat patrolman, the 68-year-old Oestreicher had more sense than to think he could shoot it out with what he presumed to be two professional killers—no doubt "mechanics" from one of the Mafia families. The only thing to do was get out of their way and call for help. His heart pounding, Oestreicher turned and ran as fast as he could to the north-south hall on the west side of the floor. Coming to an inset with a water fountain, he got down by the fountain, pulled the walkie-talkie from the case on his Sam Browne belt and frantically turned it on.

"There's a shooting going on up here on the twenty-seventh floor," he said hoarsely, holding the walkie-talkie close to his mouth. "In the offices of the Olympia Escort Bureau. Call the police and the Fire Department. There's smoke pouring out of the inner office and I seen two gunnies wearing gas masks. They're pros, carrying pieces with silencers."

The Death Merchant came to the blue-tinted door to the hall and, with a well-placed 9mm bullet, shot the lock apart. Not only did the high-velocity slug blow off the lock, but caused two large cracks to zigzag horizontally across the glass door.

Camellion and Fieldhouse didn't waste time. They raced through the door and headed for the east-west corridor.

"We can take one of the elevators," panted Fieldhouse, his voice muffled through the gas mask. "We could be on the thirty-eighth floor before they realized what was happening. Hell, that watchman ran faster than a ten-year-old passing a cemetery."

Following Camellion around the corner of the central hall where the elevators were located, Fieldhouse assumed that his partner was going to follow his advice until the Death Merchant began punching all the "down" buttons, except on the middle elevator, whose lights showed that the car was rising.

"We'll confuse them," Camellion said calmly. "They expect us to go down, not up. Let's make them think we're going down. They could be waiting for us to start down; then they could throw the master power switch in the basement. How'd you like to be trapped in an elevator between floors?"

"The service stairs, right?" Fieldhouse said, looking up and down the corridor.

The Death Merchant's chuckle gave Fieldhouse an odd feeling.

"Right—as fast as we can run!" Camellion glanced up at the red light above the elevator that was moving upward. It was already on the 17th floor. "Like the airline advertisement says, let's move our tails."

* * *

By the time the elevator had stopped on the 27th floor and three watching men were cautiously coming out with High Standard pump shotguns in their hands, Camellion and Fieldhouse were in the service tube and racing up the stairs. They were already on the steps on the 29th floor by the time the three watchmen had linked up with Henry Oestreicher and were approaching the offices of Olympia Escort Bureau.

Camellion and Fieldhouse would have been on the 30th, if not the 31st, floor, if they hadn't taken the time to turn on their PRC-8 radios, extend the antennas and repeat "Snowbird" three times each. It was possible that one PRC-8 might malfunction, but the chances of two not working properly would be synchronicity beyond the realm of all possibility.

Finally, reaching the small landing of the 33rd floor, Camellion and Fieldhouse dropped two smoke canisters and two CN grenades down the stairs. Anyone coming up that route would be in for a coughing and eye-watering surprise.

. . . The 34th landing . . . feet pounding, lungs gasping for air. Up the steps to the 35th, all the while extremely cautious, expecting exit doors above them to open and figures with guns appear.

They reached the 36th landing, raced on to the 37th, then upward to the 38th. The Death Merchant paused, took a very deep breath, exhaled, and took another deep breath, increasing his *Ch'i*.[17]

Analyze. Could some of the watchmen have guessed their plan and have taken an elevator to the 38th floor and be waiting? The Death Merchant had to consider the possibility. However, it wasn't very likely. For one thing, there weren't enough watchmen on duty. For another, most of the guards were ex-cops whose training would compel them to wait for backups, for the regular police to arrive with proper weapons—riot shotguns, tear gas, a SWAT force.

By then, we'll be in the helicopter and soaring away into the wild blue yonder. Correction! It's night. The wild black yonder. One chance in a hundred, but I've got to take it.

17. Intrinsic energy. A method of breathing by which the karateist can supercharge his system and thereby use all of his strength when he wants to. But *Ch'i* is not simple breathing. It also involves *Kata* and *Sanchin*. An understanding of both is needed in order to liberate and focus total *Ch'i*.

He pushed open the door to the hallway and looked out. Silence. Dimly glowing running lights. No one in sight. Another 150 feet and there would be safety—*Unless something goes haywire and the eggbeater isn't there!*

"I don't hear any rotor blades." Fieldhouse's voice broke the eerie silence. "Ever try flapping your arms and flying?"

"You won't hear the chopper until I open the door to the stairway to the roof," Camellion explained. "According to the blueprints, these walls are filled with something called dursilene, a material that's not only an insulator but acts as sound-proofing. Let's run for it."

"What else have we been doing?" mocked Fieldhouse with macabre humor. He thought about the hoodlums they had wasted in Soraya Duncan's office. In New York State there were two types of murder indictments: felony murder and premeditated murder. If he and Jason B. Swain were caught, they'd be charged with premeditated murder—murder one! And the Company wouldn't be able to help them. The Company wouldn't even know them!

The Death Merchant and Fieldhouse ran down the corridor that stretched to the north. As they passed the end of the center east-west hall, they heard the distinct sound of several elevators rising.

They reached the east-west corridor on the north side of the floor, raced around the corner and rushed to the short corridor in the center. Just as they reached the beginning of the short hall, a voice to their left yelled, "Halt! This is the police!"

"They're at the end of the corridor," Camellion said, "to the east. Trigger off a magazine to keep them busy while I open the door to the steps."

"Don't tell me about it!" snapped Fieldhouse. "Just do it."

While a grinning Camellion raced to the firedoor, Fieldhouse stuck his right P-38 around the corner and began pulling the trigger. He jerked back after the fifth round and reached into his shoulder bag.

Several shotguns roared, a rain of pellets hitting the northeast corner of the hall opening and sending marble chips flying outward. A few moments later, Fieldhouse tossed a tear gas grenade around the corner, then leaned down and triggered off a few more shots at the same time that the Death

Merchant opened the lock on the firedoor with five well-placed 9mm projectiles and yelled, "Let's go!"

Jerking open the door, Camellion could hear the *flap, flap, flap* of the helicopter blades and, from experience, knew that the pilot had throttled down the rotor to idling speed.

Fieldhouse ran down the 10-foot hall, rushed through the entrance and closed the firedoor, saying in a loud voice as he and Camellion rushed up the steel steps, "This is not my idea of how to spend the early hours of a Friday morning."

The door at the top of the stairs, the one that opened to the roof, was unlocked. Camellion threw it open and stepped out onto the roof, Fieldhouse, right behind him, slamming the door shut.

A hundred feet southeast of the stairway housing sat the chopper, a Bell Jet-Ranger, a multi-role helicopter with a two-blade rotor and powered by a single Allison turboshaft engine, which now was idling.

Other than the pilot in the cockpit, there were two other men, both outside the chopper, UZI submachine guns in their hands.

While running toward the Bell, Camellion pointed at the closed door of the stairs and indicated that the two men should level down on the door.

Getting closer to the chopper, Camellion and Fieldhouse saw that the men with the UZIs were James Nivens and Dennis Float. Neither man seemed nervous or worried.

Camellion and Fieldhouse were halfway to the Bell Jet-Ranger when the roof door opened and two SWAT cops stepped out. Both men wore armored vests, gas masks, riot-control helmets with face shields, and carried M16 rifles. Neither man got the opportunity to get off a shot. Nivens and Float cut loose with the UZIs, the swarm of 9mm projectiles shattering the face shields and exploding the heads within the helmets. Float then concentrated on the edge of the doorway, firing three-round bursts while Nivens pulled the magazine from his UZI and shoved in one that was extra long, one that contained 60 9mm cartridges. All the while, both men continued to back toward the chopper, keeping very low to avoid the revolving rotor blades.

Nivens got into the chopper. Camellion and Fieldhouse followed him. Float's UZI was soon empty; then Nivens took over and began peppering the door with slugs as Float climbed aboard. Nivens was still firing when the pilot lifted off the roof and started the Bell climbing straight up. By the time the police had opened the stairway door and were out on the roof, the helicopter was out of range.

Once the Butler Building was only a recent memory, the pilot switched on the red and green flashing lights, not only to serve as a warning to other aircraft but because a chopper without lights would arouse suspicion from the New York Police Department Helicopter Patrol.

Camellion pulled off his gas mask. "What's the evasion plan?" he said to the mild-looking Nivens.

"Did you have to send those two cops to box city?" Fieldhouse said angrily, his hard eyes on Nivens and Float. He answered his own question. "I know you had to, or they would have brought us down and destroyed the chopper. This mess will sure give the media a lot to write about."

"More statistics for 'Murder City,'" Float said. He turned, reached out with a big hand to make sure that the door on the starboard side of the chopper was securely latched.

"What about the escape route?" Fieldhouse asked. Neither he nor the Death Merchant had had any previous information regarding the escape route. That phase of the operation had been Grojean's responsibility. All they knew was that Float and Nivens would receive a call at the Payson Arms station. On their own initiative, they had had George Simmons, one of the "bellboys" at the Payson Arms, waiting in the Hostess Twinkies bread truck several blocks from the Butler Building.

James Nivens said, "According to the pilot, we're going about fifty miles out over Long Island Sound and put down over a cabin cruiser."

The Death Merchant made a face. "I think the plan stinks. It won't take us long to get there, but what happens if we're spotted by a police helicopter? Somebody had better have the answer."

"We asked the pilot the same question," Nivens replied. "He explained that the chopper is rigged so that he can release some of the outside skin, on both sides, from the cockpit. When he does, both sides of the cockpit will read UNITED STATES WEATHER BUREAU, HART ISLAND STATION."

92

"We can't hardly step outside to look, can we?" said Float, his good-looking face breaking out in a grin.

"We can ask the pilot," Camellion said. He got up and moved forward to the cockpit. He leaned over the right shoulder of the pilot, who looked like he should have been playing basketball instead of piloting a helicopter.

"Have you done what you have to do to make the Weather Bureau signs appear?" Camellion asked. Through the windshield, he could see countless pinpoints of light below.

"Who are you?" The pilot didn't even bother to glance around.

"Swain or the Easter Bunny, or the Ayatollah Ruhollah Khomeini! It doesn't make a damned bit of difference. I'm in charge of the entire operation. Answer the question."

"Oh, Mr. Swain!" A new respect was in the pilot's voice. "Yes, I released the aluminum covers on both sides after we were several blocks from the Butler Building. If we're spotted by one of the Helicopter Patrol's birds, they won't suspect us. And we're flying under the take-off heights of planes from John F. Kennedy Airport and Newark International."

"What about the cabin cruiser?"

"No problem. I drop down over it. You guys hop off. But don't ask me where I land. That's on an NTKB.[18] Rest easy, Mr. Swain. You've got nothing to worry about."

The Death Merchant turned and started back to the other men.

Nothing to worry about? I have plenty to worry about. I'm not any closer to solving the riddle of how the invisibility file was stolen—and why—than when I got here. I still haven't found a single clue that tells us how the Red Chinese are mind-murdering subjects. I still don't have any direct evidence that Duncan and Franzese and the rest of the scum are involved with the Third Bureau—and I don't have anything to worry about! I'm going to have to do the unexpected, something the Chinese would never dream of. . . .

18. Need-to-know basis.

Chapter Nine

Four days after Death had invaded Soraya Duncan's offices, the newspapers and television broadcasters were still keeping the story alive, stating that the cause of the shootout involved groups of rival mobsters. The mystery was why Soraya Duncan and her girls were involved. Since there had never been even a whisper of scandal about the Olympia Escort Bureau, the media was very careful about what it wrote and said about the escort service, not wanting to be involved in a million-dollar lawsuit. But that Soraya Duncan had been a hooker was public domain, and the media made the most of it, mentioning old arrest records and writing feature articles about her association with "the alleged mobster, Charles Franzese."

The morning of the shootout, the police had taken Franzese and Gindow into custody and had tried to make stick a charge of "illegal possession of weapons." The DA's office wouldn't go for it. There wasn't any direct evidence. Homicide dicks knew what had happened. A Llama Comanche .357 Magnum and a Colt .45 auto-pistol had been found 8 feet in front of Soraya's desk, but there weren't any fingerprints. The weapons had been wiped clean. There was a smudged print on the magazine of the .45 Colt. The police, however, couldn't match the print with the thumbprints of either Gindow or Franzese.

The police questioned the two hoodlums about the four dead gunmen, all friends of Franzese and Gindow. What about them? What was there to know? responded Franzese and Gindow. The six of them had been in Soraya's office playing cards. Oh! Why hadn't any playing cards been scattered around the room? Because they hadn't gotten around to playing yet, that's why. Soraya Duncan backed up Gindow and Franzese; she swore that she had given the six men permission to use her office. The police had another question: Why hadn't any of the six notified the watchmen that they were in the building? Why had they taken such pains to conceal the light in Duncan's office from the watchman making his rounds?

OK, so they had "forgotten" to notify the watchmen. Was that a crime? Concealing the light? Nonsense. The partition just happened to be there.

The fuzz wanted to know who had put the bulletholes in the files of the front row. The cops knew the answer that Franzese and Gindow would give. Hell, yes! It was the other men who had fired—and how do you question four dead men?

"We saw the two men run into Mr. Gof's office," Franzese calmly told detectives. "I didn't fire at them and neither did Mr. Gindow. We couldn't." He smiled sweetly. "We were unarmed. It was the other four who fired. Barney and I got behind Miss Duncan's desk. All we know was that there were a lot of shots. The next thing we knew, the two men in Mr. Gof's office tossed out smoke and tear gas. That's all we know."

Four dead men and four handguns. How come the police had found six weapons? Franzese and Gindow hadn't the faintest idea. They supposed that two men had carried two weapons, or one man had been armed with three. How in hell should they know? "We don't go around asking our friends if they carry weapons," Gindow sneered.

The factor in favor of Franzese and Gindow was Henry Oestreicher, the watchman who confirmed that he had seen the two gas-masked men murder Oscar Yehling, Frank Hurt and Clyde Wooten.

Franzese, Gindow and Duncan didn't have the faintest idea who the two men were. How could they? They didn't have any enemies in the world. The police released Charley Franzese and Barney Gindow.

Six days after the rubout in the Butler Building the police again wanted to interrogate Franzese and Gindow. Neither man could be found. The police hurried to Soraya Duncan's plush apartment. She, too, was missing. Some quick checking on the part of the police revealed that Gregory Gof was no-where to be found. The Olympia Escort Bureau was closed. Four of the girls who had worked for Soraya had also disap-peared.

Every day, Richard Camellion drove to the Payson Arms disguised as Allen Marion Coleman. Yet with Fieldhouse and the other Company men, he was Jason B. Swain.

On the eighth day, the Death Merchant found good news waiting for him at the CIA station on the 12th floor of the Payson Arms. Courtland Grojean had sent a long message to him, which he decoded in private. Grojean reported that the intense narcohypnosis being used on Mason Shiptonn was be-ginning to show results. Shiptonn's unconscious mind was be-ginning to remember. On his trip to New York, he had gone to the Olympia Escort Bureau. He had dated one of Soraya's girls, a young lady named Leslie Rodgers. And he had spent the night with the young woman in her apartment. That was all. Nothing unusual had happened. Shiptonn's unconscious did dredge up the tiny recall that, after he and the girl had made love and were having a drink, he had become very sleepy. The next thing he remembered was that it was the next morning. The sun was streaming in through the window and he was lying in bed beside the girl.

The counterintelligence chief also gave Camellion permis-sion to give the full facts to all the case officers at the New York station and to accomplish the mission by MEANS OF ANY PRAGMATIC APPLICATION. WE ARE NOT CONCERNED WITH THE METHOD AND/OR METHODS THAT MIGHT BE APPLIED. WE ARE CONCERNED ONLY WITH THE RESULTS.

The Death Merchant smiled as he decoded that part of the message.

Mr. G. is saying that he doesn't care whom we terminate or how we get the job done. That's fine with me.

Grojean also reprimanded him, mildly, for PERMITTING THE CHINESE TO OUT-GUESS YOU, OR COULD FRANZESE HAVE UNDERTAKEN THE TRAP ON HIS OWN? WITH THE AID OF SORAYA DUNCAN? OUR ANALYSIS IS THAT THE PLOT WAS FIRST DIS-CUSSED WITH THE CHINESE, WHO GAVE THEIR APPROVAL. WE ARE CERTAIN THAT WANG CH'EN-YI, THE CHIEF AIDE TO HSU

PING-JEN, THE RED CHINESE UNDERSECRETARY GENERAL TO THE U.N., IS THE CHIEF OF THE 3RD BUREAU IN THE UNITED STATES. WE SUGGEST YOU CONCENTRATE ON WANG CH'EN-YI.

The Death Merchant fed the message to the paper-shredder, an angry look on his face. He wasn't offended by Grojean's words. His indignation was against himself. They had outsmarted him. They had guessed that he would go to Duncan's office to have a look-see at her files. Franzese and his boys had been waiting.

I suggest I concentrate on both Wang Ch'en-yi and Hsu Ping-jen!

He left Fieldhouse's office, walked into the general conference room where Fieldhouse, Hayes and Float were waiting, and went over to the conference table. Pulling out a chair, he indicated the three other men to join him. Five minutes later, Hayes and Float had the facts, and Camellion was saying to Fieldhouse, "I'll leave it to you to tell the others, at your discretion, when you feel they have the right to know."

The Death Merchant then gave them the substance of Courtland Grojean's message, after which he asked for "round-the-table" comments.

"Not that it has anything to do with the actual mission," said Hayes, "but does the Center have any idea how the invisibility was effected? By means of some natural energy node or what?"

"Mr. G. isn't sure," Camellion said. "For that matter, neither is Admiral Stavover. As we understand it, it was done with electromagnetism. The accident was that the process opened the portal to another dimension, another time-continuum or another universe."

With a forefinger, Dennis Float began tracing small circles on the laminated top of the table. "It sounds like a lot of science fiction to me." He looked up and quickly glanced at the other men. "I'm not saying it's impossible. Ninety-nine percent of our civilization was 'impossible' only a few hundred years ago. I'm saying that it's not likely that the Navy achieved true invisibility as far back as 1943, unless it was by accident. Science didn't have the capability way back then."

Camellion put his arms on the table and folded his hands. "People said the same thing about the atom bomb until it exploded over Japan. What is or isn't possible is all a point of view."

Hayes took out a small cigar from his shirt pocket and proved that he was well read in science. "Getting back to the supposed invisibility of the U.S.S. *Eldridge,* the invisibility could be tied in with much of the work being done on the paranormal. A lot of Soviet scientists believe that all paranormal activity can be explained by concepts based solely on physics. The Soviets call much of it NBIT, the Novel Biophysical Information Transfer."

"The Soviets also reject the view of some Westerners: that parapsychology is transcendent and will never be explained in terms of physics," interjected Dennis Float. He looked at the Death Merchant. "Did the old man say anything about the ivans being in on the file swipe?"

"Negative," Camellion said. "As far as he knows—and Stavover, too—it's strictly the Red Chinese. At this point, it's academic how the Navy made the ship invisible. We could sit here for the next ten years and jabber about the Einstein-Podolsky-Rosen paradox, speculate about tachyons and multidimensional geometries and get nowhere. That's for the scientists to worry about."

Bill Fieldhouse cleared his throat. Hayes lighted his cigar. Float, shifting in the chair, acted as if he might speak. He didn't. All three were being charitable and Camellion knew it.

"What we have is zero," he said with frank honesty. "I made the decision to invade Duncan's office. We know the result. I was outsmarted. I led myself and Fieldhouse into a trap. We survived, and the police still haven't the slightest clue as to who we are."

"A good thing, too," said Float. "Two dead cops add up to murder."

"What is important," continued Camellion, "is that we haven't made one iota of progress toward finding out how Shiptonn was brainwashed. Once we know how Shiptonn was programmed, we'll have all sorts of clues as to the actual method itself. It's the method that's important. It's important because it might be the key to the 'perfect agent.' That's what Mr. G. is after."

"I don't think we're too bad off," said Dennis Float. "Soraya Duncan suspected you were an agent. If she weren't involved with the Chinese Third Bureau, she wouldn't have had any reason to suspect you and there wouldn't have been any trap waiting."

The Death Merchant said, "You are doing a lot of presuming, my friend."

"I know the faultiness of my logic," admitted Float with a wave of his hand. None of us think that Franzese planned that caper in Duncan's office on his own. He'd kill his own mother if the contract price was right, then lay bets on which way she'd fall. But he's not stupid. He doesn't make foolish moves motivated on sheer pride. I think we are in agreement that the Third Bureau gave Franzese the OK."

The others, including Camellion, nodded.

Fieldhouse commented, "There's too much coincidence involved for Franzese and Duncan not to be involved with the Red Chinese. Mr. G. said that Shiptonn shacked up with a girl named Leslie Rodgers, and she's one of the four who's missing. We know the answer to that one."

Gordon Hayes, his head tilted back, blew out a cloud of cigar smoke. "I'm inclined to think that the Chinese got rid of Rodgers and the three other girls, as well as Franzese, Duncan and Gindow. They terminated all seven as a precautionary measure."

"It's a good theory," Camellion offered, "but that's all it is—a theory. On the surface, though, it's logical. There wasn't any pressing need for Franzese and Gindow and Soraya to go underground. The police didn't have a thing on them. And why should the four girls do a vanishing act unless they were the four who lured the candidates into a mind-murder trap?"

"One girl was black; the other three Caucasian—two blondes and a brunette," Hayes said, tapping ashes from his cigar. "A little something for everybody."

"Yeah, Arabs, Latins and Japanese are supposed to get the hots for blondes," Float said with a tiny laugh. "Actually, that's a lot of hogwash."

Rubbing his hands together, Fieldhouse said, "Let's assume that everything that's been said is the truth." His intelligent eyes darted to the Death Merchant. "What can we do about it? What's our next move, now that Franzese and the rest of them are out of the picture?"

"We're going to kidnap Wang Ch'en-yi and Hsu Ping-jen,"

Camellion said in a lackadaisical manner. "We're going to black-bag'em and pull the truth out of them. We'll put the blame on the free Chinese in Taiwan. Naturally, the Taiwanese will deny any involvement. What matters is that the world won't know the difference and the Company will not be connected with the job."

Hayes and Float stared in disbelief at Mr. Swain. Not Fieldhouse, who continued to regard Camellion with calm, undisturbed eyes. He believed that Swain was capable of anything.

Hayes was so shaken that he spoke without thinking. "That's about the craziest idea I've heard yet!"

"How?" asked Fieldhouse. "How are we going to do it? We can't grab them at the U.N. The highways are too crowded, and their estate is like Fort Knox. The Commie Chinese are more paranoid about security than the ivans."

Float laughed unsteadily and leaned back in his chair. "At least we won't have far to go, if we try their estate. It's less than two miles south of here, right off Fort Washington Avenue, on 162nd Street."

"It can't be done," Hayes said, finality in his voice.

"It can and it will," the Death Merchant said firmly. "Let's get to work. . . ."

Chapter Ten

During the next three weeks there were those times when the Death Merchant was almost tempted to agree with Gordon Hayes. Methodically, the Death Merchant and the COs of the New York City Company station had begun at the beginning. They first investigated the possibility of grabbing Wang Ch'en-yi and Hsu Ping-jen at United Nations headquarters.

No way! Not only were guards all over the place, but, according to information supplied by Grojean, there were special security guards at all street approaches to U.N. headquarters. These guards, although not visible, were an added protection against fanatical terrorists. Many "visitors" were also security guards.

Putting the grab on the two Chinese at the U.N. was just that—impossible. . . .

There was also the matter of the Red Chinese guards. At all times, Hsu Ping-jen and his supposed aide, Wang Ch'en-yi, were surrounded by 3rd Bureau security goons. A grab on one of the routes that the Chinese take from the U.N. to their compound in northwest Manhattan, or vice-versa? Even the Death Merchant had to admit that any attempt in traffic was doomed to failure.

Hsu Ping-jen and Wang Ch'en-yi traveled in a limousine that was reputed to have bulletproof glass and to be armored. A car, full of 3rd Bureau agents, preceded the limo; another car followed.

What remained was a complexity that added up to a complicity.

What remained was the Red Chinese estate on 162nd

Street, a 26-room brownstone in the center of 18 fenced-off acres. Again, there were any number of obstacles. Day and night, guards patrolled the grounds. The fence—2-inch chain-link, fabric Number 11 American wire gauge—was 10 feet high and guarded by pressure-sensitive alarms. How many microwave or infrared detectors were hidden on the grounds, in the thick shrubbery and the trees? At night, in case of an emergency, the grounds could be flooded with light.

The Foolish Bunch of Idiots, better known as the FBI, was another problem, at least in front of the estate. There was always a car full of Feds sitting in front of the house, the agents taking down the license plate numbers of any car passing through the gates of the Red Chinese compound.

During the second week, the Company arranged for a private aircraft to fly over the estate at 12,000 feet and take motion pictures with twin high-resolution cameras. During the same week, on Tuesday, a Hostess Twinkie bread truck, moving west on 162nd Street, passed the Red Chinese estate. At the very same time, a step-in Reising Dry Cleaning Service van moved west on 163rd Street. In the rear of each van were several highly trained technicians and a device known as an acoustic verifier (A-V), a very technical instrument that was part of an audio countermeasures service system. The purpose of the A-V was to detect the presence of protective systems— infrared, microwave, capacitance proximity, etc. There was a small model A-V, but it could only be used at close range. By using the large models, the two trucks could do a better job of triangulating the devices.

All during this time, a lot of "squirted" (a hundredth of a second) radio messages went back and forth between the New York City Company center at the Payson Arms and the Center at Langley, Virginia.

Toward the beginning of the third week, the Death Merchant put the final touches to the plan, which Fieldhouse had facetiously dubbed OPERATION: RIDICULOUS. Often, in a joking manner, he referred to the invasion of Soraya Duncan's office as "The Wyatt Swain gun battle at the OK Building."

Fieldhouse and the other case officers had never been enthused about OPERATION: RIDICULOUS. When Camellion told them about that part of the scheme that called for a helicopter to take off from a cabin cruiser moving north in the Hudson River, they were downright horrified.

"God!" exclaimed Gordon Hayes. "Another chopper deal!" He snubbed out his cigar with an angry motion and stared fierce-eyed at the Death Merchant, who was sitting in a vinyl upholstered armchair eating kumquats and drinking cocoa. "How can a cabin cruiser, with a chopper on its stern, move up the Hudson without anyone remember seeing it?" he demanded.

Float, Nivens and Fieldhouse stared at Camellion, who finished eating a kumquat before answering. "The Bell will be covered with a canvas," Camellion said. "The rotor blades won't be attached until just before take-off. We'll send a closed radio signal as soon as we grab the two Chinamen, and the chopper will land in the yard in back of the house. Air-recon photos show that's the best place for it to put down."

"Well, you and Mr. G. have certainly been doing a lot of planning," snorted Nivens. "What happens after we get the goons aboard? We fly back to the cabin cruiser?"

"You know, it could work!" Fieldhouse chortled unexpectedly. "The Hudson is a wide river. We're going to pull off the operation on a moonless night. The Bell can return on a closed beam, the same way it finds us. It's so damned daring that it's mind-boggling. The police won't know what to think."

"I'll say one thing," grunted Float, draping one leg over the arm of a couch. "The Commie Chinamen won't expect us to attack their compound, not at three o'clock in the morning. I'll concede we'll have the element of surprise on our side."

"The helicopter will not return to the same cabin cruiser." Camellion put down the cup of cocoa on an end table. "It will put us down on a much smaller cabin cruiser. The pilot will then sink the chopper in the Hudson and come aboard with us."

No one said anything. Float glanced uneasily at Nivens and Hayes.

Fieldhouse, watching Camellion through narrowed eyelids, asked, "What about the larger cruiser?"

"There'll be only three men on board the *Angel Face*," Camellion explained in a calm voice. "They'll set explosive charges, then leave in a motor boat. Ten minutes later, *Angel Face* will become a memory. This will not take place until after we've black-bagged the two Chinese. Let's look at the map. I'll show you."

Camellion got up and went over to the conference table. The other men were soon crowded around the table and looking down at the large map.

The Death Merchant put his finger on a red circle. "Here is the Communist Chinese compound, and here—" his finger moved up "—is the George Washington Bridge, less than a mile north of the compound. Up here will be the *Angel Face*, two miles north of the George Washington Bridge. You'll notice that Englewood Cliffs is northwest, across the Hudson in New Jersey. The men from *Angel Face* will put ashore here, on the New York side, at this recreation area in Inwood Hill Park. A car will be waiting for them. They'll be taken to a safehouse in the Bronx."

"Hell, since they'll be so close to the Center, they could just walk over here," joked Float. He quit smiling when no one looked up from the map and laughed at his attempt at humor.

"I didn't know we had a safehouse in the Bronx," said Nivens.

"Grojean is setting it up," Camellion said. "Don't ask me where. I don't know either. He's moved a lot of men into the area for this operation."

"What about the smaller cabin cruiser, the one we'll be on?" asked Fieldhouse, fumbling for his cigarettes.

"The *Blue Shadow* will be a mile behind *Angel Face* or a mile north of the George Washington Bridge. The Hudson is almost a mile wide at that point. There'll be no moon, so who's going to see us? As for any nitwits on the beaches, they'll be too stoned on booze or freaked out on drugs to see anything or to give a damn—or too busy making love."

Gordon Hayes' chocolate face became one big concern. "What about any stray Coast Guard boats that might come our way?"

"We'll have to sink them with rockets," Camellion said coldly. "There's too much at stake for us to be worried about human lives, including our own."

Fieldhouse stared directly at the Death Merchant. "I think

104

you had better explain that remark. This is not supposed to be a suicide mission."

"I'm referring to capture by the New York police," Camellion said easily. "Not very probable but still possible. We'd be older than Methuselah before we even came up for parole. I'd prefer death. You could sit in the clink or take your L-pills."

For a moment Fieldhouse stared at Camellion; then he lighted his Vantage and, with the other men, looked down at the map. Four blocks north of the Communist Chinese estate was the Presbyterian Medical Center. Several blocks east was Broadway. A short distance to the south was Riverside Drive and its cutoff that merged with the Henry Hudson Parkway. Not quite half a mile south of the compound was a boat basin branching off the recreation area west of the Henry Hudson Parkway. A quarter of a mile south of the boat basin was the North River Water Pollution Control Plant.

Fieldhouse tapped the boat basin with the tip of his finger, a sudden thought stabbing at his brain.

"Look, Swain. If you tell us next that the *Blue Shadow* is going to put into this basin, I'm going to believe you're not playing with a full deck. I'll tell you another thing, too. There's only one man who could come up with a crazy scheme like this: the Death Merchant."

The other men jerked up from the map and stared at Camellion, as if trying to look past the greasepaint and special plastic-putty cosmetic on his face. *Which is why none of you have ever seen my real face!* But Camellion only smiled and said, "Who I am is not important. All that matters to me is getting this job done."

"Where will the *Blue Shadow* put in?" Fieldhouse regarded Camellion levelly. "Turning into the Harlem River will be too dangerous. There's too many NYPD patrol boats in that cesspool."

"We'll go south on the Hudson to the Upper Bay. We'll dock in Gowanus Bay just below south Brooklyn. We'll wait until the afternoon before we smuggle off the two Chinese."

"How?" asked Dennis Float.

"You'll know when the time comes," answered Camellion. Leaving the table, he walked over to where he had draped his coat over the back of an easy chair, the gaze of the other men darting after him.

"All we need is those idiots in Congress to suspect that the Company had a hand in the operation," James Nivens said slowly. "Then they'll pass more laws restricting the gathering of intelligence information."

Fieldhouse dropped into an easy chair. "When will we meet the three Chinese-Americans?"

"Two days from now," Camellion said, putting on his coat, "at the Bronx Zoo. You and I will meet them. All three are contract agents and are not to know the location of this Center. They'll be staying at a hotel in Chinatown and will meet us the night of the operation. I'll explain the situation fully when I return tomorrow afternoon."

Fieldhouse glanced at the clock on the wall. "Why not now? It's only a bit after one. Or isn't it any of our business?"

"I'm going to the Butler Building and close 'Mr. Swain's' office," Camellion said. "Tell your folks at Bedicker Supply to pick up the furniture tomorrow. No use wasting good office furniture."

Hayes laughed. "Hell, why not keep the office open, now that you've rented it? Who knows when we might need it?"

"No," Camellion said flatly. "It's too risky. Mr. G. has ordered the office closed." He paused and switched to the voice of the Mr. Swain who had presented himself to Mr. Ellsworth, the manager of the Butler Building. "After all, Mr. Swain doesn't want an office in a building where gun battles take place in the middle of the night. . . ."

Chapter Eleven

During the early part of the twentieth century (and up to the 1920s), 162nd Street and the surrounding neighborhood had been reserved for the wealthy. Unfortunately, an inch of time cannot be bought by an inch of gold. The passage of 75 years had brought many changes. Horses and carriages no longer moved over the cobblestones. The cobblestones were gone, having been replaced by concrete.

Not that the area had degenerated into a slum, or even a second-class neighborhood. Houses and grounds were well maintained, but most of the old mansions were gone. They had been torn down and replaced with modern buildings, some larger, some smaller than the originals. However, a few of the stately old houses still remained. They were in excellent condition, either covered with new coats of paint or with this or that type of siding. If constructed of stone, they were newly cleaned and calked.

For example, the stone mansion and grounds at 256 162nd Street. The house had originally been built in 1899 by Thomas Magnus Bimms, the founder of the Bimms Department Store chain. His son had sold it to a New York mobster in 1931. The mobster had sold the house in 1938 (he needed quick money to beat an income-tax rap) to a wholesaler who dealt in cheap mail-order jewelry. The jeweler had doubled his profit by selling the mansion to the Chung-Hua Jen-Min Kung-Ho Kuo or, in English, the People's Republic of China.

Before the Chinese had moved in, they had had the stones sandblasted and a chain-link fence erected around the prop-

107

erty, except in front. There, an 8-foot-high wall of decorative glass brick had been built. The grounds had been renovated, new bushes and trees planted. However, the neighbors had not been happy when the gazebo had been replaced with a 9-foot statue of Mao Tse-tung. There wasn't anything they could do about the concrete monstrosity. The Chinese compound had a diplomatic status. As such the house and grounds were considered a part of the People's Republic of China.

No one knew how the Red Chinese had remodeled the inside of the mansion; the Chinese had brought workers from China to do the job. However, the Company had calculated the number of people living inside the house. Other than Hsu Ping-jen, the Red Chinese Undersecretary General to the U.N., and Wang Ch'en-yi, his chief aide, there were 14 other officials and aides—all minus their wives and children who had remained in China. There were the 3rd Bureau security people, the cooks, house guards and maintenance people. The CIA estimated there were between 35 and 40 people living in the mansion.

At 3:06 in the morning, a Hostess Twinkies bread truck drove through the dark alley between 162nd and 163rd Streets. James Nivens slowed the truck when it was behind number 255 on 162nd Street and, one by one, four men jumped from the opening on the right side. Dressed entirely in black—even their utility caps were black—each man wore a shoulder bag and carried an Ingram submachine gun, to which a Sionics silencer was attached.

The bread truck continued east. So did the four men, moving by the side of the alley as fast as they could.

In the lead, the Death Merchant knew that now the risk was enormous. Quite by chance, a New York Police Department patrol car might turn down the alley. Should that happen, there would be two dead cops and a riddled police car, but the mission would be finished.

Camellion felt uneasy. The operation had gotten off to a bad start at 4:30 the previous afternoon. James Sheng and Robert Tse-i had become ill with food poisoning and had been taken to the hospital. Fortunately they were not in serious condition. Joey Ming, who had not eaten the same kind of meal, was the only Chinese-American with Camellion. The two men were Bill Fieldhouse and Dennis Float.

For five hours, with plastic-putty, greasepaint, liners and other materials of the makeup trade, Camellion had worked on Float and Fieldhouse's face, then on his own. The result was that they looked every bit as Chinese as Joey Ming, who, in his early 30s, was a karate instructor in San Francisco. If he survived the night, he'd be $15,000 richer by noon of the same day—all tax-free.

Facing the alley, in the rear of the Chinese estate, was a 10-foot strip of grass and short weeds. Just beyond the strip was the chain-link fence. Fifteen feet inside the fence was the row of white poplars planted by T.M. Bimms as a windbreak. Emil Risenwitz, the jeweler, had planted the poplars on the east and the west sides.

The Death Merchant and his men ran to the east end of the strip and stopped 3 feet from the fence. While Float and Fieldhouse scanned the forward area through Nite-Sight scopes and Joey Ming watched the rear, Camellion took two metal devices from his shoulder bag, each about half the size of a cigar box. Called an SCOR, each device was a microwave Sub-Carrier Override Relay. One SCOR was "positive," the other "negative." It was their silent signals that would nullify any protective device on the fence for a distance of 20 feet.

Camellion pulled out the telescoping antenna of one SCOR, placed the device within a foot of the fence and turned it on. He extended the antenna of the second SCOR, put the box 8 feet to the left of the first one and flipped its switch to "on."

"What do the two of you see?" he whispered to Float and Fieldhouse, taking a long-handled pair of heavy-duty wire snips from a ring-link on his belt.

"Four guards, each man with a sub-gun slung over his shoulder," whispered Fieldhouse. "Walking in pairs. The four of them are never at the back of the house at the same time. You know what that means?"

"First the fence," Camellion said, then went to work with the powerful wire snips. Within several minutes, he had cut a section 4 feet high and 4 feet wide, but leaving two of the strands of the Number 11 American wire intact, one strand at the top, one at the bottom, to serve as "hinges."

The danger that anyone would see them was practically nil.

109

There was no moon. Even if there had been a big, bright full moon, the thick foliage of the white poplars served as a shield between Camellion and his group and the house.

The summer night was very quiet, except for the monotonous calls of love-happy male crickets. Therein lay the danger, in the stillness. Air-recon photos proved that the distance from the fence to the rear of the house was 265 feet. Now there was the danger that the "door" in the fence might make a noise when Camellion pushed it inward.

He tested the wire. Slowly then, he pushed the left edge inward. Gradually the door opened.

"I'll go in first," he whispered. "Bill, keep watching the guards till the rest of us are inside. All of you be careful. Don't rip your shoulder bags or clothes on the wire. The ends are sharp."

He stooped and moved quickly through the opening. Float and Ming came after him, then Fieldhouse. Guardedly, Camellion pushed the section of stiff wire back into place. Pulling Webber-4b dart guns—all except Joe Ming—they crept to the poplars and, in a position that gave them a full view of the rear, lay down in the grass.

The Death Merchant took the Nite-Sight scope from Float and looked over the yard. The Chinese had done a good job. There were four mimosa trees, two on each side of the curving white flagstone walk, and two pink flowering cherry trees. Flowerbeds arranged in the pattern of Chinese symbols—from the air they spell "peace"—*the hypocrites.* There were Oriental poppies, Chinese "lanterns," pink parfait peonies, giant orange cannas and pink climbing roses on trellises. All very orderly and beautiful—*Until one sees that stupid statue of fatass Mao.*

"Terminating the guards would be a cinch if it weren't for the FBI in front," Float whispered.

Camellion, studying the situation through the infrared scope, didn't reply. Float was only half-right. The Company could have gone to the director of the FBI and requested that he pull the agents away from the house. The CIA hadn't and couldn't, the first because the CIA and the FBI hated each other's insides; the second because such a request, whether honored or not, would have been as good as a confession that the CIA was planning something very special for the Communist Chinese.

Camellion watched and saw two guards walk around from the left side of the house. They walked slowly across the rear, and were starting to move up the right side when they met the other pair of guards who were headed toward the back.

"See what I mean, Swain?" said Fieldhouse. "There's no way we can terminate all four at the same time."

"How can you even aim in this darkness?" There was awe and admiration in Joe Ming's heavy whisper. Ming had seen plenty of action in Vietnam and was used to danger of the worst kind. These men were different from anyone or anything he had ever known. Ming detected they were even more ruthless and deadly than the Viet Cong, especially the one called Swain. He was something else! There was an unreal, unnatural quality about him, a kind of preternaturalism that made one sense that he had done this type of covert work many, many times. What made Swain so eerie was that he seemed to understand Death as well as Life.

"Listen," Camellion whispered. "I'll shoot the first two I see. After that, you and I, Bill, will run to the back of the house. You wait about eight feet back from the left corner. Stay as close to the house as you can. I'll take the right corner. The moment the next two guards turn the corner, whether on your side or mine, kill them. Float, you watch through the scope. You and Ming come ahead when you see me motion. Any questions?"

"The light in that one room downstairs," whispered Fieldhouse. "It's on in a room in the glassed-in porch. What do you think it is?"

"I can't see through drapes behind glass," Camellion said. "It might be another guard station, or where the outside guards take a break. Who knows? We'll find out when we get inside the house."

Float asked, "What about the FBI agents out front? They'll think something is wrong when no guards pass in front of the house."

The Death Merchant chuckled. "Who cares what they think. There isn't anything they can do about it! Bill, give your infrared scope to Float and get set."

Camellion cocked the Webber dart gun, picked up the

Nite-Sight scope and again started watching the rear of the Red Chinese mansion. Once more two guards walked around from the left side of the house. The Death Merchant raised the Webber and, still looking through the Nite-Sight scope, sighted in his mind and aimed by instinct. He didn't fire. As soon as the guards had walked across the rear area and had turned the right corner, he began to count. He had reached 12 when the two other Chinese security men turned from the right corner. He waited until they were 6 feet from the corner, then pulled the trigger of the Webber-4b six times in rapid succession.

All six needle-darts struck the two targets. Unconscious within a single flicker of time, the two Chinese 3rd Bureau guards sank to the ground. In five seconds they would be dead from the poison that was a combination mixture composed of venom from the Australian tiger snake and from the deadly bushmaster of South America.

Camellion placed the infrared scope on the ground, jumped to his feet, pulled one of the silenced SIG Model 210-2s[19] and, with an equally quick Fieldhouse, raced across the grass, around the flowerbeds, toward the house, Camellion racing to the right, Fieldhouse to the left, their Ingram submachine guns strapped across their backs.

There was a 99-percent chance that the last two security agents would come to the back from the left side of the house. Just the same, they might decide to turn and come back the other way, in which case—*I'll be waiting for them.*

Camellion stepped into a flowerbed of peach-tart petunias and waited. To the left, Fieldhouse, who had also drawn one of his SIG Model 210-2s, crouched in a bed of lemon-lime gladiolas.

The two guards, talking in low tones, came from the left. They turned the corner, walked a few feet, suddenly saw the two corpses of their comrades on the ground—and died from the two darts that Fieldhouse pumped into each of their bod-

19. *Schweitzer Industrie Gessellschaft*—Swiss Industrial Society. The SIG is the choice of many commando groups and is reputed to be the best-made handgun in the world. Its price is $1,400 and going up. Actually the SIG is no better than a 9mm Browning auto-loader.

ies. Wordlessly, they sank to the ground, two more ciphers in eternity. . . .

Camellion, who had seen the two Chinese drop, turned to the north and motioned with his hand. He stepped out of the flowerbed and, in a low crouch, crept toward the center rear of the large stone house; soon he was with Fieldhouse. A half a dozen seconds more and Float and Ming joined them. As a group, they moved toward the door in the glassed-in porch, a bit to their right.

Motioning for Ming and Float, who had their Ingrams ready, to get behind him and Fieldhouse, Camellion put his foot on the first concrete step. He shoved the Webber-4b into its chest holster, went up the other four steps and very gently gripped the iron handle and pressed down on the thumb latch. The door was unlocked. He didn't have to be told why. The Chinese 3rd Bureau guards were ignoring procedure—*Why bother to lock the door? There are other guards inside the lighted room. Why make them bother to get up and unlock the door? This is going to be easier than shooting fish in a small barrel.*

And it was. Camellion easily pushed open the door and saw that beyond was a tiny foyer that contained two openings, one ahead to the left, the other, in the east wall, to the right.

The voice called out in Mandarin Chinese—a voice from the right—after the Death Merchant and his men were inside and Ming was cautiously closing the door. No one but Ming could understand what was being said; yet from the intonation, the speaker was asking a question.

Joe Ming whispered nervously to Camellion, "He wants to know why we've come in so early. What should I tell him?"

"Fieldhouse, you and Ming cover the left door," hissed the Death Merchant. "Float, come with me."

Ming and Fieldhouse moved to the north wall. Camellion—Float several steps behind him—raced to the left.

Kuo Mo-tsu, the guard who had called out, walked toward the door, a puzzled expression on his face, as if wondering why neither Hsin Ch'iao and P'an Wan-chu—or could it have been K'ang Li Chou and Wau Di'how?—had not answered. Shen Kung remained at the table, drinking a cup of mint tea and smoking a mild American cigarette.

Kuo Mo-tsu was too surprised to yell a warning when he

saw Camellion and Float—two strange Chinese dressed entirely in black and armed to the teeth. An instant later, Kuo Mo-tsu was too dead to do anything. He tumbled to the floor with Camellion's 9mm SIG slug in his chest.

A horrified Shen Kung was trying to get to his feet when the Death Merchant's second 9mm SIG bullet caught him 4 inches below the hollow of the throat. The impact of the high-velocity hollow-pointed projectile smashed him backward and, as he started to fall, his left arm knocked against an electric can opener on a counter. The plugged-in cord prevented the can opener from falling to the floor; instead, it banged against the side of the counter, making a loud noise.

Camellion and Float turned, raced out of the kitchen and rejoined Ming and Fieldhouse, the latter of whom whispered, "There's a long hall in there. The stairs seem to be toward the center. Two guards dozing against a wall in front of the stairs, unless that noise in the kitchen woke them."

"How's the light?" inquired Camellion. He pulled the second SIG auto-loader from its hip holster and thumbed off the safety.

"Only three small bulbs in fixtures on the walls. Same kind of bulb as in here."

"I'll take the point. The rest of you watch the sides," ordered Camellion. "Ming, Float: Keep an eye on the rear."

Dong Bi'ling was leaning back in a chair, its two front legs off the floor. Chi Ki-yu, in another chair, was also dozing, his head hanging down, his chin on his chest. The noise of the can opener hitting the side of the counter served as the unusual interruption that awakened both men, who sat up with a start and glanced at each other.

"Did you hear a noise?" Chi Ki-yu, got to his feet, looked around and listened. Dressed in an American sport shirt and slacks, he wore a Chinese Tokarev automatic (a copy of the Soviet TT M1933 Tokarev) in an open holster around his waist.

"I thought I did. I'm not sure." Dong Bi'ling did not carry a pistol. He was armed with a T-56-1 assault rifle, which he now picked up and held loosely in his hands. He was peering down the back of the hall and Chi Ki-yu was looking up the stairs when Camellion and his three men appeared at the south end of the hall.

Dong Bi-ling didn't have the necessary time to analyze what he was seeing; neither did Chi Ki-yu. The Death Merchant opened fire with both SIGs as Fieldhouse pulled the trigger of the deadly little Ingram machine pistol, loud *baziittttttssssss* coming from the three silencers.

One of Camellion's slugs stabbed Dong Bi'ling in the chest a split second before two of Fieldhouse's 9mm Ingram projectiles punched him in the chest and started spinning him toward Chi Ki-yu, who had caught an SIG slug high in the left side of his chest and three Ingram bullets in the right side of his chest. Shot to pieces, both dying Chinese struck the wall in front of the stairs and slid to the floor, leaving long smears of blood on the cream-colored wallpaper.

"Ming, Float, check the rooms off the hall," Camellion ordered in a low voice. "Kill anything that moves. Do it fast and do it quickly."

He and Fieldhouse ran forward, Bill whispering, "They may be good Communists, but they sure believe in having the best. If this carpet were any thicker, we'd need snowshoes!"

They paused for a moment and glanced at the two dead men.

"What a bloody mess we made of them," Fieldhouse said.

"At least from now on, they'll have a permanent place to stay," Camellion said, looking up the carved walnut staircase.

They checked the rooms off the front of the hall—a conference room, what appeared to be a small ballroom, a sitting room, another conference room—all empty. Camellion and Fieldhouse turned, hurried back to the side of the stairs and met Dennis Float and Joe Ming.

"All the rooms are empty," Float whispered. "The entire downstairs must be empty."

"We'll go up the stairs," said Camellion, who was in the process of shoving fresh magazines into the SIG auto-pistols. "Keep to the side of the steps so they don't squeak. Joe, don't forget your part, what you're supposed to say when the time comes."

"I haven't forgotten," Ming said, surprised at the calmness in his voice.

They started up the stairs, Camellion and Ming on one side, Fieldhouse and Float on the other. They were halfway up the stairs when they found that Fate can be not only fickle but downright sadistic.

Two Chinese, who had been walking down the north side hall, suddenly appeared at the top of the stairs. Both men carried Czech M-25 submachine guns, the stocks folded against the sides of the chatter boxes.

Astonishment flickered over the faces of the Chinese, the dumbfoundedness instantly turning to hate and determination. Both men attempted to turn the muzzles of the sub-guns downward. Instantly, both men died. The Chinese on the left took three of Camellion's SIG slugs—two in the chest and one in the stomach. The 3rd Bureau boob was bounced into infinity by nine of Fieldhouse's Ingram projectiles that literally ripped open his stomach. Amid tiny bits of cloth and a fine spray of blood, he fell back, the TNT shock contracting his finger on the trigger. The machine gun roared, a stream of 9mm slugs spewing upward and tearing into the ceiling. The fat was in the fire. The rest of the Chinese would have had to be dead—*If they didn't hear that roaring!*

Chapter Twelve

Now it was a run for life, a race again Death. Camellion and his men charged up the other half of the steps, Camellion saying in a loud voice, "Punch your radio-signal buttons the first chance you get. Not now, you don't have time. Bill, Denny—take the left rear side, the first door. Joe and I will take the right. You know what Ping-jen and Ch'en-yi look like. Don't kill those two prizes."

It took them only 10 seconds to reach the upstairs hall and see that the earsplitting roar of the Czech machine gun had awakened the entire upstairs. The main lights of the hall suddenly came on, flooding the area with brightness. Excited shouts and yells and a fearful babble of voices emanated from rooms up and down the hall, which to the Death Mechant was the worst possible place in which to indulge in a firefight—*Too many doors! Too many avenues of approach to watch! A man would have to have more eyes than a spider and more arms than an octopus!* The only thing that could save them was speed, a swiftness that would give them the advantage of a first strike.

"Hurry up!" Camellion snapped. "Get inside the first rooms. Do what you have to do, hit the signal button and put on your gas masks."

Their faces ferocious, Fieldhouse and Float rushed to the first door to the left. Fieldhouse reached out, gingerly turned the knob, pushed open the door and jumped to one side. The door was not quite all the way open when Float raked the inside with a horizontal spray of Ingram slugs. Across the hall, Camellion and Ming, without firing, rushed in low through another door.

117

Float and Fieldhouse, storming into the room to the left, saw that they had hit the jackpot, that they had entered a dormitory-type bedroom, so large it could have qualified as a small barrack. Cots were lined up against the wall. More cots were stretched out in two rows toward the center of the room. On the walls were *ta tzu pao* posters with propaganda slogans in modernized Chinese.

Float's streams of slugs had killed three 3rd Bureau agents who had been getting out of bed, and had turned the rest of the men into terrified animals. But cornered animals are always the most dangerous.

What seemed to be dozens of Chinese were in various stages of undress. Some were still in pajamas. Others had been pulling on their pants when the 9mm slugs had started singing. Several of the goons, stepping into their pants, had tripped and were on the floor, struggling to get up. Yelling in fear and rage, those who could tried to reach for weapons.

"Go screw a sapsucker, you slant-eyed slobs," snarled Fieldhouse.

He and Float opened fire, the Ingrams chattering furiously, dozens of 9mm projectiles flying across the room. Yelling in pain and confusion, the Chinese spun and twisted from the impact of projectiles that were made of 95.5 percent gilding metal, to insure the most maximum expansion upon contact with the target. Down they went, some to the floor, others falling back on the cots, red blood dribbling out of blue-black bulletholes in yellow flesh.

Two of the almond-eyed goons did succeed in grabbing weapons. One man got off a shot with the Chinese version of a 9mm Browning auto-loader. The 9mm bullet burned within an inch of Float's left arm. Ki-li Woo's only chance was gone. A second later, he was riddled with boat-tailed bullets, his chest one big bloody mess as he pitched to the floor.

Shih-ying Wong, firing frantically, triggered off a blast with a Red Chinese-type 50 submachine gun. The dozen 7.62mm projectiles would have chopped Fieldhouse in two if he hadn't spotted the man and ducked to one side as he swung the Ingram toward him.

Wong's burst of 7.62mm slugs missed Fieldhouse by a foot and stabbed into the wall. Fieldhouse's burst raked Wong across the face and throat, the impact exploding his head and sending pieces of flesh, chunks of bone, blood and part of brain splattering outward in all directions. He went down with a stream of blood spurting a foot from his shot-out throat.

"Down! Get down!" Fieldhouse gasped to Float. They ducked to the side of a chest of drawers and Fieldhouse handed Float his now-empty Ingram and pulled an SIG. "Reload them, then punch the signal button and put on your gas mask. I'm worried about what's behind the door on the other side of this chest of drawers."

While Float reloaded the Ingrams with trembling hands, Fieldhouse kept his eyes on the bodies in front of them. Some of the Chinese, not yet dead, were moaning piteously. Fieldhouse, thinking of an older brother who had died in the Korean War, couldn't have cared less.

With his right hand he reached down to the small, box-like device secure in a leather case on his belt. He extended the 2-inch antenna and pressed the red button on the top of the Davis-Impulse-Signal-Transmitter, a device that was similar to a bumper-beeper, only the DIST had a much stronger signal and a far greater range. Finished with the DIST, he pulled a Federal Labs M-183-6003 gas mask from his shoulder bag, took off his black utility cap, slipped the mask over his head and face, then returned the cap to his head.

Very quickly Float was ready. He handed Fieldhouse a fully loaded Ingram, activated the DIST on his own belt and put on his gas mask. Just in case one or more of the Chinese on the floor might be faking, Fieldhouse pulled a CN grenade from the shoulder bag, pulled the pin and flipped the tear gas canister to the middle of the room. Gas began hissing, but none of the Chinese coughed. There weren't any moans either.

Fieldhouse and Float moved around to the other side of the chest of drawers, Float creeping backward to watch the open door to the hall. They came to the door in the other wall and, his back to the wall, Fieldhouse reached out with his left hand, turned the knob and pulled the door open.

The roar of two submachine guns and two streams of slugs that sizzled through the opening made Fieldhouse jump back and curse. The damned Chinese were waiting.

"What do we do now?" Float whispered urgently.

"We use a grenade, that's what we do," Fieldhouse said angrily, reaching into the Musette bag on his left hip.

"Suppose Wang Ch'en-yi and Hsu Ping-jen are in there?" protested Float. "If we kill them, Swain won't—"

"Swain can go diddle a dodo bird! I'm not committing suicide for him or anyone else." He took an MK3A2 offensive grenade from the bag and pulled the pin.

The Death Merchant and Joe Ming found five terrified women in the room they invaded. Three were trying to hide under the bed, but they came out when they saw that the black-clad invaders had spotted them. The other two pulled the covers up to their chins, their eyes almost popping out of their sockets.

"We are the Free Chinese of Taiwan!" shouted Joe Ming, with all the dedicated fervor of a political fanatic. "We are here to take Hsu Ping-jen and Wang Ch'en-yi as hostages. Where are they, you Communist pigs?"

Screams and shouts from across the hall made the women cringe in greater fear, all except one in bed, who spit out a rapid stream of Chinese, her voice as contemptuous as her eyes. The Death Merchant, his eyes on the door across the room, to his left, knew that she was telling them where to go—and the place was not "up."

Joe Ming leaned close to Camellion and whispered, "She said they wouldn't give the time of day to 'lackeys of a degenerate society'. Now what?"

Camellion's face did not change expression. He sighed, lifted the SIG in his right hand and pulled the trigger. The silencer made a *bazitttt* sound, and a bullethole the size of a dime appeared just above the bridge of the woman's nose. Without a sound, she fell back against the headboard, her eyes wide open, the cover falling from her breasts.

The other woman in bed screamed, threw up her arms and began to jabber wildly in Chinese. Trembling, the women on the floor looked up pleadingly, silently begging for their lives.

The woman in bed stopped speaking. Ming again leaned close to Camellion, who had holstered one SIG and was pressing the button of the DIST on his belt. The woman stared at the device, thinking it might be some kind of bomb.

"She said that Hsu Ping-jen and Wang Ch'en-yi are in a

bedroom at the other end of the hall, a corner room across from us," Ming said in a low voice. "She said they and I-Cheng Loi, the military attaché at the U.N., share a bedroom."

"Ask her about the other rooms up here. Tell her if she lies, we'll come back and burn her and the rest of them alive with a thermate grenade."

Joe Ming spoke rapidly. The woman, almost crying, answered. Joe asked her more questions. She quickly replied, then burst into tears.

"Women are in the room next to this one, the household help," Ming said. "Across from us are the Third Bureau bastards. Next door to the room across from us are some officials. Down the hall are the bedrooms of other big shots and several bathrooms. I believe she's telling the truth."

Camellion thought for a moment, then said, "Turn on your signal set and put on your gas mask." He noticed the bars on the windows and thought of how the Chinese had trapped themselves. The bars had been put there to prevent any member of the Red Chinese staff from defecting in the middle of the night—*The bars are certainly doing their job.* "And tell those pigs that if they stick their heads out the door after we leave, we'll blow them off."

Ming spoke rapidly in Chinese, and the woman in bed and the women on the floor quickly nodded their heads, one of them uttering a little cry of alarm when she heard the crashing sound of submachine guns roaring across the hall.

"You think they got our boys?" whispered Ming, adjusting the gas mask over his face. . . .

Of course not! The Cosmic Lord of Death is active, but He'll stick to his agreement. . . . Camellion said casually, "Keep these lovelies covered. We'll know soon enough what's happening over there."

Camellion was slipping on his gas mask when the grenade exploded, shook the entire house and rattled loudly the windows of the room in which Camellion and Ming were standing. The women screamed, two of them on the floor once more trying to crawl under one of the beds.

The door to the left opened, but the two Chinese women screamed at the sight of Camellion and Ming, stepped back and jerked the door shut.

"That grenade was your answer," Camellion said to Ming in an easy manner and took a CN grenade from his bag. "Keep your eyes on these Commie bitches. If one sneezes hard, kill her."

He got down on one knee, placed the tear-gas grenade on the rug and unscrewed the silencers on both the Ingram and one SIG auto-pistol.

Ming watched him from the corner of his eyes, a puzzled expression on his face. He soon found out what the Death Merchant had in mind.

In the corner bedroom at the opposite end of the hall, Hsu Ping-jen, a roly-poly, graying man in his 60s, was on both knees by the side of a bed, the side closest to one of the two barred windows. In his right hand was a Llama .45 auto-loader. His hand was very steady, for Ping-jen had been tempered by blood and death and violence, by hardship and intrigue. At 13 years of age, he had made the "Long March" with Mao. He was used to danger and was not afraid to die.

By the side of another bed knelt Ch'en-yi and I-Cheng Loi. A heavily muscled man with square, angular features, Wang Ch'en-yi had a 9mm Beretta machine gun trained on the door to the hall.

I-Cheng Loi—short, heavyset, as bald as a rock—held an Austrian Steyr machine gun on the door that opened to the other bedroom. Beyond that door was a bathroom that opened to the large bedroom that had just been shaken by an explosion.

"Who can they be?" Loi whispered hoarsely to Ch'en-yi. "Whoever heard of terrorists attacking the property of a foreign nation in the United States?" He spotted a bottle of *huang chiu* wine on a small table and wished he had the sweet wine with him.

"Be quiet," Wang Ch'en-yi said coldly. "There is always a first time. All we can do is wait. Perhaps Kuan-hua Ling and the others will kill them before the terrorists get to us.

Having removed the noise suppressor from the Ingram and pushed in its double-rod stock and pad, the Death Merchant could now use the small machine gun as an auto-pistol, since the magazine, inserted into the grip, was just behind the trigger and the trigger guard.

Standing up and moving to the side of the door, Camellion pulled the pin from the CN grenade, reached out and opened the door a foot. Slugs did not *wang* through the wood. Confident that none of the Communist lice were going to zero in, he opened the door wider and tossed the grenade. He took another grenade from the bag, pulled the pin and flung it down the hall. What he did with the third grenade surprised Ming. Camellion flipped it to the floor between two of the beds. If Ming was astonished, the women were horrified. They started to gasp and cough. The single woman in bed rolled to the floor and, unmindful of her nakedness, started to stumble to the window.

"The gas will keep them out of mischief," Camellion said. "Let's move out."

Regardless of the drifting tear gas in the hall, Camellion and Ming had no trouble finding Float and Fieldhouse, who were waiting just inside the door of the room across the hall from the first bedroom containing women members of the Chinese mission.

"We wasted most of the Third Bureau men," Fieldhouse said, his voice muted by the gas mask. "We counted eighteen cots in there."

"What about the grenade?" Camellion asked, listening to sirens in the distance. They were still too far away for him to know if the police cars were headed for the Red Chinese compound.

"Five jokers were in there," Fieldhouse said. "They opened up with machine guns. I told Float I wasn't going to commit suicide for you or Mr. G. or anyone else. The grenade killed three of them. We finished off the other two. Have you guys found out anything about Ch'en-yi and Ping-jen?"

"They're in the corner bedroom, to our right, at the end of the hall," Camellion said, his voice not betraying the concern gnawing at him. The Cosmic Lord of Death was always on his side, but Time hated his guts and was forever his main enemy. There were many gods in the universe. Among those gods, Time was the most powerful and the most ruthless. Always it marched onward, second by second.

Fieldhouse's eyes reflected concern through the wide-angle Clearvue lens of the gas mask. "How are we going to get them out alive? Killing them would be as easy as pissin' into rainwater. But getting them out alive is something else."

"Why not try a ruse to get them to surrender?" Float suggested. "We could tell them that the U.S. has declared war on China and that if they surrender, they won't be harmed."

"That's a dumb idea," Fieldhouse said. "They know we're killing everyone out here. Why should they believe we won't terminate them?"

"It's worth a try," Camellion said, watching Joe Ming place the silencer from his Ingram in a long slot pocket in his black coveralls. He turned and stepped out into the hall, an Ingram in his right hand, an SIG in his left. He started down the hall, the others following, Ming and Fieldhouse going to the left.

The four hurried past the top of the steps and entered the next length of hall, Camellion and Float watching the three doors to the left. All four could hear the *flap-flap-flap-flap* of a helicopter's rotor blades, the sound gaining in volume with each second.

What ordinarily would have been the unexpected was not. The first two doors to the left suddenly swung inward. Coughing, two men stumbled out of the first doorway. At the same time, three more, all dressed in pajamas, emerged from the second. All five carried weapons.

Mi-do Chenngi and Ru-teng Lin, the two men from the first doorway, were so close to Ming and Fieldhouse that the four of them almost collided. Nonetheless, Ming and Fieldhouse had the decisive advantage; they wore gas masks.

Camellion and Float, taking advantage of the split-second lag time, ducked to their right, then to their left, and darted toward the three Chinese coming out of the next doorway.

The very fast Ming—practically nose to nose and toe to toe with Ru-teng Lin—used the SIG in his left hand to knock Lin's right arm upward, while with his right knee he smashed Lin viciously in the groin. Concurrent with Ming's action, Fieldhouse ducked to the left and threw himself against the wall to avoid Mi-do Chenngi, who was desperately attempting to swing down on him with a Chinese T-56 assault rifle. The T-56 A-R roared, the long barrel spitting out a hot stream of

7.62mm projectiles that came so close to Bill that one bullet cut through the top of his utility cap and knocked it off his head. The slugs from Fieldhouse's Ingram were more accurate: They blew up Mi-do Chenngi's chest, the grand slam of lead creating a tiny cloud of ripped pajama cloth.

The T-56 fell from Mi-do Chenngi's hands and he started to go down, some of his chest bone and rib bones showing through ripped, bloody cloth and flesh. A snarling *duddle-duddle-duddle* from Ming's Ingram and Ru-teng Lin, already in agony from the knee-lift to his groin, gurgled up a cup of blood, his dying legs dancing backward from the four 9mm slugs that Ming had put into his stomach.

Rui Tseng Lin, one of the Chinese from the other doorway, triggered off a round from an American AMT stainless steel Hardballer auto-loader. Pang-liang Jen and K'ang Bo-shin also tried to *whack* out Camellion and Float. Jen almost succeeded, the slugs from his Mikosi 7 machine pistol (a copy of the Russion Stechkin M-P) rocketing between Float's left side and left arm, one tearing through the coveralls at the armpit, but the slug leaving the flesh untouched.

As for the .45 Hardballer bullet, it tweaked the left shoulder seam of Camellion's coveralls, barely ripping the tough twill.

In back of Jen, Bo-shin attempted to use his Czech-75 auto-pistol, but he was a moment too late. Camellion and Float were firing, chopping the three Chinese into bloody mush with Ingram and SIG slugs. Within seconds the three 3rd Bureau agents were dead and lying crumpled on the hall rug.

Camellion stabbed the SIG into its holster, scooped up the Czech-75 pistol, thumb on the safety, dropped the pistol into one of the flap pockets of his coveralls and said in a low controlled voice, "Float, watch the doors on the right. Ming, Bill, check the two rooms on the left. I'll check the last room."

It took only a few minutes to discover that the three bedrooms were empty and that a helicopter was hovering several hundred feet above the Chinese mission.

They turned their attention to the three doors on the right side of the hall, throwing so many slugs into the hinges and locks of the first two doors that both doors fell inward. The middle room was a bathroom. But when they heard muffled sounds from the first room, they knew the Chinese inside were waiting, biding their time.

From one side of the shot-apart doorway, Camellion tossed an offensive grenade, then quickly made himself small against the wall. After it exploded, he charged through the smoking doorway, his chattering Ingram moving back and forth, his last seven 9mm slugs slamming through the bathroom door to his left. The explosion had torn the door off its hinges. He wondered about the other bathroom door, the one that opened into the bedroom occupied by Wang Ch'en-yi and Hsu Ping-jen. He wasn't, however, going to risk taking a look, not within the narrow confines of a bathroom.

His ammunition had been wasted. The walls and ceiling, the five beds and the floor, were splattered with blood and viscera, the wallpaper newly plastered with bloody pieces of cloth held in place by gore. From the condition of the dismembered corpses, it was difficult to ascertain whether there had been five or six men in the room. They weren't trained in survival or they wouldn't have been clustered in a group. The poor halfwits. The grenade fell in the middle of them.

The Death Merchant left the room of death, looked for a moment at the last door on the right side of the hall and motioned to Fieldhouse, who took a position by the wall to the left of the door. Camellion waited by the right while Float and Ming went into the room directly across the hall, walking over the bodies of the men clogging the doorway. Camellion and Fieldhouse turned their heads toward the wall, away from the door, as Ming and Float dissolved the wood around the lock and the hinges with several magazines of Ingram slugs. Ming and Float quickly drew back out of sight as the door fell inward and crashed to the floor.

Camellion didn't get a chance to call out to the Chinese inside the bedroom and offer them a chance to surrender. There were several loud *booms* from a .45 auto, and the furious, frantic chattering of several submachine guns, the hail of slugs thudding into the sides of the doorway. Immediately, from the room across the hall, Ming and Float poked out their Ingrams and triggered off a dozen rounds each, shooting high to avoid hitting the three Chinese.

Several moments later, Camellion and Fieldhouse each

flipped a CN grenade around the doorway into the bedroom. The Death Merchant quickly followed with a smoke canister. When he heard all three grenades hissing, he darted through the door, going in as low as humanly possible. Fieldhouse was a mini-moment behind him.

Due to the tear gas and the smoke, the room appeared to be a solid mass of rolling and tumbling purple tinged with white. Very rapidly, however, the smoke obscured the four lights in the ceiling fixture, so that the room was plunged into darkness.

Almost on their knees, Camellion and Fieldhouse listened to the gasping and coughing of the three Chinese, who had dropped their weapons in a frantic effort to breathe. They couldn't see, their eyes tightly closed as protection against the tear gas and because the "soapsuds effect" had forced them to close their eyes.

Camellion and Fieldhouse first kicked the weapons out of the way, then went to work on the Chinese. Only Wang Ch'en-yi tried to fight, a short-lived resistance that ended when Camellion punched him in the stomach with a short *Nukite* stab.

Once Camellion and Fieldhouse had the three Chinese out in the hall, Camellion said, "Chicken Little, you're wanted in the hen house!" and threw I-Cheng Loi down the stairs. He didn't care that he might have killed the man. He hadn't. Loi crawled away on this hands and knees, coughing so hard it was a miracle that his head didn't snap off.

Their Ingrams reloaded, the Death Merchant and Fieldhouse went down the steps. Behind them were Ming and Float, each with a hand on the collar of the Chinese in front of him, the muzzles of SIGS pressed against the spines of the coughing and stumbling Chinese, who wore gaudily colored silk bathrobes that resembled pizza explosions.

Ming jerked on Wang Ch'en-yi's bathrobe collar and warned in *pai hua*, or modernized Chinese, "Try to escape and I'll put a bullet in both your feet. We have nothing to lose but our lives, but when we go to hell, you and that other worthless piece of rotten dog meat will go with us."

Even before the six men reached the bottom of the stairs, it was evident that the New York police had arrived, and judging from the dozens of *ah-ou-a ah-ou-a ah-ou-as* getting closer and closer, more patrol cars were on the way. Bright beams from car spotlights were raking across the front of the large stone house, the columns of light crisscrossing in the darkened downstairs rooms. The paradox was that the police were helpless. They didn't dare set foot in the yard, much less enter the Red Chinese mission. To do so would be a violation of international law and would lead to serious consequences. Only the head of the Chinese mission, or one of his aides, through his authority, could give permission for any Americans to enter. The irony was that Hsu Ping-jen, the head of the Red Chinese delegation to the U.N., was a prisoner of the Death Merchant and his merry band of three, all of whom, with the two Chinese, were moving toward one of the rear doors of the large house, the same door through which they had entered.

They came to the end of the hall and hurried into the small foyer. The Death Merchant cracked open the rear door and looked out into the backyard—more cop cars in the alley, their beams raking the trees, the flowerbeds and the rear of the house. One of the beams almost caught Camellion full in the face, but he jerked back in time and closed the door.

"Why not throw a couple of thermate grenades back there, just before we leave?" suggested Joe Ming, jerking his head toward the bottom of the stairs at the end of the hall.

"Oh no," Camellion said. "A fire would give the police a chance to bust in, on the theory they were saving lives."

"He's right," Float said. "The New York cops love to beat in doors."

Camellion and his men were mildly surprised when Wang Ch'en-yi, righting to focus his eyes, spoke up. "Who are you men? I demand to know," he said in a thick, grating voice. "You look Chinese, but don't sound Chinese. Who are you?"

Encouraged by hearing Ch'en-yi's voice, Ping-jen drew himself up straighter and, with tears streaming down his cheeks, faced Camellion and Fieldhouse. "I shall demand that the Security Council of the United Nations investigate this outrage, this barbaric breach of international law, this terroristic gangsterism."

Joe Ming clicked his tongue impatiently. "Shut your damned mouth, you Communist pig," he growled in Chinese and jammed the muzzle of the SIG against the back of Wang

128

Ch'en-yi's beefy neck. "From now on keep your filthy mouth shut, or I'll break off your teeth with this gun."

The Death Merchant regarded Ping-jen with alert curiosity. "You do that, poker-nose. Complain all you want to the United Nations Gasbag Society. But you'll do it from a coffin unless you obey our orders and do exactly as we tell you. We've taken a vow to commit suicide if we fail, if we don't escape in that helicopter. We'll go quickly by bullets. You two will go slowly, by thermate. For a minute you'll be able to see the flesh melt off your bones."

"Let's get on with it," Fieldhouse said forcefully. "In less than five minutes we'll either be dead or *zooming* up and up and away. I'm anxious to find out which." He watched the Death Merchant press the button on top of the DIST on his belt. Deliberately, Camellion pressed the button two more times. Three times: the signal for the pilot in the Bell helicopter to get ready to rev down.

The Death Merchant, recognizing that Hsu Ping-jen was less brave than Wang Ch'en-yi, took a few steps, motioned to Float to get to one side and grabbed the back of Ping-jen's collar with his left hand.

"I'll take over this Chinese blossom," he said to Float. He reached around the side of the frightened Chinese official and jammed the muzzle of the Ingram against the man's right cheek. "When we get outside, the police will want to know what is going on. Tell them that you and Ch'en-yi are prisoners of the Fourth Commando of Free Nationalist China. Tell them that if they fire a single shot, we'll kill the two of you. Do you understand me?"

"Yes." Hsu Ping-jen looked as if he were holding his breath.

"If you ask for help in any way, you and Ch'en-yi will die," Camellion added. "Your whole staff is dead upstairs. We'd just as soon kill you and ourselves as sneeze."

"With this!" grinned Fieldhouse, and showed Ping-jen a thermate grenade.

"Float, open the door," Camellion said. "Let's find out whether we live or die. The three of you stay close to Ch'en-yi. If he tries to speak, shut him up."

Float opened the door, then stepped back. Camellion, holding Hsu Ping-jen firmly by the collar, pushed the Chinese official through the door. At once, several beams from spotlights bathed Camellion and Ping-jen in brilliance, and a voice called out over a bullhorn:

"This is the New York police. Identify yourselves. If you are members of the Chinese mission, do you require assistance? Do we have permission to enter and examine the four bodies lying on the ground?"

"Get ready to pull that pin," Camellion said, glancing quickly back at Fieldhouse, who completed the charade by replying, "My finger is looped through the ring. One tug, three seconds and we'll all go up in white fire."

"Identify yourselves!" the voice, coming through the bullhorn outside the rear fence, again said.

"Answer them, Ping-jen," Camellion said harshly, thinking that at that very moment the cross-hairs of a dozen scoped SWAT rifles were trained on him and his group. One nervous trigger finger on one dumb cop—*And the men in the chopper will slaughter them!*

"I-I forgot the n-name of your group!" whispered Ping-jen frantically.

Camellion, feeling the man trembling, jabbed him in the side with the Ingram. "The Fourth Commando Group of Free Nationalist China—you idiot! And tell them that one of us is ready to detonate the thermate grenade if they don't comply. Now! Shout it, son of a sick sow."

Ping-jen did. In a loud voice, he gave his name, explained that he was in charge of the mission, that he and Wang Ch'en-yi were hostages of the Fourth Commando Group of Free Nationalist China, and that, "If you fire one shot, they say they will kill us and commit suicide. One of them has his finger in the ring of a thermate grenade. Don't enter and don't shoot. They mean what they say."

"Tell them to take the lights off us and for the concealed SWAT gunmen to lower their rifles, or I'll have the chopper open fire," Camellion said. "Tell them if they get cute and try for a head shot, the helicopter will cremate them with napalm"
—*The police might think we're bluffing, but they don't dare take the chance. We might be telling the truth. . . .*

Camellion had only half-lied. There wasn't any napalm, only two braces of .30-caliber Brownings on both the port and starboard sides of the Bell and six rocket pods, to be used, if necessary, against police patrol helicopters. It would be necessary. Three police choppers were in the area, hovering at about 500 feet, a mile and a half away.

Ping-jen relayed Camellion's order. Immediately the spotlights were turned off and six policemen, outside the fence, made a great show of putting down their scoped M16s. The Death Merchant smiled—*Those poor dumb fools. Don't they know that we know that six or seven more M16s are trained on us?*

He said to Ping-jen, "Tell them we're going to move out and that our helicopter is going to land. Tell them to order the police helicopters to remain where they are, or this whole damn block will go up."

In a voice shaking with fear, Ping-jen shouted Camellion's message in his perfect but slightly accented English.

Came the voice through the bullhorn. "We will not interfere. You are free to leave. Do you require lights in order to land your craft?"

"No!" Camellion yelled back. He faked a heavy accent. "But if there is one shot fired, our people above will kill at least fifty of you before we die. Do you understand?"

The voice that came through the bullhorn was both angry and frightened. "We understand. No one will fire. Just get the hell out of here."

"Keep as close together as you can," Camellion said to the others. With Hsu Ping-jen, he started down the steps. "Mr. F., once we're twenty feet from the house take out your penlight and signal the Bell. The pilot will come down at about the center of the yard. That's where we're headed."

The group of six, in a tight knot, moved forward, down the steps and across the yard, the Death Merchant not daring to turn his head or remove the Ingram which, at a slant, was shoved against Hsu Ping-jen's neck, the muzzle of the short barrel pressed just in back of the man's right jawbone.

"Stop. I'll signal the chopper," Float said hoarsely. He reached into his pocket, pulled out the Air Force-type penlight, held the tip upward and worked the button in the other end, the red light blinking, "land."

The Bell Kiowa, several hundred feet above the house, began to descend. A powerful spotlight on the nose was switched on. The rotor increased pitch. The craft swung to one side and, with the beam of the spot raking the backyard, the pilot descended rapidly, the single blade creating a loud *wap-wap-wap-wapping* noise.

The terrific downdrift whipping at them and furiously fluttering the leaves of the trees by the back fence, the Death Merchant and his group did not quicken speed. They couldn't. Three of the men were moving backward, and, if they hurried, there was too much danger that police marksmen might try for headshots, although such a tactic was impossible, due to the manner in which the four "terrorists" and their two prisoners were moving. Camellion, behind Hsu Ping-jen, crouched half a head lower than his prisoner. Fieldhouse, in the center of the group, was protected by Ming and Float, who, crouched lower than Wang Ch'en-yi, were moving backward, holding the 3rd Bureau chief by his collar and left wrist. Ch'en-yi was also moving backward, the fierce downdraft of the chopper blowing his black hair.

The Bell landed on its extra-high skids — two rocket pods on each brace of the skids. Two more pods were on the nose, on either side of the cockpit.

Both the port and the starboard doors were open, in each opening a brace of twin caliber .30 T152 machine guns fastened on a bar swivel, a ski-masked man standing behind the protective armor plate mounted over the weapons.

Richard Camellion and Courtland Grojean had not missed a trick. With the pilot, copilot, two gunners and Camellion's party of five, there would be ten people on board the small craft. Add to that the weight of the four Browning machine guns, the six pods and their contents, the load would be 58 pounds over the maximum limit. There was leeway, however. Tests had been conducted at the Company's "Farm." The Bell could lift off. Once in the air it would not have any difficulty, although it wouldn't be able to win any races.

The Death Merchant and his men climbed aboard, keeping Wang Ch'en-yi in front of them, Camellion waited with Hsu Ping-jen. With his back still facing the port opening of the Bell, Camellion reached up with his left hand and Fieldhouse swung the wire and its loop into his hand. Camellion dropped the loop of wire over Ping-jen's neck and tightened it; Fieldhouse then drew in the slack.

"I'm going aboard," Camellion said to Ping-jen. "Try to

run and the piano wire will decapitate you. After I'm on board, I'll tell you to climb in. Don't move until I tell you to. Understand, pig face?"

"Y-Yes."

It took only a few minuteds for Camellion and Ping-jen to get inside the craft and brace themselves with the other men. The pilot revved up; the Allison 250-C18 turboshaft engine roared and the two-bladed rotor started to spin faster and faster. For several seconds the craft hesitated, as if protesting the extra weight. Then the Bell lifted off, the ground, the Red Chinese mission house and the dozen or more police cars falling away, growing smaller and smaller as the helicopter clawed into the big, wide bowl of black sky.

The two men who turned away from the Browning machine guns did not remove their ski masks. For that matter, neither did the pilot and copilot. All four were Company men from the Q-Department[20] and, for reasons of security, didn't want Camellion and the other CIs to see their faces. All the four men aboard the chopper knew was that "Good Queen Bess" was in charge.

"Which one of you is 'Good Queen Bess?' " one of the ski-masked men asked.

"I am," Camllion said. "Get rid of those police choppers!"

"There'll be a lot of damage below from burning debris," the man replied. "There are a lot of houses and SROs[21] down there."

The Death Merchant didn't hesitate. "Shoot'em down. We can't be concerned with any damage that might occur. The overall result more than morally justifies the means."

"None of you are Chinese!" Wang Ch'en-yi suddenly burst out angrily. "You're—"

"I am," Cammellion said. "Get rid of those police choppers!" him "just right" with a short sword-ridge hand blow in back of the right ear.

"Goddamn it," complained Float. "Now we'll have to

20. There isn't any official "Q-Department" within the CIA. Strictly a Company designation, the term refers to case officers or contract agents who indulge in assassination and/or extremely dangerous undercover operations.

21. "Single room occupancy" hotels.

stretch the sonofabitch out on the floor. Why did you have to knock him out? There's little enough room as it is."

Easing the unconscious Wang Ch'en-yi to the floor, Fieldhouse laughed like a little boy who had just dunked the girl's pigtails in the inkwell. "Don't worry about it. I'll sit on him."

In the meanwhile, the Q-Man who had spoken to Camellion had moved to the cockpit and was giving the pilot the Death Merchant's order. The pilot nodded and picked up the mike to the small speaker fastened to the inside top center of the chopper.

"Hang on back there," the pilot said in a calm-as-dust voice. "I'm going to swing around and blast the police helos tailing us."

The men hung onto the overhead handholds, including the terrified Hsu Ping-jen. True to his word, Fieldhouse was sitting on the chest of Wang Ch'en-yi and bracing himself and the prisoner by holding onto the side of one of the metal benches.

Doomsday for the three police helicopters and the six men inside the Hughes OH-6 Cayuse eggbeaters. The three police whirlybirds tried to veer wildly away from the Bell Kiowa, for the police on the ground had warned them about the rocket pods on the "terrorists' " craft.

The doom of the three police choppers was sealed.

One, two, three streaks of fire shot out from three pods of the Bell. Three beam-rider air-to-air Alkali missiles streaked toward the police choppers whose desperate pilots were trying every trick in the book to avoid them. Their efforts were useless.

The first Alkali struck the closest police Cayuse, and the craft changed into an exploding ball of brief, bright red and orange fire. That was all. Blazing wreckage, much of it trailing sparks, began falling to the city below.

Blammmmmmmmm! A half-mile to the west of the first explosion, the second police chopper dissolved in a monstrous explosion of fire.

Blammmmmmmmm! This third explosion was a mile to the east, and the third helicopter became a fireball, its flaming debris falling behind the mess that had been the other two choppers.

134

"God!" exclaimed Joe Ming, pulling off his gas mask. Toward the front of the chopper, he had witnessed the destruction of the three police craft. "They went in a hurry, didn't they?"

The Death Merchant's low voice was somber. "Almost as fast as the whole world will go in the next world war"—*A glorious day it will be for the Cosmic Lord of Death!*

He braced himself as the pilot swung the Bell around and headed west, then looked at the other gunner in a ski mask who hadn't said a single word since they had come aboard.

"How did the take-off and everything else go out there on the river?" Camellion asked. "Any trouble?"

"Everything went off as planned," the man said. "Your signal came in nice and clear. But we had it close back there, hanging over the house. If the police had opened fire . . . "

"They didn't, and that's what matters. We're up here; they're back there."

The man looked at his wristwatch. "We'll be dropping you guys off in about eight minutes. By now, *Angel Face* is at the bottom of the Hudson. We didn't use high-powered explosives. We used nine barrels of fast-acting fire-acid. It can eat through an inch of steel in six minutes. . . . Mr. G. wanted it tested."

The other man in the ski mask said, "Our only problem now is the police choppers. We can handle three more. After that . . . " He shrugged and nodded toward the .30-caliber Brownings. "After that we'll have to depend on them."

Dennis Float laughed and felt the chopper lurch slightly upward as the pilot released the three empty rocket pods to get rid of the extra weight.

"Hell, you don't know the 'efficiency' of the New York police. With three of their choppers shot down, it will take them a week to figure out what to do. Christ, there aren't even enough cops in Midtown, and that's the income heart of the city. I doubt if we'd see another police helicopter if we flew for another hour."

Joe Ming asked an unexpected question. "Say, Swain. That pistol you picked up in the hall, back at the house. What's so special about it?"

"It's a Czech-75," Camellion said, barely able to see the

135

other man in the darkness. "It's too damned bad it's made by the Commies. It's one of the finest pistols in the world."

The Bell roared toward the Hudson, flying at 1200 feet. There was another danger that no one had mentioned: the possibility that the helicopter, even though it was flying with its warning lights on, might collide with another plane from one of the numerous airports in the area. They were flying right smack at the bottom within a triangle of airports, at the northwest side of the triangle. To the northwest, in New Jersey, was Teterboro Airport. At the southwest base of the triangle was Newark International Airport. Slightly to the southeast was the peak of the triangle, John F. Kennedy International Airport. Slightly northwest of JFK Airport was the north side of the triangle, La Guardia Airport, in north Queens, just below Rikers Island. Then there were the smaller airports on Long Island—Grumman Bethpage Airport, Long Island MacArthur Airport, Brookhaven Airport and Suffolk County Air Force Base. All it would require was for some small plane to get off course and collide with the Bell. The only redeeming feature was that Camellion and the other men would never know it. Death would be instantaneous.

Thinking about it, the Death Merchant wasn't really concerned. No one lived forever. Whether he died within the next ten minutes or lived to be a hundred was purely relative.

The only thing that counts now is getting this mission completed.

Chapter Thirteen

Neither Camellion nor the other men had expected this new development: that the Chinese were building a small working model of the invisibility device. And in the United States to boot!

The rest of the plan had gone smoothly. After destroying the police helicopters, the Bell Kiowa had headed for the Hudson River. The drop to the deck of the *Blue Shadow* had been perfect. Within five minutes the Bell was at the bottom of the Hudson, the pilot and copilot and two gunners safely on board the *Blue Shadow*. In the darkness, the *Blue Shadow* had then proceeded south to Gowanus Bay, just below south Brooklyn, and there the cabin cruiser had docked.

At 1:00 that afternoon, the two drugged Chinese, whom Camellion had made up to look like Occidentals, had been helped off the *Blue Shadow* by other "drunken" men and taken to a car. The car had driven off; the *Blue Shadow* had quietly pulled out of its slip and cruised off. A few hours later, Wang Ch'en-yi and Hsu Ping-jen had been smuggled into the Payson Arms in two drums marked INDUSTRIAL DETERGENT.

Camellion and the Company men hadn't wasted any time. They took the two Chinese to a soundproof room where a Company doctor shot them full of narcohypnotic drugs, mainly cyclazocine and naloxone, both of which, acting on certain centers of the brain, deaden free will.

Under intense questioning by Camellion and Dr. Delton— the session took four hours—Wang Ch'en-yi and Hsu Ping-jen revealed how Mason Shiptonn had been programmed.

Four of the girls had been involved with Soraya Duncan and Charles Franzese in the scheme. Once the "target" was selected, the girl would slip the man a drug that, after sex with the girl, would put him into a deep sleep. During this sleep, a Chinese doctor, trained in hypnosis, would inject a specific drug into the victim, a drug that would make his mind open completely to suggestion. Wang Ch'en-yi and Hsu Ping-jen did not know the name of the drug nor the full procedure of the programming. The only fact of which they were certain was that the mind-control program was effective for only six months, after which the victim would have no memory of the narcohypnotic procedure.

Why had Mason Shiptonn stolen the BLUEPRINT: INVISIBILITY file?

Speaking slowly like a robot, Wang Ch'en-yi had explained that something had gone wrong with the programming. Shiptonn had been instructed to photograph the contents of any file he considered to be of the utmost importance. Why he had stolen the file was anybody's guess. The Chinese didn't know.

Where were Duncan, Franzese, Gindow, Gof and the four girls—murdered to keep them quiet?

Now came the big surprise. The eight were hiding out at a house on one of the numerous islands off the coast of Maine —on Chelsworth Island, in Chandler Bay, 8 miles from the coast. They were waiting to be taken to Red China where they would assist the 3rd Bureau in apprising the Chinese about American habits and customs.

It was also on Chelsworth Island that a small working model of the invisibility machine was being constructed. The machine would be completed in another two weeks, after which the device and the eight Americans would meet a Chinese freighter in the Atlantic and sail off to the People's Democratic Republic of China.

Unless Richard Camellion and the Company stopped them.

"It seems to me that's not much of a problem," Gordon Hayes said, his big hands flat on a nautical chart of the coast of Maine. "Navy SEALs can slip in at night and polish them off in no time. What's all the fuss about?"

Dennis Float and James Nivens, reclining on a steel-frame settee, nodded, their eyes on the Death Merchant, who was at a card table decoding the latest message from Courtland Grojean.

Bill Fieldhouse, cleaning a SIG automatic pistol, said, "One of the difficulties is that we don't know the full narcohypnotic procedure used by the Red Chinese. If we wipe them out now on the island, how do we know they won't try it again in another part of the world?"

George Simmons, hardeyed, a wide-shouldered man in wire-rimmed glasses and a trimmed beard, crushed out his cigarette on the conference table.

"You guys are forgetting Chou Wen-yuan, the doctor who administered the drug and performed the hypnosis. He, too, is on the island hiding out. If we could grab him, we'd have the full secret of the mind-control program. As I see it, what choice do we have? We've got to make a strike against Chelsworth Island."

Simmons looked around to find support for his contention, but the faces of the other men remained deadpan and noncommittal.

After a short pause, Dennis Float finally spoke, "The real danger is that if something went wrong, we'd be up to our ass and eyebrows in the worst kind of trouble. The press all over the world is screaming about the 'terrorist' attack on the Chinese mission house, and how terrorism has finally come to the United States. The Red Chinese are raising hell in the U.N. and the Free Chinese on Taiwan are screaming 'We didn't do it!' all over the place."

"We can't hardly use the Fourth Commando of Free Nationalistic China a second time," Hayes put forth, "not on a little hunk of an island that has nothing to do with the Red Chinese. We try that and the FBI and other intelligence agencies are going to put two and two together and they won't come up with five."

"You're right on that score." Fieldhouse leaned forward. "But unless Mr. G. says otherwise, we have no choice but to hit the island. It's not larger than a couple of city blocks and there's nothing there but that big old stone house that the Chinese have rented through half a dozen fronts." He glanced at the Death Merchant, who had gotten up from the card table and was walking toward the smaller officer. Camellion entered the office, turned on the paper-shredder, inserted the several sheets into the slot, waited until the papers were destroyed, then returned to the conference room and sat down in a high-back swivel tilt chair.

"What did the old man say?" Fieldhouse said with an air of defiance. "Do we hit the island or don't we?"

"We do, within the next three days," Camellion said. "There's a Viking 57 motor yacht on its way to New York right now. With it are six SEALers and all the necessary equipment."

"I don't swim," George Simmons said significantly.

"How large is a Viking 57?" Float demanded briskly.

The Death Merchant reacted with the precision of a computer.

"Don't worry about the size of the vessel," he said. "It's big enough to get the job done. We'll meet the *Wild Goose* day after tomorrow, at Fleet Point in Great South Bay, just south of Long Island."

"So we play the 'fishermen' bit again?" Gordon Hayes said.

"That gives us the rest of today and tomorrow to get Hsu Ping-jen and Wang Ch'en-yi to Washington," Fieldhouse said, his tone informative rather than reproachful. "Damn it, we still can't be sure those two told the truth, although Dr. Delton is positive they did."

"Uh huh, it all sounds good, but what do we do in the meanwhile, until the *Wild Goose* gets here?" grunted James Nivens.

"We plan the attack on Chelsworth Island," Camellion declared. "It's got to be fast, sure and without a single mistake. I want Chou Wen-yuan—*alive*. . . ."

Chapter Fourteen

From the stern of the *Wild Goose,* the Death Merchant could see the wake churned by the twin propellers of the cabin cruiser. The hot sun was bright on the water, and there were only a few puffs of clouds on the eastern horizon.

Camellion had seen a lot of coasts, but none could compare with the coast of Maine. In the number of miles of shoreline, formed by its involutions, there were beaches, nooks, harbors and cliffs, all of them broken in a mishmash that had a strange, quiet beauty. The consequent allurements always accompanying such coasts could never be forgotten by one who is fascinated by that mysterious and ever-beautiful wonder, the sea. In many places along the shore were huge elms and pines and birches, all towering above a carpet of wildflowers. There were also those places where there was no shore, not as such . . . no sandy beaches, only jumbled rocks over which breakers broke with loud crashing roars.

Chelsworth Island won't be that difficult, speculated Camellion. From what they had been able to learn about the island, on such short notice, it was high above the water and shaped like a gourd, with a small, natural harbor where the neck curved outward. The north and the east sides of the island, having no accessible harbors, were nothing but tumbled masses of boulders that moved all the way down to the shoreline. Along the southwest end, toward where the neck of the bottle curved, was a long stretch of sandy beach. But where the island spread out into the body of the gourd, there were only rocks and the constant crashing of breakers. The length of the island, from each to west, was 2.6 miles, at its widest point 1.3 miles. The three-story house and outbuildings were in the

141

center of the widest part of the island. A road ran from the small wharf in the southwest to the house on the east side of the island.

There are a few things in our favor, Camellion speculated. *The island is 8 miles from the mainland. Gunfire can't be heard from that distance. The danger lies in the other boats in the area, from fishermen and vacationers. Let's hope the weather predictions are right and a fog does roll in.*

Camellion turned and looked at the wake and the rolling waves of the Atlantic. The plan itself was not at all complicated. The *Wild Goose* would remain 10 miles south of Chelsworth Island, far enough away so as not to arouse the suspicions of the Chinese. The Death Merchant and his people, in Emerson closed-circuit oxygen breathing systems, would leave the cabin cruisers and be pulled to the island by DPVs, Diver Propulsion Vehicles. They would sink the units in shallow water a few thousand feet east of the wharf, creep ashore, hide their breathing units and go to work. By dawn their work would be complete and they could signal the *Wild Goose* to come in close . . . if all went well.

How many of the enemy were on the island? This is what bothered the Death Merchant. Camellion glanced at his watch. Thirty minutes past four in the afternoon—*We'll know in another 10 or11 hours.*

He turned from the stern and for a moment glanced at the radar antenna mounted on the mast of the superstructure. The antenna consisted of two major components. The slender horizontal scanner at the top, which housed the antenna's sending and receiving unit, spun around at the rate of 20 times every minute, sweeping the water as far as the horizon with its SHF radio beam. The bulkier fixed unit underneath contained the driving motor and cables for carrying impulses to and from the sending and receiving unit and the scope below.

Moving with the roll of the vessel, Camellion walked down the steps into the main lounge where Captain Edward Klimes and John Dilman, one of the two members of the crew, were pouring over a tidal current chart.

Both men, Company contract agents, had smuggled weapons into Cuba, and were not strangers to danger of the worst kind.

Captain Marion DeCrow, the leader of the six SEALs, was sitting on a settee berth. A man who looked as if he had been blasted from concrete, DeCrow could have been a hardcase from some state prison. Just as tough as he looked, he had the habit of calling everyone "mate." He didn't know what the deal was in regard to Chelsworth Island; all he knew was that he was to follow the orders of the man called Jason B. Swain.

The Death Merchant glanced from the cold-eyed DeCrow to the other two men. "I presume there's no trouble, Captain? We are on course and we will arrive on time?"

Captain Klimes and John Dilman were not sure, but both felt that Camellion's questions were not so much queries as they were orders. And to Klimes, there was that strange "something" about the man called Swain. One could not look into his eyes without feeling a certain chill, a certain type of warning. There was something alien there, something that didn't belong.

"We are on course, Mr. Swain," Captain Klimes answered in guarded tones. "And the weather is on our side. Calm for the next few days. We'll be in position by one-thirty tomorrow morning—ten and seven-tenths nautical miles south of the island. That's where you want to be, isn't it?"

"Yes, that is correct." Camellion looked at DeCrow. "Have your men ready to go at one. We'll use silencers, smoke and tear gas grenades and thermate. But no grenades. The explosions could be heard from the mainland."

"I understand," conceded DeCrow. "It's Chou Wen-yuan that concerns me. There might be a lot of Chinese on the island, and we don't even know what Wen-yuan looks like. We're not going to have time to run around and ask each one his name. We could knock off Wen-yuan by accident, mate."

"We'll have to play it by ear," Camellion said indulgently. He sat down on the left extension berth and pulled up the pants legs of his sky blue jumpsuit. All we want is Chou Wen-yuan and any of his assistants, if he has any. The rest are to be eliminated and their identities totally destroyed with thermate."

"Including the four broads?" DeCrow raised an eyebrow.

"Including the Queen of England if she's dumb enough to be there," Camellion said ruthlessly. "If any of your boys have

143

scruples about terminating women, you'd better have a heart-to-heart with them."

"Forget it," snapped DeCrow. "We'll get the job done."

"Just so you do." The Death Merchant got to his feet. "I'm going forward and grab some shuteye with the other men."

Captain Klimes made a motion with one hand. "One thing, Mr. Swain. You're aware that the U.S. Coast Guard patrols these waters?"

"So what? You're licensed," Camellion said, "and Dilman and Evers, your two crewmen, are 'sportsmen fishing.' You don't have a problem. Should one develop while we're on the island, with the Coast Guard cutter, sink 'em."

Camellion didn't wait for a reply. He headed for the bulkhead that would take him to the forward cabin in back of the anchor rode and the chain locker. With 14 people on board, plus equipment, every square inch of the cabin cruiser was filled, and each man had the feeling of being a two-legged sardine.

The Death Merchant walked through the bulkhead thinking of the Red Chinese experiments in mind control. The CIA, through grants to various universities, was conducting its own experiments—*But, are the Red Chinese ahead of us? We must find out.*

At 1:00 the next morning, Camellion was 8½ hours closer to learning the secret. Having been briefed, the men were in their wet-suits, a type of rubberized suit that permits entry of water into the suit, where it is trapped and warmed by the body, thereby creating an insulating layer. During the summer months, the water off the coast of Maine was warm, and the eleven men—the six SEALs, Camellion, Float, Fieldhouse, Hayes and Simmons—would only be swimming at a depth of 25 feet.

The men slipped into their breathing systems, strapping the two tanks on their backs, then testing the two breathing bags and the mouthpiece assembly with the non-return valves and the two-way off/bag valve.

Each man wore coral shoes, necessary for divers who operate in shallow water and/or when crawling onto a beach. The shoes were constructed of canvas uppers attached to thick rubber soles and were designed to protect the feet and ankles when working around sharp objects. A standard face mask and depth gauge completed each man's outfit. The only other piece of equipment was a watertight plastic cylinder, 12 inches in diameter and 38 inches long. Each cylinder contained each man's weapons and grenades. Captain DeCrow's cylinder also contained seven 5-pound blocks of TNT and electric detonating timers.

There were no lights on the deck of the *Wild Goose*. No moon in the sky, only countless blue diamonds of stars overhead. There were three boats miles to the east, two moving south, one northeast. Yet once their eyes were accustomed to the darkness, the men had little difficulty. The SEALers climbed down the stern ladder into the water and expertly received the eleven Diver Propulsion Vehicles that Camellion and the other men lowered over the side. Each DPV, 9 inches in diameter and 34 inches long, was nothing more than an electric battery-powered device, with a propeller, a wire-mesh propeller guard and two long protruding handles for the diver to hold on to.

The Death Merchant and his men climbed down the stern ladder into the water, and Camellion and DeCrow, the only two with underwater Nite-Sight devices, adjusted the instruments. They and the other men also checked their AN/PQC-1, or UTELs. The UTEL was a device designed to allow a swimmer to communicate with a submarine, a surface craft or another swimmer. While using UTEL submerged, a swimmer could receive voice transmissions; he could transmit by means of a "lung microphone," either imbedded in a face mask or attacked to his neck. In the case of Camellion and his men, the lung mikes were attached to their necks.

With the Death Merchant and Captain DeCrow forming the bottom point of a V, the men dove to a depth of 20 feet, turned on their DPVs and headed north toward Chelsworth Island, the water, entering their wet-suits, soon turning warm due to the temperature of their bodies.

The world of water was darkness, blackness and the *whirring* of the propellers of the DPVs. It was an alien world in which Man was not suited to live.

Every few minutes, Camellion called out over the UTEL

145

for positions, a homing signal, which each man answered by giving his initials.

Steadily the distance to the south side of the island decreased until, 48 minutes later, they were approaching shallow water, for Chelsworth Island was actually a submerged mountain, the island its peak.

Camellion and DeCrow checked their depth gauges, looked at their wristwatches, shut off their DPVs, swam to the surface and had a long look through their Nite-Sight scopes. Right on target. They were less than a mile from shore. Directly ahead was the midway point between the dock and where the larger part of the island jutted south to form the main body of the gourd. Two cabin cruisers were moored at the dock.

"We'll sink the DPVs a hundred feet from shore," Camellion said. "We'll swim the rest of the way, arm ourselves and then take care of anyone who might be on the boats. What's your opinion?"

"A good plan," DeCrow said. "Let's do it."

They worked very quietly, very quickly and with expert precision. Forty minutes more and the men had hidden their face masks, UTELs, air tanks and plastic cylinders in a grove of pine trees near the shore. Even in the darkness the men could see that there was an inexhaustible quality in the landscape, but they weren't interested in the sights of nature.

Still in their wet-suits and keeping to one side of the dirt road that led from the dock to the main house, they crept toward the two cabin cruisers moored on either side of the dock. One was a Trojan Meridian, a long-range, offshore cruiser; the other was a Hatteras 46 convertible.

The Death Merchant and his men stopped 100 feet from the rear of the two cabin cruisers. For a long time Camellion and DeCrow studied the two cabins through the infrared vision scopes. Not a single light. The two crafts looked deserted.

"Maybe they are deserted?" suggested Clayton Brode, one of the Navy SEALers. "Man, it would be simple to lob in a couple of thermate grenades."

"Yeah," grunted Gordan Hayes, "and the explosions and fires would be heard and seen for miles."

"It isn't likely that they'd leave those two boats unguarded." Fieldhouse's tone was determined and business-like. "There're no guards outside, so they must be inside the cabins."

"Two men to each boat," the Death Merchant said. "Bill, you come with me. DeCrow, take one of your people."

"Why two?" inquired George Simmons.

Camellion gave Simmons a long, pathetic look. "One to hold the flash, the other to pull the trigger. Willie, you handle the flash."

Camellion and Fieldhouse crept out of the wooded area and advanced toward the dock. The Death Merchant held a silenced Backpacker Auto Mag in each hand. Fieldhouse carried a 4-cell Kel-lite in one hand and a silenced 9mm ASP auto-pistol in the other.

DeCrow and Harlon Wiseman advanced with them, Wiseman carrying a Kel-lite and a BDA Browning with silencer attached. Captain DeCrow held an Ingram submachine gun, a Permann noise suppressor jutting out from its barrel.

The cabin cruisers were hardly moving in the quiet water. There was not a single sound from either boat. The four men reached the 40-foot-long dock and crept toward the stern end of each boat, Camellion and Fieldhouse moving toward the Trojan Meridian, DeCrow and Wiseman concentrating on the Hatteras convertible.

"Keep the flash off until we're in the main cabin," whispered Camellion. "I want to take one alive if possible."

Together, he and Fieldhouse leaped lightly from the dock onto the stern deck of the Trojan Meridian, the boat bobbing slightly from their weight. They turned and headed for the stern-cabin door. Fieldhouse turned the knob and pulled open the door. The Death Merchant plunged in first, Fieldhouse right behind him and raking the bright beam of the flashlight over the berths on the port and the starboard sides. A man was lying on each bunk.

"What the hell?" muttered the man on the port side, the flashlight beam snapping him into wakefulness. His right hand then dove for a revolver under a pillow.

One of the Death Merchant's Auto Mags made a *bazitttt*

147

sound. The man's body gave a huge jerk, relaxed and fell back to the bed, the .44 Jurras Magnum bullet leaving a hole in his right side the size of a midget's fist.

The man in the bunk on the starboard side—big, beefy and dressed only in undershorts—threw up both hands when the beam hit him full in the face and Camellion snarled, "Move and I'll scatter your brains all over this cabin. How many more of you are on this boat?"

"Just me and Roscoe," the man said hoarsely. "And you've knocked him off."

"Who do you work for, the Chinese?"

Asked Fieldhouse, "Soraya Duncan and the rest of the scum—they're at the house?"

"B-Blackeye. Blackeye Franzese. Me and Roscoe, we both worked for Blackeye. All of them . . . they're all up at the house."

"How many Chinese?" demanded Camellion. "How many altogether?"

"God, I don't know." The man blinked furiously against the light, his manner becoming more and more desperate. "Fifty, sixty! I don't know. I've never counted them. Listen, we can make a deal. We—"

The AMP in Camellion's left hand buckled, made a *ba-zitttt* sound, and the man, stark astonishment on his face, fell back, an enormous bullethole in his broad, hairy chest. At the same time there was a slight *pinging* sound as the big .44 bullet bored all the way through his body and struck a rivet head, then glanced off and buried itself in the mattress of the bunk.

Without a word, Camellion and Fieldhouse checked the forward cabins, found that they, too, were empty, then hurried back to the stern deck. Reaching under the cocktail table, Camellion pulled open the cover to the engine compartment. While Fieldhouse kept watch, Camellion put the Diesel engine out of commission with a couple of well-placed .44 AMP projectiles.

"Decrow and the other guy have just jumped up from the deck of the other boat," Fieldhouse muttered, then signaled to the two men with several flashes of his flashlight. Several moments later, Camellion and Fieldhouse were on the dock with

DeCrow and Wiseman, DeCrow reporting that they had not found anyone on board the Hatteras cabin cruiser.

"We took care of the engine," DeCrow said. "That boat will never run without an extensive repair job. What did you two find?"

The Death Merchant told him, finishing with the possible number of ". . . fifty or sixty of the enemy at the main house. How does that grab you?" Camellion gave a little laugh, cocked his head to one side, and glanced in the direction of the house.

DeCrow and Wiseman were not amused. "Look, mate," said DeCrow, "the yoga philosophy states that one should accept all things. The Zen Buddhists also endorse a don't-expect-too-damn-much attitude."

"So what?" Camellion stroked his chin. "The Chinese philosophy of Taoism supports the same philosophy."

"So eleven men attacking forty or fifty or sixty is ridiculous," growled DeCrow, who was standing beside Wiseman and looking as massive and powerful as a giant steamroller. "Danger is one thing. Suicide is another."

"It's no big deal," Camellion said persuasively as he and the three other men moved from the dock toward the men hidden in the trees. "We'll place two men on each side of the house. Three of us will go inside. That's all there is to it."

"Yeah? Which three?" DeCrow demanded indignantly.

"I and two volunteers," Camellion said with quiet conviction. "I don't want anyone going in with me who's carrying on a love affair with life. First, let's wait until we see what the house looks like."

Keeping off the winding dirt road, they proceeded east in a T formation, Camellion, Fieldhouse and DeCrow forming the cross of the T. Progress was very slow, not only because of the extreme caution used by the Death Merchant, but because the island's terrain was uneven and heavily wooded. There were maples and basswood trees in tiny groves, and majestic elms forming a wonderful canopy between earth and sky, their great trunks lending dignity and character.

There were small hills and long slopes and, in numerous places, tiny gullies on which and in which grew beech and

149

white birch. In other areas the distinctive and frond-like foliage of locust trees appeared. Wild blackberries and raspberry bushes were in abundance—and so was poison ivy. Everywhere were dandelions, daisies and choke cherries.

At length, Camellion and company came within sight of the target—the house that had been built in a clearing protected by spruce and oaks. At once, the Death Merchant and his men saw that they had been misinformed, in that the house contained not three but two stories.

Studying the house through the night-vision binoculars, Camellion remarked, as if talking to himself, "It's not the typical old-style Maine house."

"More than that," whispered Gordon Hayes. "It's damned weird."

Camellion did some reflecting. The typical old house in Maine was a one-story dwelling with one chimney, a square front entry and a room on each side. The roof would always have a good pitch and the chimney, unless modern, would always be large. Such a house would usually date in the eighteenth or early-nineteenth century.

As for a large house, a person born and reared in Maine would think of an eight-room dwelling with four chimneys, two in each side wall, this coming into fashion at the time of the Revolution and continuing to about 1820. At the time of the Revolution, the interior of such houses was carefully done with a good deal of panel work about fireplaces and stairways, and with large and excellent cornices of wood.

The house ahead, built in the shape of a rectangle and of the revived Gothic period of 1830, was constructed of stone, with the roof above the second story not having too much slant. Outside, there was little wrought-iron ornamentation, in contrast to earlier houses. The main entrance was square-fronted. There were two chimneys, one large one on the west side of the house, the second on the north side of the large structure.

It was the addition to the house that made the entire structure seem entirely out of place. A story-and-a-half building had been added to the east side of the stone house. A hundred and fifty feet long, the addition was constructed of sheets of galvanized iron, the roof flat. The house was dark, but Camellion and his men could see lights through small windows in the new building, the front of which contained three doors, two ordinary sized ones and one large enough to admit a tractor and trailer. A low humming issued from the new building.

To the east of the laboratory was a 100-foot-tall electric-generating tower, the wind-driven propeller 40 feet in length. The top halves of two other wind towers were visible from behind the house.

"Now we know where the lab is and where the Chinese are conducting their experiments in invisibility," Fieldhouse said laconically, "and we know how they're getting their electric power."

"They brought the magnets from the mainland," the Death Merchant said, "which is entirely academic at the moment." He looked at the tense faces around him. "I need two volunteers to go with me into the house. Who's it going to be?"

"Count me in," Bill Fieldhouse said with a crooked grin. "I'm as nutty as you are."

"Include me." Gordon Hayes' black face also broke out in a smile. "Although I don't understand why we don't charge the lab and get it over with. Duncan, her four whores, Franzese and his crowd are sleeping up a storm at this hour."

"I don't want Franzese and his gunmen coming in at us after we're in the lab," Camellion said. "I want to drive everyone in the house to the lab and get them together."

"That makes sense," DeCrow commented. "We can deploy men on the four sides of the house, to make sure no one escapes, then attack at a given signal. We'll keep our walkie-talkies open, with the volume just loud enough to be heard. What do you say, Swain?"

"Good enough," Camellion said. "One more thing: Don't take the silencers off your weapons until we charge the lab. Should anyone try to flee the house or the lab and you fire, the noise will give away your positions without the sound suppressors." He glanced at Hayes and Fieldhouse. "You two all set?"

"As ready as we'll ever be," Hayes said matter of factly.

While Captain DeCrow began deploying his men, Camellion, Hayes and Fieldhouse started to move west through the trees, their goal the west side of the house.

As they moved, the Death Merchant thought of one of the messages he had received from Grojean, one that had been

151

included in one of the numerous coded radio transmissions. The message was burned into his mind: PREPARE TO GO TO NORTH IRELAND.

I'm as anxious to go to North Ireland as I am to hear that I've contracted the Rumanian crud!

Chapter Fifteen

God smiles on those mortals who have the foresight to help themselves. Wearing gas masks, Camellion, Hayes and Fieldhouse moved out from the trees and crept to the west side of the stone house. His Ingram strapped to his back, the Death Merchant tried to raise the bottom section of one window while Hayes and Fieldhouse, Ingrams in hand, huddled by the side of the fireplace chimney and kept watch.

The window was of the old-fashioned kind: an upper and a lower section, with nine individual panes in each section and a lock-latch at the top of the lower frame.

The window was locked. Camellion tried another window. It, too, was locked.

"What now?" Fieldhouse regarded Camellion gravely.

"Maybe the front door is open?" said Hayes, meaning the remark as a sick joke.

"Well, if God shuts one door, He always opens another," Camellion said and pulled one of the .44 Backpacker Auto Mags from its hip holster. "Get set to crawl in."

With the butt of the Auto Mag, he smashed one of the small window panes over the latch, the glass falling to the floor with a loud noise.

"Kiss my butt!" exclaimed Fieldhouse in surprise. "Why not send them a telegram and tell them we're coming?"

"I never thought of that," joked Camellion. He reached through the opening, unlocked the window, then pushed the bottom section upward. He pulled the second Auto Mag, threw one leg over the window sill and crawled in, Hayes and Fieldhouse hurriedly crawling into the room after him.

They found themselves in a darkened sitting room filled

with Windsor chairs and settees. In front of one settee was a cherry sofa table. On a side table was a lead crystal hurricane lamp. A highbacked rocking chair was close to the archway on the east side of the room.

The Death Merchant and his two men were three-fourths of the way across the room when they heard low voices and saw the side glow of approaching flashlights from the hall beyond the next large room.

Old Rattle Bones, you're going to have a ball tonight! Camellion got down in front of a Queen Anne wing chair as Fieldhouse rushed to the right edge of the archway, Hayes to the left side.

The two men who had been sleeping in the living room and were on their way to investigate the sound of falling glass had as much chance as an ice cube in the center of a blast furnace. They were in the dining room and only 8 feet from the archway when Hayes and Fieldhouse leaned around the edges of the archway and fired off a short burst each. The noise suppressors on the Ingrams went *bazittttt* and the 9mm projectiles, stabbing into the midriffs of the two doomed men, pitched them backward. One corpse knocked over a chair and fell across the solid cherry dining-room table. The other dead, dumb dunce slammed into a cherry and pine sideboard and slid to the floor, both dead men creating enough noise to wake the dead 5 miles away.

"Cripes! We might as well have brought a brass band!" mumbled Hayes resignedly.

"Yeah," Camellion said happily, sounding as if he was enjoying himself. "Any jackass can kick down a barn, but it takes a damned good carpenter to build one. Let's do some fast moving."

They moved into the dining room, paused long enough to toss a couple of CN canisters into the hall ahead, and then charged forward, almost bumping into five men.

Sleeping in rooms on the second floor, the five men had pulled on their pants, grabbed pistols and rushed down the stairs, only to have one of the tear gas grenades explode almost at their feet. Hampered by the gas beginning to sting their eyes and clog their lungs, the five did the best they could under the circumstances.

Claude "Icepick" Childs, a bushy-haired hoodlum from the

154

Bronx, snapped off a round from a Swiss Luger. The Death Merchant ducked and the 7.65mm bullet burned air several inches over his right shoulder. One of Camellion's AMPs went *bazitttt*, and Childs' head almost jumped from his neck as the .44 Backpacker bullet blew out his throat and almost decapitated him.

Big Mike D'Alberto and Riley "The Rube" Bender were next to find out how it felt to be dead. D'Alberto, with a Ruger .357 Magnum, and Bender, his right hand holding a Smith & Wesson .38 revolver, were about to blast away at Fieldhouse and Hayes when the Death Merchant fired both Auto Mags simultaneously.

Two *baazitttttttttsssss* from the silencers on the two Auto Mags, and D'Alberto's head exploded with a loud *plop*, the instant disintegration showering George Saint Nicholas and Robert "Gentleman Bob" Rubach with blood, parts of skin, pieces of skull bone and blobs of gray brain matter. Reflex triggered the Ruger revolver and it roared like a mini-cannon. The bullet, going upward, passed between Gordon Hayes and Bill Fieldhouse and broke the globe of a New Bedford hanging lamp.

Riley "The Rube" Bender went down with an enormous blue-black bullethole in his chest, blood pouring out of the gaping wound and, running downward, soaking into the waistband of his trousers. The .44 Jurras slug had gone all the way through his body, and there was another yawning hole in his back, between his shoulder blades.

To prevent anyone else from coming down the stairs, Fieldhouse was triggering off a long burst of Ingram slugs at the same time that Hayes was cutting George Saint Nicholas in two with a burst of 9 mm projectiles and "Gentleman Bob" was getting set to cut down on Hayes with a stainless steel Vega .45 auto-pistol.

Only the Death Merchant was a split second faster. His left Auto Mag exploded, the .44 Magnum slug striking "Gentleman Bob" in the right shoulder, the TNT impact tearing off his arm and sending it, the Vega .45, and "Gentleman Bob," a giant spurt of blood gushing from where his arm had been connected to the shoulder, flying.

Upstairs, toward the south side of the house, they heard a short shriek of agony and assumed that a woman had appeared in a window and that one of DeCrow's SEALs had wasted her.

"Gordon, keep an eye on the stairs," Camellion ordered. "Willie, let's check the rest of the downstairs."

"Make it snappy," growled Hayes. "I get lonesome by myself."

"Don't worry," kidded Camellion. "The people in here aren't against us; they're merely for themselves."

The Death Merchant and Fieldhouse moved quickly through the large, old rooms—the living room, another sitting room, a kitchen, a pantry, a library with empty book shelves, but with a polished carved horse, 3 inches long and made of copper carbonate. Camellion picked up the horse and dropped it into one of the compartments of his shoulder bag.

All the rooms were empty, including the sunporch on the east end of the house—an unusual sunporch in that it didn't have any glass in the window frames. Instead, there was a wall of Galvanized iron sheets and a solid steel door with a latch-lock.

Through clouds of tear gas, for Camellion and Fieldhouse had dropped five canisters of CN, they hurried back to Gordon Hayes and saw that the gas had drifted upstairs and had filled the hallway—*But why isn't there any coughing?*

Or could they all be wearing gas masks?

"Gordon," the Death Merchant said, "cover me. Bill, watch the east end. No telling what might come through that door on the sunporch."

Camellion raced up the stairs, taking three steps at a time. He paused at the top, looked first to the left, then to the right. Nothing but gas. But not a single cough from any room—*And if they have their heads hanging out the windows, the SEALs would have shot them off. So either they weren't up here, or, if they were, they got out another way. But how?*

Camellion moved east, to the right, constantly turning, watching every door. Then his eye caught sight of the rumpled end of the rug where the hall ended. He hurried to the end of the hall, pulled back the rug and saw the trapdoor. He holstered one of the AMPs, then, standing to one side, bent down and pulled open the metal trapdoor. There it was; the wide, round mouth of a smooth aluminum tube, the kind used in schools in case of fire, to help children on the second floor escape. All one had to do was jump in and slide down.

That's what happened to Soraya Duncan, Franzese, Gindow and the rest of the trash. They slid down the tube into the lab. That's just dandy. I want all the rotten apples in one basket. Now I have them.

He took a CN canister from one of his shoulder bags, pulled the pin, dropped the grenade down the chute, dropped the trapdoor and hurried back to the stairs, keeping to one side of a wall and now exposing himself.

"Don't fire," he shouted loudly. "It's Swain. I'm coming down."

"Come ahead," Hayes called back.

Camellion rushed down the stairs, pulled the walkie-talkie from the case on his belt and contacted Captain Marion De-Crow.

"Have any of them tried to make a run for it?" Camellion asked.

"No, but one of my guys knocked off some slut opening a window. How's it in there with you guys?"

The Death Merchant gave DeCrow a full report, then asked how long it would take for DeCrow and his five men to use grenades against the outside doors of the lab and attack.

"I thought you said explosives were out? What happens if they hear the noise from the mainland, or if some passing Coast Guard cutter stops to investigate?"

"I've changed my mind," Camellion said. "It's speed we're after. Anyhow, by the time anyone figures out what's happened and shows up, we'll be long gone."

"You're in charge." DeCrow's voice came back over the set. "How do you want to do it?"

Chapter Sixteen

If there is any truth to the axiom that misery loves company, Soraya Duncan and the three young women with her had more than enough associates who were equally wretched. All four women, dressed only in lace-wrap enfolds, were huddled behind some crates in the northwest corner of the lab, Marge and Yolanda on the verge of hysteria.

Charles Franzese, Barney Gindow and nine of their men—most of whom were in pajamas or, having on only pants, naked to the waist—were scattered out toward the center of the large building, not far from the two rows of giant coils, all eleven hoodlums with either pistols or revolvers in their hands.

Doctor Chou Wen-yuan, the psychiatrist, Doctor Lin T'ien Cho-ko, a physicist, and the other Chinese had taken positions behind platforms filled with magnets; others were behind strange-looking machines and other electrical equipment. All were armed, many with submachine guns.

Gregory "Steel Fingers" Gof was behind the weird-looking device that Dr. Cho-ko called the "Space-Bender"—a repugnant little monster armed with a Heckler and Koch V70 machine pistol.

For any number of reasons, every individual in the laboratory was worried. First of all, no one knew how many of the enemy were outside. There was the problem of tear gas, and there were only ten gas masks, and ten of the Chinese were wearing them.

The people in the laboratory did the only thing they could do: they waited, watching all the entrances . . . hoping for the best but knowing the worst would soon arrive.

"I hope to hell you know what you're doing!" Gordon Hayes watched the Death Merchant finish wiring the five fragmentation grenades together and then attach a remote-control electric detonator.

"Hell, quit your complaining," kidded Fieldhouse. He shifted uncomfortably. The rubberized wet-suit was made for comfort only in the water. "Think of the good job you have. A grand a month pension at the end of ten years, and you work for an equal opportunity employer. Hell, man! Life's a ball."

"Chicken crap! Don't give me that jive, you turkey," mocked Hayes with a fake sneer. "Damn few of us live long enough to collect that grand. Those who do spend half of it on booze and the other half on taking the 'cure.' Equality of opportunity only means an equal opportunity to prove unequal talents. Like I said, chicken crap!"

"Right on, brother," Camellion agreed and placed the five grenades at the bottom of the steel door in the center of the sunporch. "Now let's get back and make the cats on the other side start paying their dues."

"Yeah—in blood," said Fieldhouse.

Camellion and the other two men ran to the end of the east hall, their divers' coral shoes making their footing very firm and certain. They got to the side of the inner wall. The Death Merchant reached into one of the compartments of his right shoulder bag, took out a small black box, opened the cover and waited while Fieldhouse took two grenades from one of his bags and Hayes made ready to pull the pin of a smoke canister.

"You two set?" Camellion smiled within the gas mask.

"Do it," Fieldhouse said.

Camellion did it. He turned on the device and pushed the red button.

The explosion could have been Mount Vesuvius erupting. The five grenades exploded in an enormous sheet of fire and a thunderous concussion. The steel door and sheets of galvinized iron sailed inward and upward while glass fell from every window in the house.

Several moments later, there were more explosions, these from the outside, from the front of the laboratory as Captain

DeCrow and his men lobbed grenades against the two ordinary-sized doors.

But the Death Merchant and the two men with him did not charge; neither did DeCrow and his five SEALs. Inside the building, the Chinese and the American mobsters, deafened and shaken by the explosions, waited, their weapons trained on the three smoking openings. None of them expected what happened next.

There was another leviathan explosion, and the huge door in front vanished in a ball of smoke and fire. Sharp pieces of galvanized metal rocketed inward and clanged loudly against machinery, the 10-foot-tall coils and the giant magnets.

"They're going to kill us all!" screamed Yolanda Ware. Utterly possessed by fear and hysteria, she jumped up and, shrieking like a drunken banshee, started running across the lab. She was 50 feet from her former position when the second half-pound of TNT exploded in the center of the north wall of the building, the terrific crash throwing metal-like spears and ragged plates. One piece knifed into the back of one of the hoods and killed him instantly. Another piece flashed inward like a giant discus and decapitated Yolanda Ware. Her head jumped a foot from her neck, her eyes fluttering. Then the head fell to the floor, and so did the corpse, blood gushing from the guillotined neck. No one felt sorry for the girl. She had taken her chances and had lost.

CN canisters and smoke grenades sailed through the large torn gash in the north wall and through the three openings in the front of the lab. To the west, the Death Merchant tossed two frag grenades through the rent where the steel door had been. Fieldhouse followed with two smoke canisters, MH-8Ca jet black stuff; Hayes lobbed in three CN canisters. Another frag grenade sailed through the large opening in front, on the south side. Two more frag grenades and several more smoke canisters made their short journeys through the ragged, twisted opening in the north wall.

Only then did the Death Merchant and his men charge—Camellion, Hayes and Fieldhouse from the west end; Captain DeCrow, Ridgeway and Thompson from the north side; Brode, Wiseman and Koerner from the large entrance in front. Float and Simmons charged in from the doorway in

160

front, the one west of the large opening. All eleven kept low and zig-zagged, advancing in no discernible pattern.

Due to the thick black smoke, drifting lazily through the air, and the clouds of tear gas, it was almost impossible to distinguish friend from foe; and although greatly outnumbered, Camellion and his ten men had the advantage. The SEALs had been trained in more than underwater demolitions; they were also members of the 16th Arrowhead Black Beret Unit—men trained for quick-strike-and-kill situations. The four Company men were also experts in ultimate violence. But the expert of experts was Richard Camellion, who, in eleven years, had killed literally thousands of people . . . some by methods that medical science, in the West, would insist was impossible, yet were yoga techniques that were ancient before the time of Christ.[22]

The firing of weapons was a cacophony of sound right out of hell, a dissonance that ripped at the mind and tore at one's sanity. There was the stink: the acrid odor of burnt cordite and TNT mixed with the clawing, clogging, sooty stench of smoke and the stinging sweetness of tear gas. None of this bothered Camellion and his men or the Chinese, all of whom were wearing gas masks.

The Death Merchant and his men had removed the noise suppressors and were using their Ingrams the same way they were using their pistols—as auto-loaders, having set the Ingram machine pistols to fire three-round bursts.

With slugs skimming by his wet-suit, some even grazing the black rubberized material, Camellion began firing once he was 6 feet inside the lab, the Backpacker Auto Mag in each hand roaring. Blackie Tower, a moonfaced moron, and Peppi Calcimine, a pimp who loved to beat working girls with coat hangers, went down with .44 JHP slugs having bored big, bloody tunnels through their chests and backs.

To Camellion's left, Bill Fieldhouse darted, ducked and dodged a burst of 9mm slugs from a Chinese wearing a gas mask and a blue smock. Before Chi Teh Pi could correct the angle of fire and Bill could swing around, Gordon Hayes mut-

---

22. No doubt the deadly yoga technique of *Pingala*: intense concentration that, if properly applied, can kill a person, either by stroke or heart attack.

tered, "You monkey-faced mother-frigger!" and stitched Chi Teh Pi's left side with Ingram slugs that turned his heart and lungs into bloody mush. Then Hayes cried out in pain and anger when a .38 Special bullet raked his left thigh on the outside, the lead cutting through the suit and slicing into the skin; but, expert that he was, he didn't permit the pain of the deep graze to interfere with speed. He turned slightly and fired, the *duddle-duddle-duddle* of the snarling Ingram punching three holes in the chest of the man who had fired at him.

To the north, Captain DeCrow, Walter Ridgeway and Gene Thompson got off short bursts that killed four Chinese technicians and Harry Jomuskie, one of Charley Franzese's triggermen. Bloody and dead, the Chinese went down like broken tree trunks struck by lightning. Jomuskie, blood dripping from his mouth onto his fuzzy beard, spun around, dropped the Astra .357 revolver, had a fleeting thought of his mother, died and fell across a mass of thick cables that led from the banks of magnets to the Space-Bender machine.

DeCrow, Ridgeway and Thompson tried to race ahead, but when enemy slugs began coming too close, they darted to their right and sought safety behind several large crates, on the sides of which were stencilled: MAGNETORESISTORS, STAMFORD ELECTRICAL CORPORATION, DAYTON, OHIO.

Across the laboratory, Harlon Wiseman, Martin Koerner and Clayton Brode had stormed in firing, had killed three Chinese, critically wounded Buck "Funny Money" Cerone and then had jumped behind a magnetohydrodynamic generator that hummed with power.

Dennis Float and George Simmons had fired off bursts, but their slugs hadn't struck any of the enemy. Crouched behind a heavy metal workbench that had been overturned by concussion when the large door in the center of the south side had been blown, the two men looked out on what could have been a Paris flea market after an auction sale riot. Everywhere the concrete floor was littered with trash and debris, with fragile equipment that had been slammed to the floor by concussion and broken. Glass, fractured bakelite and cracked field-effect tubes lay in piles. Several open cases had overturned and hundreds of nickel-cadmium cells lay scattered amidst nuvistors, those small vacuum tubes with cantilever-supported cylindrical electrodes that eliminated the need for mica supports.

Like the rest of the Death Merchant's men, Float and Simmons could guess the position of the enemy from the furious coughing going on; yet through the drifting smoke and gas, they had caught glimpses of the blue-smocked, gas-masked Chinese and realized that not all of the enemy could be detected by sound.

Float tossed another smoke canister ahead, then he and Simmons charged forth, their hands filled with Ingram subguns and SIG auto-loaders.

Dr. Chou Wen-yuan, the psychiatrist and specialist in mind murder, was with Lin T'ien Cho-ko, the fairly young physicist who had gotten his Ph.D. at MIT. Both men wore gas masks and were close to the Space-Bender, the device that, although yet untested, could teleport objects from point A to point—to point *where*?

Surrounded by technicians and by experts of the Chinese 3rd Bureau, the two scientists had no illusions about their fate. Already the lab was completely divorced from any objective reality, and to think that they could win and that the experiment would ever be completed was as absurd as asking a victim of shell-shock to describe in exact detail the bursting of an artillery shell. The hourglass could not be reversed. . . .

The two scientists accepted their fate with the stoicism of their ancestors. They would fight to the bitter end. They had chosen to ride the tiger; now they could not dismount.

Only 40 feet to the west, they heard the snarling of submachine guns and the enormous *Beroommms* from what must have been very large pistols. To the left, they heard Chi Ul'kuei, one of the technicians, scream and fall backward, blood dripping from the front of his smock. To the right, only 3 feet from Dr. Cho-ko, there was a loud *plop* as the gas mask, face and head of Li Hsiao-p'ing, one of the 3rd Bureau agents, exploded from the impact of a .44 Backpacker bullet.

Doctor Wen-yuan thought of the American gangsters who had taken positions by the coils. No matter that they would die. Once at sea, the 3rd Bureau would have killed them anyhow, them and the women. The Americans were no longer needed. However, it would have been necessary to have them disappear forever. Peking wanted no evidence left behind.

Doctor Cho-ko felt only a deep bitterness, not only because

he knew he was going to die, but because he realized that he would never complete the experiment. In another four days he could have finished the project. He could have completed spectral analysis, magnetograph tape readings and electromagnetic profiles. He could have opened the door to another universe!

But none of it was to be. Yes, reflected Cho-ko, Confucius was right: *He who offends against heaven has none to whom he can pray.* . . .

If Confucius had known Soraya Duncan, the old fool would have said that *A stupid son is better than a crafty daughter* (he did anyhow). A born survivor, Soraya was not about to accept death as her fate, not if she could help it. Huddled in the northwest corner with Marge Baker and Donna Jean Kirol, Soraya could hardly keep her eyes open. The two other women were in the same fix. Breathing through handkerchiefs didn't help much either. Nevertheless, Soraya knew there was still a chance for life. A very slim one, true. Just the same, it was still possible that she and Marge and Donna Jean could slip unnoticed through the large tear in the center of the north side wall.

Soraya had spotted DeCrow, Ridgeway and Thompson when the three SEALs had stormed through the mutilated north wall. Wisely, however, she had not fired at them with the little .25 Bauer automatic she held in one hand, more than realizing that she was not a match for even one man, much less three, all armed with machine pistols. Logic also told her that sooner or later the three men would storm forward and leave a clear field for her and the other women. The fighting was going on toward the west and the southwest. In the smoke and confusion, who would notice her and Marge and Donna Jean?

Gasping for air through the wet handkerchief she held over her mouth, Soraya discreetly looked out from behind the crate and saw that the three men in black swimsuits were darting and dodging and weaving toward the south. . . .

"Now's our chance," Soraya whispered to Marge Baker, a blonde who was so sexy she could have given an erection to a stone statue; and to Donna Jean Kirol, a 22-year-old brunette who was equally as shapely.

"W-We'll never be a-able to make it!" gasped Donna Jean weakly through tears.

All three women were a mess, their wraparounds torn and dirty, their faces smudged, their hair uncombed.

"Would you rather stay here and have them find us and kill us later?" Soraya whispered savagely.

"N-No."

Soraya shook Marge Baker by the arm. The blonde was so paralyzed with fear her eyes resembled two large marbles about to pop out of her head. Tears flowed from her eyes and spittle from her mouth.

"You Goddamned chippie!" Soraya shook her again. "Did you hear me? When I say, 'Run,' you run. Do you understand me?"

Dumbly, the young whore nodded.

Again, Soraya looked around the edge of the crate, then, motioning with the pearl-handled .25 Bauer, forced the two other women out ahead of her.

"Now run for the opening in the wall," she said hoarsely.

Run they did. Donna Jean first, then Marge, Soraya right behind them, to make sure they didn't falter or change their minds. What Soraya hadn't counted on was how much stress the human nervous system can withstand. A human being can stand up to a tremendous amount of pressure; yet when a certain borderline is reached, there occurs what psychiatrists call "nervous decompensation." This is the critical psychic crisis. What follows is the mental crackup. The victim goes all to pieces.

Nervous decompensation struck Marge Baker when she and Donna Jean and Soraya were halfway to the ripped opening in the north wall, her hysterical crisis triggered by several richocheting machine-gun slugs that struck the Space-Bender machine and were making exceptionally loud and long-ringing whines.

The breaking point! Marge stopped, put her hands to her head and started shrieking, screaming at the top of her lungs, her sudden, unexpected shrill screeching causing Soraya and Donna Jean to pause in alarm. Her caterwauling also attracted the attention of Walt Ridgeway, who was behind a large wooden crate filled with homopolar magnets. The screaming was coming only 30 feet behind him and, as highly trained as he was, he turned and fired by instinct. Captain DeCrow and Gene Thompson—20 feet to the right of Ridgeway and protected by other crates—reacted in a similar manner. They, too, spun and fired.

Nine-millimeter Silvertip HP projectiles ripped into Marge Baker's chest and stomach, the slugs switching off her screaming and her life. Her corpse was falling toward the north wall when 9mm bullets tore into Soraya Duncan. One slug tore off her left breast. Another struck her an inch below the navel. A third bullet tore through her left eye, cut through her brain and tore out the back of her skull. Donna Jean Kirol caught two slugs in the lower part of the body, the bullets giving her a free hysterectomy. A third slug knifed into her belly and flattened out against her spine. Bloody and useless, the three corpses lay there . . . fitting food for hungry maggots. . . .

The Death Merchant, lying almost flat behind an overturned tool rack, was not pleased the way the fire-fight was going, even if the Chinese were assembled in the middle of the lab, crouched down around various pieces of equipment surrounding the Space-Bender mechanism. What bothered Camellion was that Charley Franzese and most of his gunmen had moved to the rows of giant coils that were to the northwest of the Chinese. Should DeCrow, Ridgeway and Thompson charge from the north side, and Camellion and Hayes and Fieldhouse from the west, both groups would be caught in a crossfire and cut to pieces. Float and Simmons and the three SEALs to the south could not be expected to make the charge alone.

The problem was not complicated. The Death Merchant knew that he had to move the mobsters to the Chinese, or vice versa.

Lying next to Camellion, Bill Fieldhouse was thinking along the same lines. Bill turned his head and glanced at Gordon Hayes, who was 10 feet to his left, down behind a mess of some kind of wrecked electrical equipment. There was the time factor to be considered, too.

Fieldhouse said to Camellion, "How are we going to do it, Swain?"

A blast of slugs from the Chinese glanced off the thick end of the tool rack.

166

"The coils are only twenty-five feet to the northeast of Hayes," Camellion said darkly. "Tell Hayes to pitch two thermate grenades at the coils while you cover him and I cover you. Make sure your Ingram is fully loaded. Tell Gordon not to toss until I give him the 'Go.'"

While Fieldhouse relayed the orders to Hayes, Camellion slipped an extra-long magazine into the Ingram, one that contained 64 9mm Silvertip cartridges. *Good bullets*, thought the Death Merchant. *Take the thin aluminum alloy cap from the nose of a Silvertip bullet, cap it with pure or almost-pure lead and you get a fine bullet that is less expensive to make. It's also very accurate, expands very rapidly, doesn't drag on feed ramps and has the added advantage of an additional 5 percent velocity at identical pressure for conventional jacketed bullets of the same weight.*

Fieldhouse said, "I'm set. So is Gordon."

"I'm going to toss a smoke canister at the goons," Camellion said. "Tell Hayes the second it goes off to throw the first grenade."

"Right. Damn these wet-suits. I feel like I'm inside an oven."

Camellion reached into one of his kit bags, took out a smoke grenade, pulled the ring and flipped it expertly at the Chinese ahead. The small round cylinder hit the floor. One-two-three seconds. Thick black smoke began to pour out of the canister.

Simultaneously, Camellion reared up slightly and began raking the Chinese with short bursts while Fieldhouse began a concentrated firing in the direction of the coils and Hayes tossed the first thermate grenade.

Absolutely beautiful! The loud hissing that was the explosion of the thermate grenade was only the prelude to the exquisitely gorgeous burst, as resplendent as a large shining flower opening its blue-white petals to the morning sun. But no flower on earth can do what thermate—a mixture of thermite, barium nitrate and sulfur—does: burn at almost 5,000° Fahrenheit.

Hayes tossed the second TH3 incendiary, and, amid hideous screaming coming from the direction of the coils, it also expanded into a lovely flower whose petals glowed with a blue-white brilliance.

167

Camellion smiled slightly within the gas mask—*Dominus Lucis vobiscum! Who says that Death can't be splendid?*

Thermate, turning to molten iron, becomes like the inside of a volcano. The two TH3 incendiaries had fallen short because of the angle at which Hayes, unable to rear up, had been forced to throw. However, some of the molten fire had splashed on the coils and three of the hoodlums.

Sam "The Man" Fulsims caught fire full in the face, and while the flesh melted from his head and turned his face into a dripping mess of flesh and a grinning skull, "Little Davy" Lubeck and Santos Alluala rolled on the floor, their pajama bottoms on fire, rib bones beginning to glisten white as the molten iron consumed flesh. Other liquid fire dribbled on the coils, which began to arc blue lightning back and forth.

The horror that invaded Charley Franzese, Barney Gindow and the two other mobsters was a confusion that possessed even their sense of taste and smell, a storm of the mind that was bitter and sweet, perfume and vomit. Like being stabbed and stroked with a feather—all at the same time.

Gagging at the sight and the smell of roasting flesh, the four men darted toward the group of Chinese assembled around the Space-Bender. Bernie Hall didn't make it. Five of Fieldhouse's 9mm projectiles caught him in the hip and the right side and knocked him to the floor with the force of a sledge hammer.

Slight laughter in his voice, Fieldhouse said, "Well, Swain, we have them all together. Why don't we just finish off the entire group with thermate?"

"We don't know what that strange-looking machine might do, if we tried that," Camellion said. "We're fooling around with a power we know nothing about. The thing might explode or make this whole place and us vanish into non-time and non-space."

"Damn! 'Dimension-X'!"

"Precisely."

"That might happen anyhow when we get in close."

"We have to take the chance. And I want the head Chinese, provided they don't get killed."

Fieldhouse's voice was filled with puzzlement. "How will you know who they are?"

"Instinct." Camellion thought of the enemy trapped

168

ahead—*Horatius at the bridge! Leonidas at Thermopylae!*
Hitler in his bunker! You Communist pieces of trash are fin-
ished! "I'm going to give the signal to attack."

He removed the walkie-talkie from his belt and punched
the button, slowly, four times. He and Fieldhouse then started
to reload their weapons, Camellion an Ingram and one Auto
Mag, Fieldhouse an Ingram and his 9mm ASP auto-loader.

At length, Camellion pressed the button two more times on
the walkie-talkie. The red light began flashing and the special
buzzer began sounding as the various men answered. They
were ready. . . .

The Death Merchant and his men first tossed six smoke
grenades. Then, as a group, they charged—from the west, the
south and the north . . . moving low, racing in crooked angles. And the enemy knew they were coming. Pistol and
machine-gun slugs tore through dark smoke in an attempt to
find the invaders. Hot metal grazed rubberized swimsuits, the
projectiles then *zinging* on their way, either to die in screaming ricochets or thud into wood or plastic or some other
substance the slugs could penetrate.

The Death Merchant and his men closed in, sprinting the
final feet when Clayton Brode caught a 7.63mm slug in the
left side of his chest. Another bullet, this one a 9mm, stabbed
him in the stomach. With a cry of pain and shock, Brode
went down, blood starting to bubble from his open mouth.
Death began to rock him gently in bony arms. . . .

The firing of pistols and submachine guns! Coughing! Then
metal clanging against metal! Shouts! Grunts! Groans! Now it
was man to man, with neither side having time to reload, even
though some of the Chinese and the three American gangsters
tried.

Let us go to work! Camellion slammed one of the Chinese
across the temple with the barrel of the AMP Backpacker
and stabbed another in the throat with the stubby barrel of
the Ingram machine pistol while delivering a right-legged
Yoko Geri Kekomi side-thrust kick to the groin of a third
man. All three pieces of Red Chinese trash made a nose-dive
for the floor, one dead from a crushed skull, one choking to
death, the third in such terrible agony that he wished he could
die.

The man called Richard Camellion was not too concerned. Not only was he a 5th-degree black belt (*Godan*), but he had a very personal arrangement with the Cosmic Lord of Death. Camellion knew that his time would come. And he knew when—*But today is not the day.* . . .

With lightning speed, he dropped the Ingram and holstered the AMP Backpacker, preferring to have his hands free, except for one item he wore on the second finger of his right hand—the Deadringer, worn like a ring. Designed by Chris McLoughlin, a master of death in his own right, the Deadringer was an actual knife, like a diminutive push dagger, the double-edged blade 1⅝ inches long and spearpointed. Of high-quality steel, the deadly little dagger could be worn with either the blade pointed outward and away from the knuckles—for cutting, slashing or thrusting—or toward the palm for more subtle application.

Camellion preferred to wear the Deadringer, snug on his finger, with the blade pointed outward—the non-reflective steel blade inflicting hideous damage on some of the Red Chinese trying to bring him down. He used a left-elbow *Empi* stab to wreck the celiac (solar) plexus of Yeh Bo L'ang trying to come in behind him, a high *Fumikomi* front stamp kick that landed solidly on the sternal angle[23] of Wang Wen-hung, one of the top men of the Red Chinese 3rd Bureau in the lab. The pain didn't do anything to Wang Wen-hung. The sudden shock did. It killed him. He was still falling when Camellion used a *Mawashi Geri* rear roundhouse kick that barely reached Nanki Hiso, who jumped back—straight into the path of Bill Fieldhouse. At the same time, as Camellion's left hand shot out to grab the wrist of Liu Ki Cho'i'pi, who was coming at him with a knife, he used his right hand in a very fast *Seiken*, the blade of the Deadringer slicing through the jugular notch of the man's neck. Blood spurted. Cho'i'pi gur-

23. The sternal angle is the point where the manubrium (the upper part of the breastbone) and the body of the sternum come together, about 2 inches below where the collar bones meet at the base of the throat. This is a weak spot in the sternum, and if attacked with a powerful blow to the "sternal shield" over the heart . . . bronchus, lungs and thoracic nerves can be broken, producing intense pain and shock to the circulatory and respiratory systems.

gled, wished he had stayed home in China and started to fall into the final blackness.

Nanki Hiso, although an expert in *Hsing-i* and *Shaolin*—Chinese boxing—was no match for Bill Fieldhouse, who was not only a past master in *Pentjak-silat* (the national defense form of Indonesia), but an expert in *Kun-Tao* (Chinese: "fist-way") and in Okinawa *Karate-jutsu*.

Hiso tried to spin away from Fieldhouse, who, when killing, worked with an astonishing coolness and precision. As fast as Hiso was, Bill—even with the extra weight of the shoulder bags—was much faster. He let Hiso have a right-legged Patagonian purr-kick, the piston of his foot caving in Hiso's left side and forcing broken ribs to stab into the man's left lung. Fieldhouse began using his legs and feet the way a boxer uses his fists. A blink of an eye! He powed Hiso with a left-legged *Ko-ja* dynamite kick that landed on the side of the man's head and broke his neck—spun with the speed of a top and kicked another Chinese full in the face, the rubber sole of the coral shoe breaking the goof's jaws, nasal bones and the orbital bones around both eyes.

Another Chinese, knowing he was facing a murderous, methodical expert, jumped back, raised a knife with a double-edged blade; he was about to throw it at Fieldhouse when Gordon Hayes spotted him and tossed his own knife while Yao Bi'Pong was drawing his knife-arm back. The blade of Hayes' Quicksilver knife buried itself in the right side of Bi'Pong's throat. A river of red poured from the mouth of Bi'Pong, sinking as though his legs were melting out from under him.

Terrified at Bi'Pong's sudden, bloody demise, Tasi Ko-shek—first-in-command of the 3rd Bureau agents on Chelsworth Island—took three steps backward, tripped over a piece of shattered equipment, righted himself, turned and came face to face with a mean-eyed man who, underneath his M-17 gas mask, looked as if he had just escaped from a Federal prison.

DeCrow had just cut the throat of a Chinese technician with a knife whose handle was shaped like brass knuckles. Now DeCrow stabbed Tasi Ko-shek in the stomach, pushed the knife upward, then out. All in the same motion, DeCrow lashed out with his left leg, in a *Sokuto Geri* sword-foot kick that almost wrapped Ch'en Ch'inn's colon in knots around his spine. The kick, however, had thrown DeCrow seriously off balance. Ko-shek—his guts hanging out—fell, and so did Ch'en Ch'inn. So did DeCrow—going down on his butt and falling slightly to the right. He didn't fail to see the two men rushing in to take advantage of his position. However, it was the Chinese who got the surprise—the last of their lives. De-Crow had dropped his Ingram MP, and his holstered .45 Safari Enforcer auto-pistol was empty. That left only the little stainless steel COP[24] in an open holster on his belt, just in front of his walkie-talkie.

"Goddamn Orientals!" snarled DeCrow, his right hand whipping down toward his belt. Out came the COP, his finger starting to pull the trigger as he swung the unique pistol toward the first charging man.

The pistol roared and the first Red goof caught the flat-pointed .357 bullet in the stomach. Traveling upward at a steep angle, the bullet plowed out his back between his shoulder blades, the terrific impact lifting him several inches off the floor.

The COP roared again and the second attacker caught the bullet in the chest, the collision between projectile and body knocking him back against several of his Comrades, who were throwing themselves at George Simmons and Martin Koerner. Three more Chinese were coming at Koerner and Simmons from the right.

Koerner went down first, his head caved in by a length of steel table leg swung by a fat-faced freak with a bald head. Groaning, Simmons started to sag, with a screwdriver buried in his stomach and the long blade of a pocketknife in his right side. But one of the Chinese went down with him, Simmons' own Vindicator buried in his gut, right up to its black Micarta handle. But Jo Pen-mu, the fat-faced bald bastard, didn't really have any victory to celebrate; neither did Lan Fu'lii, the 3rd Bureau agent who had stabbed Simmons in the stom-

24. An unusual weapon, the COC (Compact Off-Duty Police) has four barrels, the chamber of each filled with a .357 Magnum cartridge. All four cartridges are fired by a rotary-hammer double-action ignition. The weapon is just 5.5 inches long, 4.1 inches high, 1 inch wide and weighs 28 ounces.

ach with a screwdriver. DeCrow, getting to his feet, had seen what had happened. He now fired the third barrel of the COP. Jo Pen-mu's porcine face vanished in an explosion of flesh, bone and blood, the .357 Magnum slug blowing off his head. The fourth barrel of the COP discharged its projectile, which struck Lan Fu'lii in the left rib cage, tore through his heart and lungs and went on its bloody way through his right rib cage.

The other two Chinese who had been in on the killings of Simmons and Koerner turned toward the sounds of the two roars, then tried to duck down, not knowing how many shots DeCrow had in the weapon. Their evasive action was useless. Walter Ridgeway and Gene Thompson, nearby, went for Kung Ji Kang and Nu Wa Chin.

Ridgeway grabbed Chin by the left wrist, jerked on the man's arm, kicked him in the stomach, then slammed him in the throat with a *Yon Hon Nukite* four-finger spear thrust, his fingers crushing the thyroid cartilage. Nu Wa Chin would die from suffocation within 40 seconds.

Gene Thompson went to work on the other goon, landing a left-handed *Haito* ridge-hand chop to the man's right cheek. A right *Seiken* forefist to the man's stomach. And when Kung Ji Kang doubled over in agony, Thompson finished him off with an expert *Tsumi-Saki* tip-of-toes strike kick that landed squarely in the middle of Kang's solar plexus. The dog eater would be with his honorable ancestors within a few minutes.

All this time, Gregory Peter Fluggmeyer, or Gregory "Steel Fingers" Gof, had kept crouched behind the lid of a crate, next to the Space-Bender. He had exhausted the ammunition of his H&K V70 machine pistol and knew that in spite of the strength in his arms, he was not a match for any of the attackers. He was simply too short. By keeping his face close to the floor and breathing through a handkerchief, into which he kept spitting, he had been able to breathe; and since none of the tear gas had come close to the Space-Bender, and because gas rises, he could still see through his one good eye. Now and then, he would risk looking out from behind the lid. Each time that he did, he saw that his own position was becoming more and more precarious. More and more Chinese were dying. Sooner or later the enemy would find him and Dr.

173

Cho-ko and Dr. Wen-yuan, both of whom were on the other side of the 8-foot-in-diameter device, down behind sheets of the south door that had been blown inward.

Gof's luck went all bad when he peeked around one edge of the lid and Dennis Float saw and recognized him. There was no mistaking the ugly patch, the ugly face, the thick lips and crooked nose. Float's face twisted in hate. Yes, sir. There was Soraya Duncan's "little brother." *Ugly little sonofabitch! Here is where you get yours!*

Float had covered the 8 feet and was jerking aside the lid as fast as an icepick can stab through an eyeball. Gof let out a howl of surprise and, as Float leaned down, tried to grab the Company man's wrists with his powerful hands filled with steel fingers. Float, however, had anticipated such a move. At the last moment, he quickly raised his arms and, with his right knee, kneed Gof straight in the face, the big slam breaking Gof's nose and some of his upper teeth. Before the grotesque dwarf could recover from the pain and shock, he found himself being jerked upward and raised high above Float's head, squirming in a horizontal position. In one fleeting moment of blind, rushing panic, he felt not so much pain as stark horror over his own approaching death, only moments away. He had one final thought, one final picture of his massive head being squashed against the side of the Space-Bender like a grape. Only his thought processes did not have the time to realize that his execution was going to be carried out in another manner.

Float, in the process of bringing Gof down, suddenly got to one knee, his other knee sticking out, all the movements smoothly coordinated. Gof landed on the small of his back, on Float's extended knee. There was a dull cracking sound. His eyes glazed. His body went limp. Float pushed the corpse away, let it fall to the floor, and was momentarily struck with fear when he felt a pair of arms start to drop over his head in an attempt at either a rear strangle hold or a neck-snap.

The quick-thinking Float moved his head down, dropped to both knees, hunched himself down as far as possible and, before She Chi T'an could recapture him with his arms, rolled backward between the man's legs extended in a V position, with the bottom point of the V being T'an's crotch. Snarling in rage and frustration, She Chi T'an was spinning around when Float, on his back, jerked upward like some kind of monstrous worm, grabbed T'an in a scissors hold with his legs and slammed him to the floor.

The advantage was with Float, in that the wind had been knocked out of T'an. In a flash, Float was all over the 3rd Bureau agent, his big hands chopping vicious *Shuto* blows. In less than half a minute, the one-sided battle came to an end when Float applied a Commando neckbreaker.

Float got to his feet, paused and listened. Had he heard movement from the other side of the tall, cylindrical machine. Yes . . . he had. . . .

Charley "Blackeye" Franzese and Barney "The Pig" Gindow had managed to reload their weapons, Franzese shoving a clip into a Colt Government Model .45, Gindow using a Smith & Wesson .41 Magnum. Both hoodlums were in a bad way. While Franzese still wore his dark glasses, the smoke and the tear gas had not helped his *retinitis pigmentosa*, the eye disease from which he was suffering. The smoke and the tear gas had reduced his vision by 90 percent and, down on his knees by a table, he was helpless.

"The Pig" wasn't much better off. Gindow was hungry—he usually was. Due to his weight, he was short-winded, and the smoke had not increased his capacity to breathe. Furthermore, he was terrified. He didn't mind shooting a man. But when men shot back and fought like maniacs, that was another matter. Hunched under a workbench, resembling a big fat toad, Gindow trembled with fear.

Lyle "The Hammer" Stover, the last American mobster, was different from Franzese and Gindow. More of a fanatic than a coward, Stover (a pimp who used a small hammer to break the kneecaps of working girls who held out on the long green) knew he would never leave the lab alive. But, by God, he would take as many of them with him as he could.

Down behind a pile of overturned equipment, Stover aimed down on one of the enemy and pulled the trigger at the same time that Bill Fieldhouse ducked to avoid a *Haishu* open backhand by Kuan Shih-yin, one of the few Chinese still alive. The .45 Star slug missed Fieldhouse by an inch. But the sound of the shot did attract the attention of Harlon Wiseman, who was only 10 feet to the left of Stover and had found the opportunity to duck down and shove a full clip into the Ingram he had clipped to a ring on his belt.

An overly confident Stover was moving the Star back and forth, trying to get a clear shot at either Fieldhouse, or the Death Merchant, the latter of whom was darting and weaving toward Gindow and Franzese when Wiseman squeezed off a short burst that turned Stover's head and neck into bloody chopped-apart mush.

No sooner had he wasted Stover than Wiseman heard several shots 20 feet or so to his left, to the southeast. Ridgeway and Thompson had also heard the shots. With Wiseman, they started for the Space-Bender.

Having drawn the AMP Backpacker that was still fully loaded, the Death Merchant jumped over rubble and equipment, darting first one way and then another, all the while his keen eyes keeping track of Gindow and Franzese.

And "The Pig" finally spotted him. Wildeyed, speechless and panting, Gindow tried to swing his S & W around and up to fire at the tall man coming at him like a black whirlwind. The only sound, however, was a big *beroommmm* from the AMP in Camellion's left hand. Gindow's body shuddered from the impact of the big bullet and he slumped dead, a large bloody hole in his lower right chest. He had eaten of bread baked in blackness and had paid the price.

Charles Franzese went next . . . a born gambler who had forgotten that he no longer could break the bank. The Death Merchant's AMP roared and Franzese fell back, without a head, parts of his brain and pieces of flesh and skull bones falling around him.

Camellion looked around. Most of the smoke and tear gas had drifted away, some of it still hanging toward the ceiling— *We, the living, no longer belong here. This is now the domain of the Cosmic Lord of Death. . . .*

He caught sight of Fieldhouse, who was holding the top of his left arm with his right hand. With a nod of his head, Fieldhouse indicated the Space-Bender. In a very short time, Fieldhouse and Camellion were standing with Wiseman, Ridgeway, Thompson and DeCrow.

The six of them stared down at the dead bodies of Dennis Float and Lin T'ien Cho-ko. Float, lying on his back, had been shot twice in the stomach. Cho-ko sat slumped with a Quicksilver knife buried in his chest, a 9mm Chinese Model 51 auto-loader in his right hand.

Ridgeway had pulled the gas masks from the two Chinese and was examining Chou Wen-yuan. "He's alive, but I think his jaw is broken," Ridgeway said, his voice hollow as it came through the voicemitter of the gas mask. Ridgeway felt of Wen-yuan's throat pulse. "His pulse is good. He's in good shape."

"Man, look at the bruise on that goon's jaw!" Gene Thompson said.

"Float no doubt used a *Savate* blow on him," Fieldhouse said placidly. "Only a foot blow could make a bruise like that."

The Death Merchant, studying the two Chinese, thought of how ambition can creep as well as crawl. The ambition of the Chinese had brought them only death. Used to thinking in fourteen different languages, Camellion thought in German— *Es geht alles vorueber, es geht alles vorbei—everything passes, everything has its day*.

It was not difficult to deduce what had happened to Float. He had come across the two Chinese hiding by the side of the machine. Cho-ko had put several M-51 slugs into Float who, in one last desperate effort of will and physical strength, had stabbed Cho-ko with the Quicksilver and had slammed out Wen-yuan.

Camellion took off his gas mask, sniffed the air and looked at Fieldhouse. "How about the arm?" He began reloading the first empty Auto Mag Backpacker.

"It's a pretty good cut," Fieldhouse said. "That Chinese, the last one I had, was damned good. I finally got him with a simple old-fashioned right cross to the chin—then stomped his throat."

He noticed that a subtle change had come over the man called Swain (and Fieldhouse knew that was not his real name). He had noticed this change before and had wondered about it. It was not a nervous tension, but an intense watchfulness, a concentrated suspiciousness that, Fieldhouse felt, was directed even at him. During such a time, Swain, giving the impression of extreme guardedness, would be tight-lipped and very curt in his conversation, the way he was now.

"We'll get a tourniquet on that arm," DeCrow said to Fieldhouse and nodded at Ridgeway, indicating he wanted him to apply it. DeCrow had also removed his gas mask, and now wished he hadn't. The stink was not pleasant. Besides the odor of smoke and gas and of burnt gun powder, there was that distant malodor of Death, the peculiar sweet smell of things already starting to decay.

Fieldhouse held his arm out to Ridgeway, who had taken a tourniquet kit from one of his Musette bags. "Seven left out of eleven," Fieldhouse said slowly. "I suppose that sounds better than saying that four of our people are dead."

"At least, this time we didn't have to look into the eyes of any innocent children," mumbled Ridgeway, thinking of his days in Vietnam. "Damn it, hold your arm still."

Camellion stared down at the two Chinese by the side of the Space-Bender. *Ordnung muss sein—things must be in order.* . . . "DeCrow, Wiseman, Thompson . . . check and make sure about our people," he ordered. "If you find any Chinese still alive, terminate them. Once we're sure of our own people, we'll set the thermate and the explosives and get out of here. We're ten minutes over the schedule."

As the three men moved quickly off, Fieldhouse said, "What about Doctor Chou Wen-yuan? Is he dead? For that matter, how will we know he was even here?"

"The man with the broken jaw might be he," Camellion said.

"Uh huh, instinct, I suppose?"

"Deduction. He's in his late fifties. He's too old to be a technician, as a rule. Notice all the pens and note books in the top pockets of his smock. He's not Third Bureau. So who knows what we might have?"

"There, that should do it," Ridgeway said, finishing with the tourniquet. He grinned. "You should live another twenty-four hours at least."

"Ridgeway, you keep an eye on the unconscious Chinese," Camellion said. "Try to bring him around. Bill, go outside and radio Captain Klimes. Tell him we're about finished here and that I want him to bring the *Wild Goose* in as close as he can."

Fieldhouse nodded with an air of satisfaction. "What are you going to be doing?"

"I'm going to have a good look around and start setting the big blow stuff. After you've completed the message to Klimes, come back in here and photograph this gismo from all angles." He jerked his head toward the Space-Bender. "This has to be the invisibility machine. It can't be anything else."

Gordon Hayes was not dead. They found him when he was regaining consciousness. He had killed several Chinese, and then had slipped in a pool of blood, fallen to the floor, and had knocked himself out by hitting his head against a piece of equipment—"Or the edge of a work bench. I don't know which. And if you jokers ever tell anybody about that dumb stunt, I'll scramble your balls with a pair of longnosed pliers."

Later, as the group was placing the TNT blocks, the grenades and the thermate, wiring the arrangement so that the entire works could be detonated from one control unit, they found the dead bodies of Soraya Duncan and the other women. Soraya Duncan in particular was a grotesque sight. Her once-shapely figure had jackknifed, due to the beginning of rigor mortis, and she was in a position that morticians call an "equestrian posture," sitting upright, as though in a saddle, both arms outstretched, her cold hands holding invisible reins.

Finally their grim work was done, and they left the laboratory, glad to be free of the eerie place and its occupants of dead flesh. They moved quickly through the early dawn, DeCrow and Wiseman prodding Chou Wen-yuan along with Ingrams. His hands tied behind his back, the Red Chinese expert in brainwashing did not resist. His broken jaw was pure pain—and where could he run to?

A slight breeze rustled the leaves of maples and basswoods. And in the high branches of the elms were large blackbirds that made the Death Merchant think of Berlin's *Nebelkraehe*, or fog crows, birds that breed and nest in Poland, summer in Russia, but always winter in Berlin, Germany.

The Death Merchant in the lead, the group at times trotted down the road; at other times they literally ran, DeCrow threatening Wen-yuan that if he couldn't keep up, "We won't kill you. I'll thumb out your eyeballs and leave you. You can spend the rest of your life in darkness, remembering the last dawn you saw in the United States."

* * *

The *Wild Goose* was only 50 feet from the dock, her engine throbbing, her three man crew impatient.

"What about the *Trojan Meridian* and the *Hatteras?*" Fieldhouse asked. "We going to blow them?"

"Why bother?" Camellion said. "And we don't have the time."

They jumped into the water, removed their shoulder bags and let them sink to the bottom. Who cared what the U.S. Coast Guard might find, or the police? Absolutely nothing could be traceed to any of the men or to the Company.

Once DeCrow and Wiseman had Chou Wen-yuan in the water, they were very careful with the Chinese mental expert. They had come this far, and they weren't about to let their precious prize drown, which was a possibility if he passed out from the agony in his jaw.

The three were the last to board the vessel. No sooner were they on deck than Captain Klimes ordered John Dilman, in the wheel house, to pull away and head out at full speed.

The Death Merchant had only one question to ask Captain Klimes: "How about the Coast Guard transmissions?"

"The Coast Guard has heard some explosions, but they're not sure where they came from," Klimes said nervously. "But now with daylight, the sooner we get out of here, the safer we'll be. When are you going to blow whatever you found back there? What did you fellows find back there, or isn't it any of my business?"

Camellion steadied himself against the side of the pilot house as the vessel gathered speed.

"When we're a mile out—and it's not any of your business," he said, sniffing the air that was clean, cool and refreshing. "I'll do it from the bridge."

Turning, he headed for the stern door of the midsection cabin.

At top speed the *Wild Goose*, with its supercharged engine, headed out toward the Atlantic, Camellion visually calculating the expanding distance between boat and dock, the remote-control device in his hands.

"Are you going to stand there until noon?" an impatient Fieldhouse said. "Go on and do it."

180

"Yeah, mate. I like to hear explosions!" DeCrow laughed harshly.

"Tch, tch! Such violent people with whom I am forced to associate!" mocked Camellion.

He flipped the "on" switches of the remote-control device and pushed the red button.

All heard the monstrous explosion; none, however, saw the flash of fire. They didn't have to. They could easily imagine what had happened during that split second: the entire laboratory dissolving in a sheet of fire and smoke . . . galvanized iron and machinery, bodies and equipment splitting into millions of pieces. What the TNT and the grenades hadn't destroyed, the scattered thermate would.

There was a long silence, each man knowing that there wouldn't be any traces of the bodies . . . nothing that would really make sense, only a bone or two several hundred feet from where the lab had been. Dozens of bones wouldn't make any difference. The Maine police would have a mystery that would never be solved.

DeCrow sighed. "That does seem to be that."

"My arm hurts like hell," said Fieldhouse.

The Death Merchant listened to the steady throb of the Diesel and gazed solemnly at the dawn . . . the eastern sky a riot of redness. Belfast also had beautiful dawns—and Death—*As for manmade beauty, I'll find little in Belfast or in all of Northern Ireland*.

In Northern Ireland, the aerosol paint business was big business. The IRA painted walls white to outline British soldiers in the dark. In turn, the British Tommies would paint the walls black.

But the paint-spray business was only the second-largest industry in that troubled land where violence was an accepted way of life.

The first was the manufacture of artificial limbs. . . .

Damn Grojean! I should tell him to get someone else to go to Northern Ireland. But I won't. I'd die of boredom without action. OK. He wants a Shamrock Smash. He'll get it. . . .

More bestselling action/adventure
from Pinnacle, America's #1 series publisher.
Over 14 million copies
of THE DESTROYER in print!

☐ 40-877-3	Created, The Destroyer #1	$1.75	☐ 40-295-3	Deadly Seeds #21	$1.50
☐ 40-878-1	Death Check #2	$1.75	☐ 40-898-6	Brain Drain #22	$1.75
☐ 40-879-X	Chinese Puzzle #3	$1.75	☐ 40-899-4	Child's Play #23	$1.75
☐ 40-880-3	Mafia Fix #4	$1.75	☐ 40-298-8	King's Curse #24	$1.50
☐ 40-881-1	Dr. Quake #5	$1.75	☐ 40-901-X	Sweet Dreams #25	$1.75
☐ 40-882-X	Death Therapy #6	$1.75	☐ 40-251-1	In Enemy Hands #26	$1.50
☐ 40-281-3	Union Bust #7	$1.50	☐ 40-353-4	Last Temple #27	$1.50
☐ 40-282-1	Summit Chase #8	$1.50	☐ 40-416-6	Ship of Death #28	$1.50
☐ 40-885-4	Murder's Shield #9	$1.75	☐ 40-905-2	Final Death #29	$1.75
☐ 40-284-8	Terror Squad #10	$1.50	☐ 40-110-8	Mugger Blood #30	$1.50
☐ 40-285-6	Kill Or Cure #11	$1.50	☐ 40-907-9	Head Men #31	$1.75
☐ 40-888-9	Slave Safari #12	$1.75	☐ 40-908-7	Killer Chromosomes #32	$1.75
☐ 40-287-2	Acid Rock #13	$1.50	☐ 40-909-5	Voodoo Die #33	$1.75
☐ 40-288-0	Judgment Day #14	$1.50	☐ 40-156-6	Chained Reaction #34	$1.50
☐ 40-289-9	Murder Ward #15	$1.50	☐ 40-157-4	Last Call #35	$1.50
☐ 40-290-2	Oil Slick #16	$1.50	☐ 40-912-5	Power Play #36	$1.75
☐ 40-291-0	Last War Dance #17	$1.50	☐ 40-159-0	Bottom Line #37	$1.50
☐ 40-294-3	Funny Money #18	$1.75	☐ 40-160-4	Bay City Blast #38	$1.50
☐ 40-895-1	Holy Terror #19	$1.75	☐ 40-713-0	Missing Link #39	$1.75
☐ 40-294-5	Assassins Play-Off #20	$1.50	☐ 40-714-9	Dangerous Games #40	$1.75

Buy them at your local bookstore or use this handy coupon:
Clip and mail this page with your order